A small town in Georgia.
A family with a past.

A miniseries packed with sensual secrets
and elusive scandals.

Bestselling author Gina Wilkins continues her
unforgettable family drama,

by bringing you the wildest member of the family yet!

Former cop Mac Cordero is going undercover
one last time...to bring his proud Southern family
to its knees!

in

Yesterday's
Scandal

Enjoy the sexy, scandalous escapades of the
McBride clan, the most notorious family
in the South!

Dear Reader,

The Wild McBrides have certainly taken me for a wild ride, through six Harlequin Temptations and now this, my first single title release. It seems fitting that this story should be centered around the "wildest" McBride yet—one who possesses knowledge that could bring down the close-knit McBride clan. They've survived scandal before, but this time they will be forced to face truths that will shake their very foundation....

Sharon Henderson finds herself in the middle of this crisis, torn between loyalty to a family that has always been very dear to her, and her love for a man who needs retribution—and doesn't seem to care who gets hurt along the way. Is her love strong enough to soothe the anger inside this proud man—or will his desire for revenge destroy them both?

Hold on,

Gina Wilkins

Books by Gina Wilkins

HARLEQUIN TEMPTATION—THE McBRIDES
668—SEDUCING SAVANNAH
676—TEMPTING TARA
684—ENTICING EMILY
710—THE REBEL'S RETURN
792—SEDUCTIVELY YOURS
796—SECRETLY YOURS

Gina WILKINS

Yesterday's Scandal

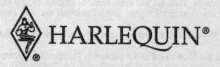

HARLEQUIN®

TORONTO • NEW YORK • LONDON
AMSTERDAM • PARIS • SYDNEY • HAMBURG
STOCKHOLM • ATHENS • TOKYO • MILAN • MADRID
PRAGUE • WARSAW • BUDAPEST • AUCKLAND

For my friends and colleagues in Novelists, Inc.,
the most supportive group I have ever met.

And for Nora Roberts, my personal hero,
who was there for me when I needed her
during this past year.

My thanks to all of you.

ISBN 0-373-83439-X

YESTERDAY'S SCANDAL

Copyright © 2000 by Gina Wilkins.

This edition published by arrangement with Harlequin Books S.A.

® and TM are trademarks of the publisher. Trademarks indicated with
® are registered in the United States Patent and Trademark Office, the
Canadian Trade Marks Office and in other countries.

Visit us at www.eHarlequin.com

Printed in U.S.A.

CHAPTER ONE

TAILLIGHTS GLOWED red in the darkness ahead of him as Mac Cordero drove along the rural outskirts of Honoria, Georgia. He wasn't deliberately following the other vehicle. They just happened to be headed in the same direction on the narrow, hilly road bordered by thick woods on the left and a rain-swollen river on the right.

Mac had no particular destination in mind. He was merely killing time on this Friday evening, delaying his return to the no-frills motel where he would be staying until he made better arrangements for the next few months. He had things to accomplish in this oddball town, and the renovation of the 1920s-era Victorian-style house he'd recently purchased was the excuse he'd use if anyone asked why he was here. The *real* reason he was here—well, sometimes that even seemed like a mystery to him.

Because it was a warm, early-June evening, his windows were down, letting in the fresh, woodsy air and the sounds of night creatures. Neither lifted his mood, nor eased the frustration that he had accomplished so little since his initial visit to Honoria several weeks earlier. He was no closer now to solving the mystery that had brought him here than he'd been when he'd decided to pursue it.

The small car ahead of him began a steady ascent up a steep, blind hill. Mac shifted in the seat of his truck. All in all, it had been an unproductive day. He was beginning to wonder if boredom was all that awaited him here. He hated being bored.

A squeal of brakes brought him abruptly out of his thoughts. His hands tightened on the steering wheel when the taillights ahead of him swerved suddenly and erratically, then veered off to the right side of the road—straight toward the river. At the same moment, a light-colored van topped the hill in the center of the road, speeding, weaving, making no effort to slow down. Acting on instinct, Mac jerked his wheel to the right, pulling his truck to the side but stopping before it went over the edge. The van sped past, disappearing behind him.

Muttering a curse, Mac didn't waste time trying to get a license-plate number, but jumped from his truck and ran to the edge of the road. The slow-moving river looked like black ink in the darkness, shimmering with multifaceted reflections of the three-quarter moon overhead. He saw no sign of the car he knew had gone over. Kicking off his shoes, he prepared to dive in.

A head broke the water in front of him as he started to jump. He heard a loud gasp for air, followed by what might have been a broken cry of pain and fear. A moment later, he was in the cold water, reaching the woman just as she went under again.

He grabbed her arms and hauled her to the surface, noting automatically that she was lightweight, slender. His hands easily spanned her waist as he treaded water and supported her until she caught her breath. It was difficult to see her features in the shadows, but he got the impression she was somewhat younger than his own thirty-three years.

Reassured that she was stable, he asked urgently, "Is there anyone else in the car?"

"No. I was alone." Her voice was a choked whisper. "It…took me a while to get out. I had my windows down, but…"

"It wasn't as long as it must have seemed to you." He was aware that she was trembling so hard her teeth were chattering. The water was cool, but not frigid. Sensing that shock was about to set in, he tightened his grip on her. "Can you swim? Are you injured?"

"I…I don't know," she managed to say, clinging to him. "I hurt, but I don't know exactly where yet."

Because it made sense to him, considering the circumstances, he merely nodded and wrapped an arm around her to help her toward the bank. He would assess her injuries once she was safely out of the water, he decided, beginning to swim with steady, rescue-trained strokes.

The bank was steep, mud crumbling beneath his hands and feet as he helped the woman out of the river. It wasn't easy to swing her into his arms and carry her up to the side of the road. Hard shivers racked her, and he could hear her teeth chattering. Damning the darkness that kept him from seeing whether she was bleeding anywhere, Mac settled her on the gravel beside the road. "I'll be right back."

He dashed to his truck, water streaming off him, his wet socks providing little protection from the rocks on the roadbed. Ignoring his discomfort, he snatched his cellular phone and dialed 911. Grabbing the lightweight jacket he'd tossed into the passenger seat earlier, he gave the emergency dispatcher a clipped summation of his situation, requested an ambulance and then hung up.

The woman was curled into a fetal ball when he returned to her. He suspected that if there was enough light, he would see that her lips were blue. She wore a T-shirt and shorts, and her feet were bare. She'd probably lost her shoes in the river. She lay in a puddle of water, trembling.

"I've called for help," he said, wrapping his jacket snugly around her. The thin fabric seemed to make no difference at all; she seemed hardly to notice it. Shock, he thought again, and shifted her onto her back, pushing her knees upward so that her legs were higher than her head.

Only marginally aware of his own soggy, chilled condition, he smoothed wet, nape-length hair from the woman's face. His eyes had finally grown accustomed to the darkness and he could make out the woman's features. Her skin was so pale it looked like porcelain in the milky moonlight. He took another guess at her age—mid- to late twenties, perhaps. Her hair looked dark, but it was hard to tell for certain. "What's your name?"

"Sharon." Her voice was faint, but coherent, to his relief. "Sharon Henderson."

"I'm Mac Cordero."

She pulled a hand from the folds of his jacket and reached out toward him. "Thank you."

He cradled her icy fingers in his larger, somewhat warmer ones. Their gazes met and held. Her eyes glittered in the moonlight. He knew his own face was in shadow, but he offered a faint smile of encouragement. "You're welcome."

She shivered again and he tightened his hand. He felt as if something passed between them at that point of contact—warmth, emotion…something. Most likely he was overreacting to the dramatic turn the evening had suddenly taken. When he'd complained of boredom earlier, he certainly hadn't been hoping for anything like this.

A dark Jeep with a flashing light on the dash topped the hill and braked to a stop across the road. The driver stepped out of the vehicle and crossed to them swiftly, kneeling at the woman's other side. "Sharon?" he said, recognizing her immediately, "Are you hurt?"

"I don't think so," she answered, but didn't sound quite convinced.

"An ambulance is on the way. Can you tell me what happened?"

"I was leaving Tressie's house after dinner. There was a van—it came out of the driveway on the other side of the hill without stopping. I swerved, but it ran me off the road—almost as if it was intentional.''

"I saw the van,'' Mac added. ''It never even slowed down."

The other man looked at him. ''Chief Wade Davenport, Honoria Police Department,'' he introduced himself.

''Mac Cordero. I happened to be following behind Ms. Henderson's car, and I saw the accident.''

''Judging from your appearance, I take it Sharon's car went into Snake Creek?''

Mac frowned. Snake Creek? Hardly a name to inspire confidence. He hated snakes. Yet he knew that even had the water been crawling with them, he'd have gone in after her. Years of training and practice had kicked in the moment he'd seen someone in trouble. You could take the cop out of his uniform, he thought ruefully, but it was a hell of a lot harder to break those old cop habits.

''My car.'' Sharon turned her head to look mournfully toward the edge of the road. ''I just made the final payment.''

Davenport patted her shoulder. ''Let's not worry about that right now, okay?''

A siren broke the deceptively peaceful silence of the night. Davenport glanced in its direction, then turned his attention back to the soggy couple in front of him. ''You said the van pulled out of the driveway just over the hill?''

Sharon nodded. ''Yes. The driver didn't even

pause to see if anyone was coming from either direction.''

"That's the Porter place. The Porters left for vacation three days ago.''

"You think the van was there to rob them?'' She sounded appalled.

The police chief glanced at Mac, who had already leaped to that conclusion, then looked back at Sharon. "I'll check that out as soon as you're taken care of. I don't suppose either of you got the number of the license plate on the van.''

"No." Mac shook his head, knowing he'd be able to provide little detail. "I thought it was more important to make sure no one was trapped underwater.''

"You made the right call.'' Davenport stood as an ambulance pulled up behind the Jeep. "I'll have more questions for you later, if you don't mind, Mr. Cordero.''

"I'll tell you everything I saw—but I'm afraid it wasn't much. It all happened too quickly.''

Two uniformed paramedics—a man and a woman—approached with swift efficiency. Only then did Mac realize that he was still holding Sharon's hand. She clung to him when he would have released her, as if he were her only lifeline in frighteningly uncharted waters. He had to gently peel her fingers away so the medics could do their jobs.

He hadn't been cold when he'd knelt beside her, holding her hand. Now, as he stepped back, he felt a chill penetrate his wet clothing. He shoved his hands into the pockets of his slacks and winced when the waterlogged fabric clung to him. Fortunately, his wallet was in the truck, so the only thing he'd ruined was a good leather belt. His shoes were still by the water's edge. He'd get them as soon as the ambulance left.

Wade Davenport returned from using the radio in his Jeep just as Sharon was being loaded onto the ambulance. "I'll come to the hospital in a few minutes to see about you," he promised her.

"All right," she answered automatically, though she was still looking at Mac. "Mr. Cordero..."

He stepped closer to the gurney. "Yes?"

"Thank you."

She had already thanked him. He answered as he had before, "You're welcome."

He watched her—and was watched in return—until the ambulance doors closed between them. Only when the ambulance had driven away did he turn back to the chief of police, prepared to answer his questions.

SORE MUSCLES CLENCHED when Sharon shifted in her seat Sunday evening, causing her to wince. She immediately regretted doing so when the man on the other side of the restaurant table frowned and asked, "Are you sure you're all right?"

Since it was at least the tenth time he'd asked in the past couple of hours, Sharon had to force herself to answer patiently. "I'm fine, Jerry. Still a little sore, but the doctor assured me that was to be expected.''

Jerry Whitaker didn't look satisfied. He seemed convinced that her injuries from Friday night's mishap were worse than the few scrapes and bruises she had told him about.

He'd been out of town for the weekend, and when he'd returned that afternoon, talk of the accident had been all over town—no surprise in Honoria, where rumors zipped from household to household with the frantic speed of a metal ball in an arcade pinball machine. Having lived here since adolescence, Sharon had learned to discount most of what she heard, but Jerry still tended to take the local gossip much too seriously.

"Tell me more about your business trip," she encouraged him, trying to change the subject. "How was the weather in Charleston?"

Her attempt at diversion failed. "Fine," he answered automatically, then returned to his questions about her. "Have you talked to Chief Davenport since I called you this afternoon? Have there been any further developments in the investigation of the Porter robbery—any leads on the van that ran you off the road?"

Resigned to rehashing it all again, Sharon looked down at her plate. "Nothing. It's as if the van disappeared off the face of the earth. If Mr. Cordero hadn't seen it, I would have wondered if I had imagined it."

Jerry's scowl deepened. "Ah, yes. Cordero-the-hero. That's what they're calling him around town, you know."

Sharon wrinkled her nose. "You're kidding. That's so corny."

"Have you *heard* some of the stories going around about what happened Friday night? Mildred Scott told me you drowned and Cordero brought you back to life with CPR. Clark Foster said you were trapped in the car and Cordero had to break a window to pull you out, nearly drowning himself. And then there's the version Gloria Capps is spreading—that you cut yourself on broken glass and almost bled to death before Cordero saved you by using his necktie as a tourniquet."

"That's ridiculous. He wasn't even wearing a necktie." She shook her head. "It's *all* ridiculous. I was already out of the car when Mr. Cordero jumped in to help me. I'm sure I could have made it out of the river on my own."

She didn't want to sound ungrateful for Mac's help, but she didn't like hearing she'd been cast as the hapless victim in so many improbable scenarios. She'd been taking care of herself—and the rest of her family—for a long time. It wasn't easy to let anyone else take charge, even briefly.

"Of course you would have made it out on your own."

Sharon didn't know whether Jerry's attitude was due more to his faith in her or his jealousy that Mac Cordero had become such a romanticized figure in Honoria. Jerry had lived in this town all his life.

He'd taken over his father's insurance office a few years ago, but an insurance salesman was rarely regarded as dashing or heroic, terms that had been applied to Cordero in the numerous retellings of Sharon's accident.

She'd been dating Jerry casually for three or four months. They shared several common interests and had passed many pleasant evenings together. She'd been aware from the start that their relationship owed more to circumstance than chemistry—there weren't many singles their age in Honoria—but she wasn't looking for romance, only occasional companionship, which Jerry provided without making too many demands in return.

"I really don't understand all this fuss over the guy," he muttered, slicing irritably into his steak. "He's a contractor, for Pete's sake. Not even a particularly shrewd one, if he thinks he's going to make a profit on the Garrett place."

"I've heard he specializes in restoring old houses. He must know from experience whether or not the Garrett house is worth renovating."

Jerry shook his head stubbornly. "That eyesore is going to require a small fortune just to make it livable again. It should have been condemned years ago. The location's not bad, even if it isn't close to the golf course, like all the best new homes. Tear it down and start from scratch, that's what I would do. Maybe even subdivide—it sits on a three-acre lot. That's enough land to put in quite a few houses and more than pay for the initial investment."

Just what Honoria needed, Sharon thought. Another tacky subdivision filled with cheaply built, cookie-cutter houses on undersize lots. "Some people love the old, the historic," she murmured. "The Garrett place was practically a mansion when it was built in the early part of the twentieth century. It must have been beautiful."

"Maybe it was then, but now it's just old." Jerry shook his head in bafflement. "I've never understood what people see in beat-up antiques when they can have shiny new things, instead."

She wasn't surprised by Jerry's attitude. He had a taste for flash. He traded cars nearly every year when the new models debuted, and was always upgrading his computers and electronic equipment. The past held little appeal for him—his eyes were firmly fixed on the future. She saw no need to remind him that she had a soft spot for antiques. It was something he just couldn't understand.

Jerry's thoughts were still focused on Mac Cordero. "The guy's just a contractor. I don't know why so many people around town want to make him into something else. The rumors about him are absurd. Why can't they just accept that he's exactly what he says he is?"

The mildest speculation cast Cordero as an eccentric multimillionaire who fixed up old houses for his own hideaways. Some whispered that he was an agent for a Hollywood superstar who wanted a place to escape the press occasionally. The most incredible story she'd heard suggested he was working for an organized-crime family preparing the Garrett house for a mobster who needed to get out of New York City.

"You know how rumors get started around here," Sharon reminded Jerry. "Because Mr. Cordero chooses not to share information about his personal life, people entertain themselves by filling in the blanks with colorful details."

"So what do *you* know about him?" Jerry's question proved he wasn't as averse to gossip as he pretended—something Sharon already knew, of course.

"I don't know anything more than you do. I didn't exactly have a lot of time for personal chit-chat when I met him. All I can tell you is he seemed very…capable," she said for lack of a better description.

As much as she hated to admit it, even to herself, she had been in trouble Friday night. Yes, she'd managed to get out of her sunken car on her own, but she'd been shaken and disoriented. She probably would have gotten to the shore on her own—at least, she hoped so—only to find herself stranded on a rarely traveled country road without a car or a phone. As frightened as she had been, there had been something about Mac Cordero that had reassured her. Maybe it was the strength of the rock-hard arms that had supported her until she'd caught her breath. Or the steady way he'd held her gaze when he'd assured her that help was on the way. Or maybe it had been the way her hand had felt cradled so securely in his.

It embarrassed her now to remember the desperation with which she had clung to the stranger who'd pulled her from the water. At the time, she'd simply been grateful to have someone to hold on to.

"Would you mind if we talk about something else now?" she asked, uncomfortable with the feelings those memories evoked. "It seems that all I've talked about for the past two days is the accident."

"Of course. So, what about your car? Have they pulled it out yet? Were you able to salvage anything?"

This time she didn't bother to hold back her sigh. There appeared to be nothing she could do to distract Jerry. Pushing her unsettling thoughts of Mac Cordero to the back of her mind, she concentrated on her dinner, answering Jerry's questions with as little detail as possible.

She could only hope something would happen soon to get the town talking about something else.

"I'VE INTERVIEWED everyone I could think of who might've seen something suspicious around the Porter place, Wade. We've put the word out all over town that we're looking for the light-colored panel van that was seen leaving the scene of the crime. We're getting nothing. Apparently, the only two people who saw the vehicle were Sharon Henderson and that Cordero guy."

Chief Wade Davenport raised his gaze from the accident reports scattered in front of him to the skinny, dejected-looking deputy on the other side of the battered oak desk. "Keep asking, Gilbert. Someone had to see something."

Ever the pessimist, Gilbert Dodson gave a gloomy sigh. "I'll keep asking, Wade, but I've talked to everyone but the chickens now."

Wade leaned back in his creaky chair and steepled his fingers in front of him. "Then maybe you should start interviewing chickens."

Shoulders slumping, Gilbert nodded and turned toward the door. "I'll get right on that, Chief."

Wade muttered a curse as his office door clicked shut. He tended to take it personally when anyone broke the law in his town. There'd been a rash of break-ins about a month ago, and the culprits had never been caught. Now there'd been another—the Porter place. They'd been quietly and efficiently cleaned out by whoever had been in the same van that had almost killed Sharon Henderson.

The break-ins were connected. Wade was sure of it, even though he had no evidence to support his hunch. There wasn't that much crime in Honoria, and there hadn't been any breaking and entering going on in almost five years. Not since the O'Brien kid and his buddies had thought it would be "fun" to start their own crime ring. Kevin O'Brien was twenty-three years old now and had done his time. The first thing Wade did when the current burglaries began was to check on Kevin's whereabouts. As far as he could tell, there was no connection this time.

Which meant he had another thief operating in his

town, victimizing and endangering his friends and neighbors. And that made Wade mad.

Narrowing his eyes, he picked up the report that had been filed by Mac Cordero, the "mysterious stranger" everyone had been gossiping about. It was interesting that the previous burglaries had taken place while Cordero was in town a few weeks back buying the old Garrett place. Now there'd been another one, only days after Cordero returned to begin the renovation project. Cordero "just happened" to be driving down that back road at the same time the Porter place was being cleaned out. Maybe there was no connection there, but Wade didn't like coincidences.

Wade's wife and kids lived in this town. It was his job to keep them—and the other residents—safe. He turned his attention to Cordero's statement again, looking for anything that resembled a clue.

CHAPTER TWO

It DIDN'T TAKE LONG for Mac to learn a few things about the woman he'd pulled from Snake Creek. Even though he didn't mingle much with the townspeople, every busybody he encountered in Honoria during the next few days—and there seemed to be many of them—was anxious to tell him all about her. He found some of the information interesting, but two comments, in particular, caught his attention.

Sharon Henderson was an interior decorator *and* a good friend of the McBride family.

The motel where he was staying was not so coincidentally located within full view of the McBride Law Firm. From the window of his room, Mac could see the firm's parking lot. He'd heard that the founder, Caleb McBride, a lifelong resident of Honoria now in his early sixties, had very recently left for a month-long Caribbean cruise with his wife, Bobbie. Their older son, Trevor, was running the law office single-handedly until Caleb's return.

Mac had watched a steady stream of clients and visitors entering and exiting the office building during the last five days he'd spent in Honoria. Some he could already identify, such as Trevor's striking, red-haired wife and two young children, and Trevor's younger brother, Trent, whom Mac had met a month ago in that same parking lot.

Late Monday afternoon, Sharon Henderson arrived at the firm.

Watching from his window, Mac recognized her immediately, though he wasn't sure how. The attractive, well-dressed woman who slid out of a nondescript sedan bore little resemblance to the wet, shivering waif he'd encountered Friday night. Her hair fell in a gleaming brown sweep to just above her shoulders and she carried herself with poised self-confidence. As she disappeared inside the law office, he told himself he could be mistaken. There was no way he could know for sure the visitor was Sharon. Even if he'd gotten a closer look at her that night, he was too far away to see her clearly now.

Drinking coffee from the coffeemaker provided in the room, he was still sitting in the uncomfortable chair watching the other building when the woman emerged again. Though he'd spent the past hour trying to convince himself he couldn't possibly have identified her, the sense of recognition hit him again the moment she walked out into the parking lot. He didn't know how he knew, but he was convinced Sharon Henderson had just dropped in on Trevor McBride.

Interesting. He'd heard she was a friend and her visit proved there was a professional relationship, as well. He wondered just how much she knew about the McBride family history...and if she shared the rest of the town's passion for idle gossip.

Maybe it was time for him to pay a call on her. He'd been thinking about doing that, anyway, for professional reasons. Now that he knew her connection to the McBrides, he had more personal motives for wanting to get better acquainted with Sharon Henderson.

"C'MON, SHARON, why can't I go? All the other guys will be there."

Sharon grimaced as her fifteen-year-old brother's voice edged perilously close to a whine. She tightened her grip on the telephone receiver, trying to get a firmer hold on her patience at the same time. "Brad, you are not going to an unchaperoned party. I know Mike Riordan's parents are out of town this week, and I don't at all approve of them allowing him to have a party at their house while they're away. As far as I'm concerned, that's just asking for trouble."

"But Mike's brother Joe is going to be there to keep an eye on things. He's a college man."

Sharon wasn't impressed. "He just finished his first year of college. That makes him barely nineteen years old. I'm sorry, but that isn't my idea of a suitable chaperon for a houseful of teenagers. The answer is no. We can go out to eat or to a movie, if you like. Or you can invite a couple of your friends over to eat pizza and play video games."

"All my friends are going to the party. No one's going to want to miss it to hang out with me."

Refusing to be swayed by his plaintive tone, Sharon responded firmly. "I doubt that everyone will be at the party. I'm sure I won't be the only adult who'll think this is a bad idea."

"Just let me go for a little while, okay? If it gets too wild, I'll call you to come get me."

"You aren't going to a party that isn't adequately supervised, and there's no use discussing it any further."

"Fine. Great. Ruin my life."

She sighed. "I'm not trying to ruin your life. I'm trying to be a responsible guardian."

"Mom would let me go if she was here."

The operative word, Sharon thought wearily, was *responsible*—something their dear, ditzy mother had never been. "Well, Mom's not here. While she's away, I'm in charge. You're just going to have to accept that."

Sullen silence was his only response.

"Be thinking about what you want for dinner tonight, okay?" she suggested, her tone conciliatory. "We can go to that new Mexican place you like so much. You'd enjoy that, wouldn't you?"

"Might as well sit at home and watch TV," he muttered.

"If that's your choice," she agreed evenly. "I have to get back to work now. I'll see you this afternoon."

He hung up without responding.

Sharon rubbed her forehead as she hung up the phone. It was Tuesday afternoon, a slow day in her home-decor shop, and for once she was grateful for the lull. Her full-time assistant was at a doctor's appointment, and Sharon was alone. Between her confrontations with her rebellious kid brother and the almost incessant calls from acquaintances still wanting to talk about the incident Friday night, she was ready for some time to herself.

With her back to the door of the shop, she slid the phone into its place beneath the counter, then turned to the paperwork she'd been looking over when Brad called. Her elbow bumped a thick wallpaper-sample book, which crashed to the floor at her feet. Muttering a mild curse, she knelt to pick it up, tucking it into the crook of one arm. What else could go wrong today?

She gasped when a man's hand suddenly appeared in front of her, offering to assist her to her feet. She hadn't heard anyone enter the shop, so it caught her completely off guard to realize she wasn't alone. She looked up and swallowed hard when her gaze was captured and held by a pair of eyes as dark and unrevealing as polished onyx.

Sharon had never considered herself a fanciful person, but the image that came immediately to mind was that of a sleek, dangerous black cat. This intriguing man was as out of place in her little shop as he was…well, in this small, sleepy town.

No wonder everyone in Honoria had been speculating about him.

Almost involuntarily, she placed her hand in his. There was an instant shock of familiarity when his fingers closed around hers, bringing back memories of how safe she had felt when he'd pulled her out of Snake Creek.

He helped her to her feet. Her voice was a bit breathless when she said, "Thank you, Mr. Cordero."

His left eyebrow rose half an inch. His voice was a deep growl that befitted the exotic animal she had envisioned when she saw him—the same voice that had echoed in the back of her mind since the accident Friday night. "I wasn't sure you would remember me."

Her smile felt wry. "I'm not likely to forget our meeting anytime soon."

His answering smile was just a slight shift at the corners of his mouth—and only added to his attractiveness, in Sharon's opinion. She hadn't gotten a really good look at him in the shadowy darkness Friday night, but now she could understand why so many women in town had been whispering about him. It wasn't often they saw a man like this.

"Six feet of sex," Leslie Anne Cantrell, the town flirt, had called him, eliciting delighted giggles from the women who'd overheard. Sharon could honestly say now that Leslie Anne hadn't been exaggerating. Any normal woman would appreciate Mac Cordero's thick black hair, gleaming dark eyes, taut brown skin and sleekly muscular build.

He wasn't a man any woman was likely to forget, she mused, no matter how they met.

Realizing abruptly that she was standing there gazing up at him, her fingers still clasped in his, she pulled her hand away and stuck it in the pocket of the navy linen blazer she wore with a muted plaid shirt and khaki slacks. Though the expression in his eyes was impossible to read, she had the unnerving sensation that he could see directly into her mind as he searched her face. "You've suffered no ill effects from your ordeal?"

"No, I'm fine. A few colorful bruises and sore muscles, but no real injuries, thank goodness."

"You were fortunate."

She nodded. "Yes, I know."

"Any word about the van that ran you off the road?"

"No. Wade—the police chief—said it seems to have disappeared. But if it's still in the area, he'll find it."

"You seem confident about that."

She couldn't help smiling. "Wade takes his job very seriously. When someone breaks the law, he doesn't rest until he catches them."

"Then I hope he catches them soon." For the first time since he'd helped her to her feet, he looked away from her face long enough to glance around her shop, Intriguing Interiors. The store was filled with rows of wallpapers and borders, shelves of order books, swatches of designer fabrics, and displays of decorator and gift items. "Nice place."

"Thank you. I bought it almost two years ago."

What might have been amusement glimmered for a moment in his eyes. "I know."

She studied him curiously. "You do?"

His mouth quirked again into that sexy semismile, making her pulse race in a manner that both distracted and annoyed her. She made an effort to focus on their conversation rather than the effect he had on her—something she would think about and rationalize later, she promised herself.

"Ever since I helped you out of that water, everyone in this town has wanted to talk to me about the accident—and you," he said ruefully.

She waved a hand toward the door. "That's my town. The rumor capital of the world. So what did they tell you about me?"

"That you're a very talented decorator. Which is one of the reasons I stopped by."

He had surprised her again. "You need a decorator?"

"Yes. I've purchased an old Victorian house at the end of Deer Run Lane—"

"The Garrett place," she acknowledged with a nod. "People have been talking about you, too."

The slight twist of his mouth this time might have been a smile or maybe a grimace, but either way, it was as sexy as all get-out. Feeling uncomfortably schoolgirlish, Sharon almost sighed.

"Anyway," he continued, "I'm completely renovating the place. I need a decorator. I'd like to keep the decor appropriate to the period of the architecture—Victorian, but not overdone. I'll want to start consultations soon so there will be plenty of time to order wallpaper, light fixtures and any other decorating items I'll need. Are you interested in the job?''

Though she loved the idea of decorating a restored historic home, Sharon felt compelled to be honest. ''I'm not really a trained decorator, Mr. Cordero.''

''Call me Mac. I understand you've decorated quite a few homes and offices around town. Trent McBride, who's doing the cabinetwork for my renovation project, recommended you. He said you're redecorating his father and brother's law offices.''

She wondered if she could ever be comfortable using his first name. She found herself rather intimidated by this man, for some reason. It was hard to imagine having a casual relationship with him.

''I do some interior decorating as a sideline for my shop,'' she admitted. ''It's always been an interest of mine, and I've taken a few decorating classes. I started out helping friends, and then other people began to request my services. But if you want a more experienced, better-known professional decorator, you'll have to bring someone in from Atlanta.''

He shook his head. ''I prefer to patronize local businesses.''

She knew he had hired local carpenters, plumbers, electricians and other subcontractors for the renovation project. She knew, as well, that he hadn't demanded a lengthy list of credentials from everyone he'd hired. Trent McBride, for example, had only just gone into business as a cabinetmaker.

"I would certainly be interested in discussing this with you," she said, intrigued by the challenge of such a project, even as she hoped she was up to it.

He leaned a forearm against the sales counter. The casual pose brought him a bit closer to her, just enough to make her self-conscious again. His smile was slightly deeper this time, giving her a glimpse of white teeth. The job he offered was looking better and better, she thought, letting herself drift for just a moment in sheer feminine appreciation.

"Maybe we could talk about it over dinner tonight?" he suggested. "The restaurant on West Charles isn't bad."

She was on the verge of accepting—just to discuss the project, of course—when she remembered her brother. There were times when she'd left him home by himself for a couple of hours, but she didn't think it was a good idea tonight. She wouldn't put it past him to sneak out and go to the party anyway—and she wasn't going to give him that opportunity. The boy throwing the party was a notorious troublemaker, and Brad was too easily led into mischief. There had already been one occasion when he'd been escorted home by Officer Dodson; she didn't intend for it to happen again tonight.

"I'm afraid I can't tonight," she said.

If Mac was disappointed, he didn't show it. "When would be a good time for you to meet?"

"I can spare a couple of hours tomorrow afternoon, if you're free then."

He straightened away from the counter. "I'll be out at the site tomorrow meeting with subcontractors. If you want to join me there, we can do a walkthrough. It will give you a chance to look the place over, too."

Definitely intrigued—and more comfortable with the thought of discussing the job at the site rather than over dinner—she nodded. "What time?"

"Two o'clock?"

"I'll be there."

He was already moving toward the door. "Until tomorrow then."

"Mr. Cordero—"

"Mac," he reminded her over his shoulder.

"I want to thank you again for helping me Friday night."

He gave her a sudden, full smile that nearly melted the soles of her shoes. He didn't smile often, apparently, but when he did—*wow*. "Not necessary. See you tomorrow, Sharon."

She hadn't given him permission to use her first name, but it would be churlish to remind him of that now. She wasn't usually one to insist on formality— but with this man, a little distance might not be such a bad idea.

He was just reaching for the doorknob when the door opened and a plump blonde bustled in, nearly crashing into Mac. "Oh, sorry," she said, catching herself just in time.

His smile fading into a more somber expression, he nodded politely. "No problem." And then he let himself out, leaving the two women staring bemusedly after him.

"Who," Tressie Bearden demanded, "was *that?*"

Dragging her gaze away from the glass door, through which she could see him walking purposefully away, Sharon cleared her throat and turned to her employee. "That was Mac Cordero."

Tressie's eyes widened. "Cordero-the-hero? Oh, man, he's even better-looking than I've heard."

Sharon frowned. "I wish you wouldn't call him that. It's such a silly nickname."

"Hey, you were the damsel in distress he rescued," Tressie replied with an impish grin. "I would think you'd consider the nickname appropriate."

Though she was tempted to argue again that Mac had only assisted her, Sharon resisted the impulse. "How did your doctor's appointment go? Everything check out okay?"

Glancing again toward the door, Tressie answered absently. "She said I'm a healthy, red-blooded woman in my prime. So I guess it must have been Mac Cordero's gorgeous dark eyes and delectable bod that made my heart rate go crazy, hmm?"

Since Sharon had been experiencing similar symptoms during the past twenty minutes or so, she couldn't argue with Tressie's conclusion. Apparently, they were *both* healthy, red-blooded women.

Now that they'd settled that, it was time to put adolescent foolishness aside and get back to work. "About those wall sconces you ordered..."

Tressie waved a hand impatiently. "We can talk sconces later. What was Mac Cordero doing here? What did he say? What did *you* say? Did you find out anything interesting about him?"

Tressie was an active participant in local gossip circles and her membership in the Honoria Community League gave her an inside track to the most juicy tidbits. Her gift of gab and easy way with people made her an asset to the shop, but Sharon sometimes found her co-worker's chatter exasperating. If she told Tressie that Mac had offered her the decorating job, the news would be all over town within the hour, and Sharon hadn't even given him an answer yet. She settled for half the truth. "He said he wanted to make sure I'd recovered from the incident Friday night."

"Really? That was nice of him."

"Yes, it was."

Tressie's expression turned speculative. "Do you know if he's married or anything?"

"No, I don't know. The subject didn't come up." For some reason, Sharon would have bet he was unattached. Educated guess—or wishful thinking? she wondered with a slight wince.

Looking disgusted, Tressie shook her head. "I'd have made sure it came up. Why didn't you ask him?"

"Because it's none of my business." Sharon

could only hope the hint got through as she moved across the shop to straighten a display of clearance items. "So why don't you call and check on those sconces? They should have arrived two days ago."

Tressie hesitated a moment, reluctant to drop the subject, but then she nodded and moved toward the telephone. As much as she loved to gossip, she was efficient and hardworking, and Sharon was still grateful that Tressie had come to work for her.

Feeling a little guilty for not telling Tressie about the decorating offer, Sharon went back to work, herself, her thoughts divided between details of her business, worry about her brother and anticipation of her next meeting with Mac Cordero.

THE MAN in the gutted-out kitchen with Mac was young—no more than twenty-six—golden-blond, blue-eyed with glasses and a little on the thin side. Picturing his own solid build, black hair, dark eyes and brown skin, Mac was well aware that he and Trent McBride could not have looked more different. No one could have guessed from looking at them that they shared a blood relationship—and no one but Mac knew about that relationship. Even he didn't know exactly how close the connection was.

"So you want a state-of-the-art modern kitchen concealed behind solidly built, period-appropriate woodwork," Trent summed up with a comprehensive glance around the large, shadowy room. The electricity wasn't turned on yet, so the only light came through the filthy windows and from the two battery-powered lanterns Mac had brought with him.

The house had been empty for years, and the deterioration was pervasive—so much that there were some who openly doubted the renovation was worth the time and expense. With his experience, Mac knew better. He'd taken on more daunting projects, and the results had been both satisfying and profitable. There were plenty of people who were willing to pay for history and quality. Of course, Mac's previous jobs had been in areas with a bigger money base and more historical interest—Atlanta, Savannah, Charleston, Birmingham. It might take a bit longer to find a buyer here. But he wasn't too worried about it. He'd come to Honoria for reasons that were far more personal than professional.

Even if it cost him every dime he'd managed to accumulate in the past few years, he would consider it money well spent if he finally got some answers to the questions that had haunted him all his life.

Because Trent was still waiting for a response, Mac nodded. "I want every modern convenience, but I don't want it to look like a restaurant kitchen. We'll use appliance garages and custom cabinetry to camouflage the equipment."

Trent seemed to approve. Mac could tell the younger man was picturing the end result as he looked around the cavernous room with its big windows and massive stone fireplace at one end. "It's going to be expensive."

Mac shrugged. "Quality costs. Of course, I'll be

keeping a close eye on expenses, making sure I'm paying fair prices and spending no more than necessary.''

Trent didn't seem concerned about the prospect of close supervision. ''I'll work up a detailed cost analysis for you,'' he offered. ''If anything unexpected comes up, we'll discuss then how to handle it.''

''That's the way I prefer to do business. I'm not crazy about surprises.''

Trent smiled a little at that. ''I could have guessed that from the few meetings we've had.''

Mac wondered how *Trent* felt about surprises. He could give him a whopper of one right now, if he wanted. But he would wait until the time was right—until he had his answers—before he decided how, or whether, to break his news to the McBrides.

A woman's voice came from somewhere in the front of the house. ''Mr. Cordero?''

Mac swiveled toward the sound, then wondered why his pulse had suddenly quickened in response to Sharon Henderson's voice. A decorator, he reminded himself. That was all she was to him. All he intended for her to be. And this was his chance to find out just how friendly she was with the McBride family.

CHAPTER THREE

MAC FOUND SHARON waiting just inside the front door, which he had left open. In marked contrast to the dull, colorless surroundings of the run-down entryway, she looked fresh and pretty, dressed in clean, bright colors. She was studying the broken, curved staircase, her expression thoughtful. "I've never been in here before," she said when he joined her. "I didn't know what to expect."

He found it annoyingly necessary to remind himself that he was only interested in her because of her interior-decorating skills and her friendship with the McBrides—not because she was the first woman he'd been attracted to in months. Dragging his gaze away from her, he glanced around the entryway. "Most of the damage is cosmetic. This place was built to last, and it has, despite the neglect."

"It's really worth saving?"

He rested a hand on an intricately turned newel post. "I wouldn't be here if I didn't think it was."

Wearing the same contemplative look he'd just seen on Trent, she glanced slowly around the big entryway and then through an arched doorway into a room that had probably served as a front parlor. "It must have been beautiful once."

"And it will be again. Let me show you around downstairs. I'd rather save the upstairs until the staircase and upper floors have been reinforced."

She glanced up the stairs, as if she was reluctant to miss anything in the tour he'd promised. But then she turned away from the staircase to follow him along the lower floor.

He led her through the parlor, the single downstairs bedroom, what might have once been a sitting room or music room, and a long, narrow dining room. Without lights, the rooms looked even more shabby and ramshackle than they actually were. The sunlight that managed to penetrate the dirty windows turned gray and dusty inside. But Mac saw the still-intact crown moldings, the repairable plasterwork, the solid-wood paneling and hardwood flooring, and he knew the house could be spectacular again. He wondered if Sharon shared his vision.

She murmured something he didn't quite catch. "I beg your pardon?"

Looking at him with an air of distraction, she motioned to the long, fanlight-topped window at the end of the dining room. "Beveled leaded glass," she said. "And look at the detail of that crown molding. You don't see work like that anymore."

Her comments pleased him, as did the expression on her face. Oh, yeah, she was seeing what could be, rather than what was. Just as he did when he looked at this place.

She stepped closer to the window to examine the

framing. "The woodwork is in good shape all through the house? No dry rot? Termite damage?"

"Some, but minimal. There are a few places where we'll have to do some reproduction work, but not many."

She moved close to a wall to peer at the darkened wallpaper that had once been a bright sunflower design, more indicative of the 1970s than the early 1900s. "I bet there are at least a half-dozen layers of wallpaper on these walls. Homeowners often used to paper right on top of existing patterns. If that's the case, I should be able to re-create original decor by studying the earliest layers."

"I counted six layers in the master bedroom. Five in the kitchen." He'd dug through all that in his initial examination of the house's condition.

"Were the early patterns distinguishable?"

"In places, yes. You'll probably want to see it, though I'm not interested in an exact reproduction of the original decor. Just a look that's appropriate for the period."

"The townspeople have always referred to this place as a Victorian mansion, but it isn't strictly Victorian, is it? More a combination of Queen Anne, Italianate, and even a little Early American craftsman influence. Sort of a hodgepodge, but it works. It must have been spectacular."

Despite her disclaimers that she wasn't a professional decorator, he was satisfied with the observations she'd made thus far. He had seen examples of her work, having learned that she'd decorated several of the businesses he'd visited in town, and he knew she had a flair for color and proportion. Now he was even more confident that he hadn't made a mistake approaching her about this project.

Her friendship with the McBrides might be useful to him later, but it was her decorating expertise that interested him at the moment. At least, that was what he told himself, though he was all too keenly aware of how nice she looked in her pale blue spring-weight sweater and fluidly tailored gray slacks that emphasized the slender waist his hands had spanned so easily.

He reminded himself again that he didn't have time for that sort of distraction now. He might notice her blue-green eyes and sweetly curved mouth, the shallow dimple in her left cheek, the graceful line of her throat or the feminine curve of her breasts beneath the soft knit sweater she wore, but that was as far as he intended to take it. He had a job to do—and the Garrett place was only a part of it.

Though his voice was casual, he was watching Sharon closely when he led her into the next room. "This," he said, "is the kitchen."

The smile that lit her face when she saw who was waiting there was full, warm and beautiful. Mac couldn't help wondering how it would feel to be on the receiving end of a smile like that from her. "Trent," she said, and even her voice was warmer now. "What a nice surprise."

Though Mac had summed Trent up as a somber, even brooding, type, the smile he gave Sharon held a natural charm with a hint of mischief. Having heard through the local rumor mills that Trent had been involved in a near-fatal plane crash that had left him with both physical and emotional scars, Mac suspected he was seeing an echo of the cocky young ladies' man Trent was reported to have been before the crash.

"Hi, Sharon. It's good to see you again." Trent kissed her cheek with the ease of long acquaintance.

Mac found himself frowning as he watched Trent's casual touch against Sharon's smooth cheek. He cleared his expression immediately, forcing himself to study the pair objectively.

"It's good to see you, too," Sharon said. "You look great."

"So do you. I was glad to hear you weren't seriously injured Friday night."

"Only a few bruises. I was lucky. So how are the wedding plans coming along?"

A glow of satisfaction warmed Trent's usually cool blue eyes. "Everything's on schedule. Annie and I will be married the last Saturday in August."

"I know your mother is looking forward to having another wedding in the family."

Trent grimaced. "Oh, yeah. She loves a big fuss—any excuse to get the family all together."

Mac stuck his hands in his pockets.

Sharon and Trent exchanged a few more pleasantries and then the conversation turned to the project at hand. "What do you think of the house?" Trent asked.

"I have to confess, I've always wanted to come inside and look around this place." Sharon made a slow circle to study the kitchen, her attention lingering on the huge fireplace. "It's something, isn't it?"

"It definitely has potential. You're doing the decorating?"

"Mr. Cordero and I are discussing that possibility."

It was beginning to irk Mac that she continued to call him Mr. Cordero in that prim, rather prissy way. It couldn't be more opposite to the warm and informal manner in which she spoke to Trent. "Mac," he reminded her, deciding it was time for him to do a little fishing. "I take it you two know each other?"

Trent chuckled. "You might say that. Sharon and I went to the prom together."

Sharon's smile turned a few watts brighter. "Trent was a senior, I was a junior. He had already been accepted into the Air Force Academy. I was so impressed, I spent the whole evening looking at him and giggling like an idiot."

"I don't remember it quite that way," Trent said gallantly.

Mac told himself he should be pleased to hear this. After all, her connection to the McBrides was one of the reasons he was interested in her. Right? And yet he still found himself changing the subject rather more abruptly than he had intended. "Yes, well, perhaps we should talk about the renovation project now."

He stepped smoothly between them and opened the briefcase he'd left on a rough-surfaced counter. "I have some blueprints and sketches here..."

Sharon and Trent moved closer on either side of him to study the paperwork in the yellow light of the battery-powered lanterns. It annoyed Mac that he had to make such an effort to concentrate on the job instead of Sharon's spicy-floral scent.

This wasn't working out exactly as he had planned.

FORTY-FIVE MINUTES LATER, Trent left, explaining that he had an appointment with his fiancée. Sharon was touched by the eagerness that glinted in his eyes as he left. For almost a year after his accident, Trent had barricaded himself in his solitary rural home, brooding and alone. He'd held his friends at a distance, seeing no one but family—and Annie Stewart, the housekeeper his mother had hired for him against his will. Now he and Annie were planning their wedding, and Trent was learning how to smile again.

Sharon was delighted for him.

Mac cleared his throat, drawing her gaze away from the back door through which Trent had disappeared. "Prom, hmm?"

She smiled. "Yes. I wore a flame-red satin slip dress and Trent wore a black tux with a red cummerbund and bow tie. I thought we looked sophisticated and glamorous—like movie stars. My mother still keeps our prom picture on the piano with all her other family pictures.''

When Mac didn't seem particularly amused by her reminiscing, she cleared her throat and turned the conversation back to business. ''At what point would you want me to become involved with the renovation?''

''You're considering taking the job?''

She practically itched to be a part of this project. ''Yes.''

''I'm glad to hear it.''

Something about his expression and the tone of his voice made her wonder why he seemed so pleased that she would be joining the renovation team he was assembling. He didn't really know her, and he had seen only a few examples of her work. Had the recommendations he'd heard really been so persuasive?

He had said it was his practice to patronize local businesses and workers whenever possible. Granted, there weren't many professional decorators in Honoria to choose from—none, actually. ''You're sure you don't want to consult a few other decorators first?'' she asked, a sudden attack of nerves making her wonder if she was being wise to get involved with this man. With this *job,* she corrected herself quickly.

He shook his head. ''I want you.''

She really wished he hadn't worded it quite that way. Something told her those three words would echo in her mind for a disturbingly long time. ''I would certainly understand if you want to at least consider—''

"Sharon—do you want the job or not?"

Clasping her hands in front of her, she glanced around the big, old kitchen. "Yes. I want it."

"And you believe you can do a good job?"

She could already picture the front parlor done in tastefully restrained Victoriana, old Oriental rugs on satiny, refinished hardwood floors, strategically placed mirrors making the small rooms look bigger. "Yes, I do."

"Then all we have left to discuss is the money," he said matter-of-factly. "I've written the decorating budget here—" he stabbed a finger on one of the sheets of paper scattered across the counter "—which includes your fee, itemized on the next line. Does that look like a fair estimate to you?"

She glanced at the figure, blinked a couple of times, then read it again. "Yes, that looks fair," she said, her voice a bit strained.

She couldn't help remembering all those wild rumors about Mac—that he was a rich eccentric, or on consignment for a celebrity millionaire, or working for a big-money crime family. As improbable as those scenarios had sounded, money didn't seem to be a problem when it came to this project. She would be compensated very generously for the sheer pleasure of helping this sadly deteriorating building become a beautiful home again.

"I'd like you to be closely involved with the project from the start," he said. "You've probably noticed I have my own way of doing things—it's not necessarily the way most contractors work, but it suits me. I assemble a team at the beginning and then involve everyone in the decision-making, utilizing their expertise in their areas. Final decisions, of course, are mine, but I'm always open to discussion and suggestions.''

"How long have you been doing this? Buying and restoring old houses, I mean.''

"Full time for almost three years now. Before that, I restored a couple of small houses as a sideline to my day job.''

"And what was your day job?''

She'd considered herself making conversation, not trying to pry, but she got the sudden feeling that Mac wasn't comfortable with her questions. "I've worked in several jobs prior to this one.''

"I see.'' She looked at her watch. "I really should get back to the shop. I have an appointment with a sales rep this afternoon.''

"I'll walk you to your car.''

She knew the layout of the house this time, so she led the way with Mac following close behind her. As she walked, she looked around again, making dozens of mental notes. She would like to return soon with a camera and sketch pad. She was so involved with her planning, she forgot to concentrate on her steps and she might have tripped over a broken board had Mac not reached out to take her arm before she reached it, guiding her around the plank.

"The floors are pretty rough,'' he said without

letting go of her. "It's even worse upstairs. Once the carpenters get started, I'm going to designate the whole house as a hard-hat zone."

"I should have been watching where I was going. I'm afraid I was too busy mentally decorating."

He chuckled. "As much as I appreciate your eagerness to get started, I wouldn't want you to injure yourself because of it."

"I'll be more careful from now on," she promised, trying to keep her tone light despite the ripples of sensation emanating from his hand on her arm.

"Good."

When he didn't immediately move away, her smile wavered. His face was only inches from hers. His dark eyes looked straight into hers. She'd never understood more clearly what it meant to be in danger of melting at someone's feet. When it came to her hormones, this man was downright dangerous.

She cleared her throat so she could speak without squeaking. "Is there something else?"

He hesitated a moment, then dropped his hand and stepped back. Without further comment, he motioned for her to continue through the house. She took care to watch her step as she walked out.

She unlocked the driver's door of the rental car her insurance company had provided until she could replace the one she'd lost in Snake Creek. Uncertain what to say, she turned hesitantly to Mac before getting in. "I'll start gathering some pictures and samples before our next meeting. I'd like to come back soon to take some measurements and photographs."

"The work crew starts tomorrow, so someone will be here pretty much all the time, Monday through Saturday. Come by anytime, but be careful around the construction."

"Thank you, I will. So, I guess I'll see you later."

"Mac," he said.

She lifted an eyebrow in confusion, wondering why he'd just said his own name. "I beg your pardon?"

"I'd like to hear you say, 'I'll see you later, Mac.'"

"Why?"

"Let's just say I like my team to be on comfortable terms with each other."

"I'm quite comfortable with you," she lied briskly.

Wearing a slightly challenging smile, he leaned against her open car door. "Then why can't you say my name, Sharon?"

He said hers easily enough. And something about the sound of it on his tongue made a funny little shiver go through her. Which was hardly a professional way to react to a business associate, she chided herself.

"I have no problem saying your name, Mac. But I am running late, so if there's nothing else, I'd better be on my way."

There was definite satisfaction in his smile when he straightened away from the door. "No, there's nothing else—for now. Drive carefully."

He didn't stay to watch her drive off, but turned

on one heel and walked back to the house. He didn't even glance over his shoulder before disappearing inside. Sharon was left staring after him. She roused herself with a slight shake of her head and reached for the key.

As she drove away, she vowed to herself that this was the last time she would allow him to turn her into a tongue-tied adolescent.

Any further exchanges between her and Mac Cordero were going to be strictly business—even though she was beginning to wonder if Mac had something else in mind.

BRAD WAS on his very best behavior Thursday evening during dinner, which pleased Sharon almost as much as it worried her. She loved her younger brother dearly, but any time he acted sweet and polite, she couldn't help wondering what he was up to.

"How are you enjoying your summer vacation, Brad?" Jerry Whitaker, who had joined them for dinner, asked encouragingly.

Looking up from the baked pork chops, rice and steamed vegetables Sharon had prepared, the boy tossed a fringe of shaggy brown bangs out of his face to look across the table. "It's okay. Better than school, anyway."

"What are you doing to keep yourself busy?"

"Baseball, mostly. Coach Cooper has practice every afternoon. And I go to the Boys and Girls Club a couple of mornings a week for tennis lessons."

Jerry smiled at Sharon. "Sounds like you've got quite an athlete in the family."

Absently returning the smile, she glanced at her brother. "Yes, Brad's very good at sports."

"What else do you have planned for summer, Brad? Hanging out at the pool with your friends? Flirting with the girls? I seem to have a vague memory of doing a lot of that back in the olden days when I was your age."

Because he knew it was expected of him, Brad chuckled in response to Jerry's exaggeration, but then his smile faded as he glanced at his sister. "Sharon doesn't let me hang out with my friends much. She's afraid I'll get into trouble."

Sharon's defenses went up when Jerry gave her a reproachful look. "That's not exactly accurate," she protested. "I certainly don't forbid Brad to see his friends. I simply ask him to let me know where he'll be and what time he'll be home."

"And I have to tell her who's going to be there, and what we'll be doing, and what we'll be eating, and—" Brad held up a finger for each point he made.

"That's enough," Sharon cut in, knowing her brother was still annoyed with her for keeping him from attending the party Monday evening.

She still felt justified in her decision, especially since she'd heard that Officer Dodson had been dispatched to send everyone home when the festivities had gotten too loud. She'd been surprised that he hadn't reported seeing signs of drinking among the underage guests. At least the kids had been smart enough not to try to get away with that—probably because they'd guessed that Chief Davenport would have someone keeping a close eye on them.

"Your brother is fifteen years old, Sharon," Jerry murmured. "You have to loosen the apron strings sometime."

Brad looked smug.

Sharon was annoyed with Jerry for undercutting her in front of Brad. Surely he knew she was doing the best she could while their flighty mother was off vacationing with a group of congenial widows she'd met over the Internet. It wasn't the first time Lucy Henderson had left Sharon in charge of the household—she'd been doing it since Sharon was a teenager, herself—but it was getting much more difficult as Brad grew older and more rebellious.

She picked up a bowl. "Have some more vegetables, Jerry."

Fully aware of the message she was really sending him, he chuckled, took the bowl and obligingly changed the subject. "What's this I hear about you working on the Garrett-house renovation?"

It had taken less than forty-eight hours for the news to get to him. Sharon wasn't sure why she hadn't already mentioned it, herself. Maybe because Jerry so rarely showed any real interest in her business, which he tended to refer to as "the little wallpaper shop." "I've been hired as the interior-design consultant. I'll help choose colors, patterns, fixtures and so on. Mac wants the house completely ready for occupancy when the renovation is completed."

"Mac?" Jerry murmured, lifting an eyebrow.

Funny how easily the name had slipped from her this time, proving that she'd already begun to think of him that way. "He doesn't care much for formality."

"I'm not sure I approve of this arrangement." Jerry seemed to be only half teasing. "Apparently he's quite the romantic figure around town. Handsome, mysterious, reportedly wealthy. *And* he's the guy who saved your life last weekend. I wouldn't want you to get swept off your feet."

Sharon forced a smile. "I'm only working for him, Jerry, not dating him."

"I'm glad to hear that. Why do you think he chose you as his decorator? Do you suppose his budget is more limited than rumors have implied?"

Aware of Brad listening to the conversation while he ate, Sharon tried to keep her tone humorous. "Are you calling me a cut-rate decorator, Jerry? Hardly flattering."

He didn't even have the grace to look sheepish. "Now, Sharon, you know I didn't mean it like that. But you must admit, you aren't a licensed decorator. Picking out colors and wallpaper patterns has been a hobby for you."

A hobby? She thought of the hours she'd spent reading, studying, poring over magazines, journals and sample books. She'd had several paid decorating jobs, including the recent remodeling of the First

Bank of Honoria and the upcoming McBride Law Firm project. Needlework was a hobby; decorating was a passion she'd had since adolescence. "He said I came highly recommended," she said simply, knowing it would be a waste of breath to argue semantics.

"I'm sure he won't be disappointed."

Had Jerry always had that slightly condescending tone when he talked about her work, or was she simply being oversensitive this evening? Whatever the cause, this conversation was beginning to annoy her as much as his criticism of the way she was watching out for her brother.

"I'll make sure he isn't," she said, and stood. "Who wants dessert? I baked a strawberry cake."

Brad and Jerry both eagerly accepted the offer.

As Sharon stood alone in the kitchen slicing cake, she found herself thinking that maybe she shouldn't see so much of Jerry for a while. She'd gotten into the habit of hanging out with him without really thinking about where the relationship was going. She hadn't liked the note of possession in his voice when he'd quizzed her about working for Mac. Was he under the impression that they had an exclusive relationship?

As far as she was concerned, she and Jerry were friends. They weren't lovers. Jerry had broached the possibility a time or two, but Sharon had always put him off. She wasn't ready to take that step, she'd told him. She didn't think it set a good example for Brad. Both were legitimate excuses, but the truth was, she simply hadn't wanted to become that intimately involved with Jerry. Something had always held her back.

Maybe it was because he'd never taken her breath away just by looking into her eyes, a small voice whispered inside her head. He had never caused a jolt of electricity to go through her with a simple brush of his hand. She had never actually reacted to any man's touch that way—until Mac.

The cake server slipped from her hand, clattering against the tile floor. The noise roused her from her disturbing thoughts, clearing away the image of Mac's gleaming dark eyes.

"Are you okay in there?" Jerry called out from the other room.

"I'm fine," she answered, her tone sharper than she had intended. She immediately regretted it. It wasn't Jerry she was angry with, it was herself. She was simply going to have to get herself under control when it came to Mac Cordero. And she was going to have to take charge of this situation with Jerry. It wasn't fair of her to lead him on.

Maybe it would be better if she simply concentrated on her brother and her business, at least for the next few weeks.

CHAPTER FOUR

MAC WAS in his motel room early Thursday evening when someone tapped on the door. He took another look at the photograph in his hand—a picture of a woman holding a tiny infant with Mac's dark hair and eyes—and then slipped it back into its usual place in his wallet before moving toward the door. He had to take a couple of deep breaths to release the pain and anger looking at that photo always roused in him. Only then could he answer the knock.

From long habit, he checked the peephole before releasing the lock. Curious, he opened the door and leaned against it, shoving his disturbing memories to the back of his mind. "Well, hello, Chief. Paying a social call?"

"Partially," Wade Davenport surprised him by answering. "Mind if I come in?"

Mac stepped out of the doorway and gestured toward the two chairs beside the window. "I would offer you a drink, but all I have is half a can of soda—and it's probably flat."

Glancing around the rather spartan motel room, Wade asked, "Are you going to be staying here long?"

Was the police chief just making friendly conversation, or keeping tabs on the stranger in town? Mac shrugged. "I've been looking for an apartment to rent for the duration of the renovation job. I talked to the manager of the complex on West Elm this afternoon. I'll probably move there next week."

Wade wandered to the window and glanced out. "Not much of a view. The McBride Law Firm's parking lot. The McBrides are related to my wife, you know. Caleb's her uncle, Trevor's her cousin."

"There usually are a lot of family connections in a small town like this one," Mac observed, following Wade's glance. He wondered if the police chief would be so cool if Mac told him about his own family connection to the chief's wife.

Turning away from the window, Wade sat in one of the chairs. Mac settled in the other. "What can I do for you, Chief?"

"Call me Wade. Seems more appropriate between colleagues, don't you think?"

"Colleagues?" Mac repeated carefully.

"One cop to another."

Long experienced at concealing his emotions, Mac kept his posture relaxed. "Cop to *ex*-cop is more accurate."

Wade nodded acknowledgment of the distinction.

"Any particular reason you've been checking up on me?"

"You've come to my town at the same time as what passes for a crime wave in these parts. Seemed appropriate."

"You always keep this close an eye on things around here?"

"That's why they pay me the big bucks."

Because Mac knew how little small-town police chiefs typically earned, he chuckled dryly. "Careful. Start talking about big bucks and I'll suspect you're on the take."

"Marvella Tucker slips me a dozen home-baked cookies about once a month. She's ninety years old, likes to drive her big old car right down the middle of Main Street. She thinks I won't ticket her if she keeps baking cookies for me."

"Is she right?"

Wade grinned and patted his stomach. "What do you think?"

"I think I need to figure out a way to get on Mrs. Tucker's cookie list."

"So what's a former vice cop doing remodeling an old house in this burg? How'd you choose the Garrett place?"

"Still checking up on me?"

"Making conversation," Wade corrected him. "I used to be with Atlanta P.D. Burned out, came to Honoria for the slower pace and better working hours. What brought you here?"

Mac lifted a shoulder. "Mine's a similar story. Got tired of working vice and decided I needed a change. Old houses have always interested me, so that's the direction I took. It's satisfying work."

"My wife and I live in a house her father built more than forty years ago. There's always something needing repairs, but I still prefer it to one of those new cut-and-paste houses. Emily says it has character.''

"Most old houses do," Mac agreed.

"You never told me how you found the Garrett place."

"I saw a photo in a real estate listing. It looked as if it had potential, so I came here to check it out. You know the rest." The answer was only partially true, but close enough not to bother Mac's conscience overly much.

"You've got the town all abuzz, you know. Nothing the folks around here like better than having someone new to talk about."

"So I gather."

"They're good people, for the most part. The gossip only occasionally turns vicious."

Mac thought Wade was being generous, considering how often the gossip had turned against his wife's family. It hadn't taken him long to figure out that the McBride name had been synonymous with scandal for several generations.

No one but Mac was aware that there was one scandal yet to be revealed. One in which he was intimately involved. One for which he deserved some sort of revenge—once he found out who to direct it toward.

"So what's the buzz on me?" Mac asked casually. "What made you think you needed to run a check?"

Wade shrugged. "What would you have done in

my position? The only stranger in town just happened in the vicinity of the very isolated Porter place when it was being robbed. No real reason for you to be out there. Last time you were in town, when you were buying the Garrett house, someone broke into Joe Baker's storage shed and took an RV and some other expensive sporting goods. I make it a practice to be skeptical of coincidences.''

Through narrowed eyes, Mac studied the other man warily, having trouble reading Wade's affable expression. He wasn't sure why the chief was telling him all this. If the guy really suspected he was involved, would he be quite so open about it? Was Wade saying Mac's law enforcement background cleared him of suspicion, or that circumstantial evidence still pointed his way? "I guess I'd have done the same in your position. But I'm not your thief.''

"That's what my hunch tells me.''

"How accurate do your hunches generally turn out to be?''

Wade grinned lazily. "Oh, about ninety percent.''

"Ten percent margin of error. Not bad. So, who's your hunch telling you to go after?''

His smile fading, Wade sighed. "Unfortunately, it isn't leading me anywhere. I literally haven't got a clue yet. Just a feeling that I've got four break-ins that are all related, and that there's something going on in my town I don't know about. And that pisses me off.''

"I'll keep my eyes open. Sometimes an outsider sees or hears something the locals miss.''

"Especially an outsider who worked vice for a number of years, I'd imagine. I'd appreciate your insight if something catches your attention."

Though he didn't really expect to be in a position to identify a local crime ring, Mac nodded.

Wade planted his hands on the arms of his chair and pushed himself to his feet. "We'll have to swap shop talk soon. Over lunch at Cora's Café, maybe. Tasted her pies yet?"

"No, not yet."

"Then you're in for a treat. She makes the best I've ever had—and I'm something of a connoisseur when it comes to desserts." With a last glance out the window toward the McBride Law Firm, he moved toward the door. "I'll see you around, Mac."

Still clueless as to the real purpose behind the chief's visit, Mac saw him out, then watched from the window as Wade drove away.

He had an itchy feeling that Wade Davenport wasn't an easy man to mislead.

"YOU SHOULD HAVE INVITED him to dinner," Emily McBride Davenport chided her husband later that evening when he mentioned his call on Mac Cordero.

Looking up from the block tower he was building with their almost-two-year-old daughter, Claire, Wade lifted his eyebrows in surprise. "Now, why would I do that? We don't even know the guy."

Watching from the couch where she'd been reading a book, Emily pushed her mop of golden curls out of her face to frown at him. "He's new to town, Wade. He's probably lonely."

"I'm not so sure about that. He seems like the self-contained sort. Probably prefers his solitude. You know he's turned down most of the invitations he's received from well-intentioned townsfolk."

"Most likely because he could tell most of them just want to pump him for personal information," Emily retorted.

He smiled as he guided the red block gripped in Claire's chubby hand to the top of the tower. "And isn't that what *you'd* like to do?"

Emily looked offended. "Of course not. I'm not interested in his personal business. I just think it would be neighborly to have him to dinner."

"I don't make a habit of bringing strangers home unless I know my family is safe with them."

Emily rolled her eyes, as she so often did when she felt Wade was being overprotective. "You like him, Wade. I could tell from the way you spoke of him."

He did sort of like him, actually—even if he wasn't quite sure he trusted him. Just because Mac Cordero had bravely jumped into a river to save Sharon Henderson's life, and just because Wade had learned that Mac was a former police officer from Savannah didn't mean the guy had no ulterior motive for being in Honoria.

He knew Mac had lied to him at least once that afternoon—when he'd said he'd come here after seeing a photograph of the Garrett house in a real estate ad. The Realtor had told Wade that Mac had approached her, asking what old homes were available in this area. He hadn't seen the house and then come here, as he'd claimed—it had actually been the other way around. So why the lie?

There was a reason Mac had come to Honoria— and Wade had a hunch he hadn't yet heard the whole story.

MAC DECIDED to have dinner at Cora's Café Friday evening. He'd been thinking about her pies ever since Wade had mentioned them the day before. Because it was a nice spring afternoon, still sunny and warm at six o'clock, he decided to walk the half mile from his motel to the café.

Honoria's downtown section had fallen victim to urban sprawl, leaving abandoned buildings and boarded-up storefronts behind. There had been some effort to revitalize the area, but the new development on the west side of town had taken a heavy toll in this neighborhood. Mac studied the shabby old stone storefronts and thought of the history and traditions that had been abandoned here and in so many other small towns.

A group of teenage boys wearing baggy clothes and fashionably surly expressions loitered on the sidewalk in front of a seedy-looking store-turned-arcade. Mac counted seven boys, none of them over seventeen, four holding cigarettes. Tough guys, he summed up swiftly—at least in front of their buddies. Wanna-be rednecks. Trouble waiting to happen. He'd seen boys this age and younger packing guns and pushing drugs on street corners in Savannah.

The boys completely filled the sidewalk, blocking Mac's path. He could step into the street to go around them, but there were a couple of cars coming and he wasn't in the mood to play dodge-the-Ford. "Excuse me," he said, focusing on the boy who looked least likely to be a jerk.

The boy started to move, but two of his pals closed around him, their expressions challenging. They were bored, Mac thought, and hungry for excitement—even the negative kind. If it were up to him, they'd all be put to work, flipping burgers, pushing brooms, picking up trash, if necessary.

Without speaking, the boys watched for his reaction to their defiance. One of them—the tallest and probably the oldest—took a drag from a cigarette and blew the smoke directly into Mac's face. Mac didn't react, his narrowed eyes still locked with those of the first boy he had approached. He kept his voice very soft. "Perhaps you didn't hear me. I said excuse me."

The boy swallowed visibly and shifted his weight backward.

"C'mon, Brad, you chicken," someone muttered. "We were here first. Make him go around."

Again, Mac kept his voice very quiet, an intimidating trick he had perfected during his years on the force. "Just step aside, and I'll be on my way."

"Don't let him push you around, Brad," one boy ordered.

"Shut up, Jimbo," Brad muttered, glancing up at Mac, who stared steadily back at him.

"Better not start anything you don't want to finish, boy," Mac advised, never taking his eyes off the teenager's tense face. The boy looked familiar, he couldn't help thinking. Something about his wide, blue-green eyes reminded Mac of Sharon Henderson.

His cheeks burning in resentment and embarrassment, Brad moved out of the way. Mac walked on at the same leisurely pace as before, not bothering to glance over his shoulder at the boys. He heard some of the other kids giving Brad a hard time for backing down, and another make an unflattering comment about Mac's Latino heritage, but he didn't react and they made no effort to purse further trouble with him.

They weren't quite as tough as they pretended to be. Which didn't mean they couldn't turn dangerous if someone didn't get them under control soon, he mused as he pushed open the door of Cora's Café. He was glad he wouldn't have to deal with them again.

AN OVERSIZE HARD HAT slipping to one side of her head, Sharon peered through the viewfinder of her camera Saturday afternoon. Ignoring the sound of hammering coming from the second floor above her, she framed a shot of the leaded-glass window in the dining room of the old Garrett house. She snapped the picture, then lowered the camera, wondering if she should try another angle.

From behind her, someone straightened her hat. A ripple of electricity ran through her, and she didn't have to hear his voice to know it was Mac. "This should fit tighter," he said.

She wasn't sure what he would see in her expression, so she fussed with her camera as an excuse to avoid turning around for a moment. "I found it sitting in a box in the entryway. It was the only hard hat I could find."

"Then I'll have to get you one of your own. This won't protect you much if something heavy were to fall."

Almost as if to illustrate his words, a crash came from upstairs, followed by what might have been a muffled curse. Sharon glanced up at the stained ceiling and smiled. "Point taken."

"How long have you been here?"

"About an hour. I've already taken photos of the kitchen and the parlor. I was just finishing up in here."

"What else do you need?"

"I was going to take a few pictures in the downstairs bedroom. I don't suppose I can go upstairs yet?"

He shook his head. "Not today. The crew's up there testing the floors and patching holes. I'm reasonably sure the structure is safe, but I don't want you wandering around up there until I'm sure."

"And when will that be?"

He shrugged. "They'll be finished later this afternoon. They haven't found any problems so far."

Although she understood his caution—after all, he was the owner of the house now and therefore liable in the case of accidents—she was still impatient to get upstairs and explore. "I'd be very careful."

His smile was pleasant but unyielding. "Next time."

"Has anyone ever mentioned that you can be awfully bossy?" she asked him a little too sweetly.

He chuckled. "Around here, I *am* the boss."

"I'll just finish up downstairs, then—boss." She turned to snap one more shot of the window, then moved toward the bedroom.

He fell into step beside her. "Getting any great ideas?"

"A few." Unfortunately, the only ideas that struck her as she entered the bedroom with Mac had nothing to do with decorating. Never mind that the room closely resembled a shadowy cave filled with dust and cobwebs. Or that one windowpane was broken, letting a warm breeze whistle through it. Or that there wasn't a stick of furniture. It was still obviously a bedroom, and she and Mac were alone in it.

What was it about this man that he could affect her just by looking at her in that smoldering manner? She hadn't blushed since high school, but she was dangerously close to it when he put a hand at the small of her back to guide her around a nail sticking up from a floorboard. The heat of his skin penetrated the thin, scoop-neck T-shirt she'd worn with jeans and sneakers for her exploratory visit here.

"The architect recommended taking out this fireplace and replacing it with doors leading out to a garden," Mac said. But even that strictly-business comment sounded oddly intimate because he had murmured it into her ear.

Grateful for an excuse to move away from him, she crossed over to the stone fireplace in question and made a pretense of studying it. "It would bring more light into the room, of course, and easier access to the outside. But I wouldn't do it."

"You'd keep the fireplace?"

She turned to look at the center of the room, picturing a big white-painted iron bed there, covered in eyelet and mounded with pillows. A rocking chair in one corner. Fresh flowers on an old chest. A fire burning in this wonderful stone fireplace. Two people cuddled in the bed—she refused to picture faces. "I would definitely keep the fireplace."

He nodded. "I had already decided to do that. I'll convert the small window in the west corner to a glass-paned door leading outside. That should provide enough natural light to brighten the room a little during the day, but I didn't want to sacrifice the fireplace."

"I'm glad. It's really lovely." She rested a hand on the heavy oak mantelpiece. "I've always wanted a fireplace in my bedroom," she mused almost to herself.

"The romantic type, are you?"

She dropped her hand and squared her shoulders. "Not particularly. I've always considered myself the practical type. A fire is a nice way to take away a chill on cold winter evenings."

"Mmm." He made it clear he didn't quite accept her self-description. "Will you have dinner with me this evening?"

She swallowed before asking, "Do you want to talk about my ideas for the decorating? I'm afraid I don't have much to discuss with you yet, since I just—"

"No," he cut in quietly. "This has nothing to do with business."

He was asking her for a date. She hadn't dated anyone but Jerry in months—primarily from lack of interest in going out with anyone else who had asked during that time.

She couldn't claim a lack of interest in Mac; the opposite was actually her problem. She was, perhaps, *too* interested in him. She supposed some people—her assistant, for example—would consider that an odd reason to hesitate about accepting his invitation. But Sharon had always considered herself a shrewd judge of people, and something told her Mac wasn't exactly what he seemed to be.

It wasn't that she was afraid of him, or even that she didn't trust him—but she was definitely wary of him. Should she follow through on her undeniable attraction to him, or listen to her instincts and avoid further complicating her life?

His left eyebrow lifted. "I didn't think it was that difficult a question."

"You aren't a member of a crime family, are you?"

"I beg your pardon?"

"According to local rumor, you're either an eccentric millionaire, a flunky for an eccentric movie star, or you're a member of an organized-crime family. The first two possibilities don't worry me overmuch, but I would definitely be concerned about the latter."

His chuckle was disarming. He didn't laugh often, and it was a pleasant sound. "I am not a crook," he assured her, the cliché making her smile. "I don't work for anyone except myself. As for the millionaire part—I'm afraid not."

Remembering Tressie's question, Sharon asked, "Are you married?"

"No. I'm single, straight and unattached. Are there any other juicy tidbits you want to quiz me about?"

"I probably haven't even heard all the talk," she confessed. "Those were just the stories that made it to my shop."

"Do you always take gossip so seriously?"

She had to smile at that. "Hardly."

"Is there anyone who would object to you having dinner with me?"

She thought of Jerry, but shook her head. "I'm not seeing anyone special, if that's what you're asking."

"So…?"

It was as good an evening as any to go out. Brad was going on an overnight campout with his baseball team, sponsored by the coach and several team dads. Having made an excuse to Jerry after her recent decision to spend less time with him, Sharon was free for the evening. She had planned to spend a little time to herself for a change perusing decorating journals and making preliminary notes for the renovation project. Instead, she heard herself saying, "All right. What time?"

His only reaction was a brisk nod—as if there had been no real doubt that she would accept, she couldn't help thinking. "Seven? I'll pick you up."

Sharon thought of the inevitable ramifications if she and Mac were seen sharing a cozy dinner-for-two in town. There would certainly be talk. Speculation. Questions. She wasn't accustomed to being the center of gossip. She'd always been the quiet and responsible type. Everyone knew her mother was a lovable flake, that her father had died of a heart attack thirteen years ago, and that her little brother tended to hang with the wrong crowd, but they had never attracted the sort of interest that the McBrides or some of the other longtime Honoria residents garnered.

"I could cook," she suggested, wondering whether her alternative was actually more or less reckless than dining in public. "You're probably tired of restaurant food by now," she added quickly, not wanting him to take it the wrong way. "Maybe you'd enjoy a home-cooked meal?"

"I would very much enjoy a home-cooked meal. Restaurant food gets a little tiring after a while." He seemed to take the question at face value. She hoped he wasn't reading more into the offer than she intended.

She nodded, hoping she wouldn't regret the impulsive invitation. She couldn't quite believe she had invited Mac Cordero into her home.

One thing she was certain of—this was the only bedroom in which they would be alone together that day.

CHAPTER FIVE

MAC FELT smug as he parked his car in Sharon's driveway Saturday evening. He would have been satisfied to buy her a meal in a crowded restaurant. Dining in her home, where they could talk privately and without interruption, was even better than he had hoped for.

He planned to make good use of the evening. He would just have to be careful not to raise her suspicion with the questions he intended to ask.

He wondered if she was a good cook. It had been months since he'd eaten a meal that hadn't been prepared in a restaurant kitchen. Although he had to admit the blue plate special at Cora's Café had been pretty darned close to home cooking—and Wade hadn't exaggerated the quality of her pies.

Sharon's house was a frame-and-brick ranch-style in a middle-class neighborhood. One of the cookie-cutter houses Mac usually disdained, but he assumed it had been chosen more for affordability than taste. Sharon opened the door almost the moment his finger touched the doorbell. Apparently, she had been waiting for him.

"I wasn't sure what you're serving," he said, holding out a bottle of wine. "I brought white."

She took it without meeting his eyes or touching his fingers. "Thank you. This is perfect. We're having Cornish hen. I hope you're hungry," she added brightly as she closed the door behind him. "I'm just putting finishing touches on dinner. It looks like it might rain later this evening, doesn't it? The weather guy said there's something like a seventy percent chance. Of course, we need the rain, but I hope it doesn't ruin my brother's camp-out with his friends. If you'd like to wash up before dinner, there's a—"

"Sharon." Mac couldn't help smiling. "Breathe."

She went still, then grimaced. "I was babbling, wasn't I? Sorry."

Her nervous chatter hadn't prevented him from noticing how nice she looked. She'd changed out of the clothes she'd worn earlier, and was now wearing a pastel yellow blouse and light khaki slacks. The pale colors accented her glossy brown hair and creamy-peach complexion. He considered telling her how pretty she looked, but he was afraid that would set her off again. Instead, he glanced around her living room, admiring the bold use of color and texture in her decorating. "Nice place."

"Thank you. Please, sit down. Can I get you anything to drink before dinner?"

He settled on the boxy, red-print sofa. "No, thank you."

"I'll just put the wine away and check on dinner. I'll be right back."

True to her word, she wasn't gone long. Mac was still sitting where she'd left him, studying the comfortable living room. "You decorated this room?" he asked to start the conversation.

Sharon perched on the very edge of a straight-backed armchair upholstered in red, gold and green stripes. "It's my mother's house, actually, but she had me do all the decorating. Mother's on vacation in Europe for the summer, and I'm staying here with my younger brother until she returns. After that, I plan to move into a place of my own—probably an apartment for a while."

"You said your brother's on a camping trip?"

"Yes. His baseball team is having a father-son camp-out. Our father died when my brother was just a baby, but they encouraged him to go, anyway. I always feel so sorry for poor Brad when things like this come up—it makes him so much more aware of not having a father, himself. It isn't easy on him."

No, it wasn't easy. Mac clearly remembered father-son camp-outs from his own youth. He'd never had a father to take him, either. He wondered if it had made Sharon's brother as angry and resentful as it had made him. And he wondered if Brad's mother and sister had overcompensated for that loss. Mac's own mother hadn't allowed him to wallow in self-pity—and he still appreciated her for that. "How old is your brother?"

"Fifteen." Seeing that he looked surprised by her answer, she added, "He's almost eleven years younger than I am. My parents had given up on having a second child, and were completely surprised when Brad came along.''

Brad. Remembering the teenager with that name on the street corner last night, Mac wondered if it could possibly be the same boy. If so, Sharon certainly had her hands full. The crowd that boy had been hanging out with looked like trouble with a capital T in Mac's opinion. ''Your brother doesn't mind having his older sister as a baby-sitter?''

Her grimace was expressive. ''We've had our differences, but we're getting along fairly well for the most part. It would be easier, of course, if he was in school, so I wouldn't have to worry about keeping him entertained during the day.''

''He doesn't have a summer job?''

''No. He's involved in several sports and he isn't old enough to drive yet, so it isn't really feasible for him to have a job now. I offered to let him work at my shop for the summer, stocking shelves, sweeping up and dusting, that sort of thing, but he was afraid he'd be bored. I don't want to ruin his summer.''

It was Mac's opinion that school should be held year-round, with break time built in throughout the year. Since few schools had adopted that schedule, he believed kids who'd reached the teen years should have jobs to keep them out of mischief and teach them a work ethic. After all, school terms had been built originally around farm life, when most of the students had worked in the fields during the summer months. They certainly hadn't sat around on their butts watching the tube, playing video games or hanging around on street corners looking for trouble with strangers. Mac, himself, had taken his first job when he was twelve.

It wasn't honest work that caused boredom, as Sharon and her brother seemed to believe, but lack of anything productive to do. Yet Mac had learned long ago that it was best to keep his opinions to himself when it came to other people's kids—or, in this case, kid brothers.

After a moment of silence, Sharon sprang to her feet. "Dinner will be ready in just a few minutes. Make yourself comfortable—are you sure I can't get you anything?"

"No, I'm fine. I'll just wash up—down this hallway?"

"Yes. Second door on the right."

Mac wandered back into the living room after washing his hands. His attention was drawn to a cluster of framed photographs arranged on an old upright piano in one corner of the room. A quick study confirmed that her brother was the boy Mac had encountered outside the arcade. *Great,* he thought with a shake of his head. Sharon's brother already hated him. Not that it mattered, he supposed. It wasn't as if anything serious was developing.

The photograph he was looking for sat at the back of the grouping. In it a young, blushing Sharon stood beside a teenager Mac might have mistaken for Trent McBride's mischievous younger brother, had he not known it was Trent, himself. His handsome face was creased with a big sloppy grin and his arm was around Sharon's waist. They had been a very attractive young couple.

He returned to the couch so Sharon wouldn't walk in and catch him snooping through her photographs, but the image of Sharon and Trent was still very clear in his mind. He knew Trent was happily engaged to someone else now, but there was clearly some sort of history between him and Sharon, even if nothing more than an innocent friendship.

She appeared in the doorway, looking little older than the girl in the photograph as she gave him a slightly shy smile. "Dinner is ready."

He followed her into the dining room, unable to resist admiring the graceful sway of her hips as she led the way. Just because he hoped to pump her for information didn't mean he couldn't appreciate spending an evening with an attractive woman.

"THIS LOOKS GREAT," Mac said, sitting at Sharon's beautifully set table a few minutes later.

"I hope you like Cornish hen. I forgot to ask what you prefer when I offered to cook."

"When it comes to food, there's very little I *don't* like," he admitted, reaching for his napkin. "Except sushi. Never developed a taste for that."

"I've never tried it. Sushi bars aren't exactly common in this area. I love most seafood, though."

"It tastes pretty much like you'd expect raw fish wrapped in seaweed to taste. I'm more of a meat-and-potatoes guy, myself."

"Then it's a good thing I prepared meat and potatoes tonight, I guess."

Swallowing a bite of creamy scalloped potatoes, he murmured, "Oh, yeah."

She seemed to relax a little in response to his enjoyment of the meal. "It's nice to cook for someone who appreciates my efforts. Brad would rather order pizza or pick up burgers than eat home-cooked vegetables."

"He'll get over that."

"I hope so. It's a constant battle to get him to eat well."

"Is your mother a good cook?"

"When she pays attention to what she's doing, she's an excellent cook. My mother's a bit of a daydreamer. An artist. She's been known to get distracted and put pepper in pudding or sugar on scrambled eggs. She even poured coffee on Brad's cereal once."

"She sounds...interesting."

"Brad teases her. He asks her how we'll be able to tell if she ever gets senile?"

Mac chuckled and took another bite of fresh asparagus. "You said she's an artist?"

"Yes. She teaches art at the junior high school."

It seemed like as good an opportunity as any to slip the McBrides into the conversation. "Trent mentioned that both his mother and sister-in-law are teachers. I suppose your mother knows them?"

"Everyone knows everyone in Honoria. Trent's mother, Bobbie, has taught at Honoria Elementary for more than thirty years. She seems to have no intention of ever retiring. Trevor's wife, Jamie, teaches speech and drama at the high school. She graduated from Honoria High, then spent almost ten years acting in New York before coming back to teach.''

"You never had an urge to teach, yourself?''

She shook her head. "I've always loved decorating. After I finished high school, I took a two-year interior-design course and some business classes at the local college. I worked in a wallpaper store for a couple of years, and when the owner decided to sell, my mother encouraged me to buy it. It was a little scary, making that investment, but Caleb McBride helped me with the paperwork and details, and so far, I'm holding my own.''

The McBrides again. As interested as he was in Sharon's own story, Mac knew he should probably start directing the conversation the way he wanted it to go. "Caleb's the attorney?'' he asked, though he already knew the answer.

"Yes. He's Trent and Trevor's father. They have a sister, too. Tara lives in Atlanta.''

"Trent mentioned that his parents are away on vacation.''

She nodded as she reached for her wineglass. "A cruise. It's their first vacation in longer than anyone can remember. Caleb's a dear, but a real workaholic—they practically had to carry him onto that ship. He had a minor heart attack a while back, and his family has been making him take better care of himself since.''

Mac took a sip of his own wine, then set his glass back on the table, keeping his tone offhand. ''I get a little confused about the relationships around here. What exactly is the family connection between the McBrides and the people who built the old house I bought?''

''Didn't Trent tell you?''

''We haven't talked much about the history of the place, just the plans I have for it.''

''Well, the Garrett house was built by Trent's great-great grandfather, I think. His grandmother—Caleb's mother—was a Garrett and I believe the house was built by her grandfather.''

''So the McBrides and Garretts are longtime residents of Honoria.''

''Oh, yes. But there aren't many Garretts left—a couple of distant cousins in Carrollton. And Caleb's the only McBride left of his generation, as far as I know.''

''He was an only son?'' Again, it was a question Mac already knew the answer to, but he wanted the conversation to unfold naturally. Casually.

Sharon seemed comfortable enough with the topic. ''No, Caleb had two brothers, Josiah Jr. and Jonah. They're both dead now.''

It had infuriated Mac when he'd first arrived in Honoria and learned that two of the older McBride brothers were dead. It had reduced his chances of getting revenge by two-thirds. His original plan had been to make someone suffer the humiliation and disgrace his mother had endured. To make it publicly known that a McBride had fathered and then abandoned a child, leaving a vulnerable woman alone to deal with her shame.

But it was hard to humiliate a dead man. And unless Caleb McBride was the culprit—which even at this early stage of Mac's investigation seemed unlikely—it didn't appear that Mac would find the retribution he'd craved for so long. But at least maybe he could finally find some answers.

"The McBrides don't seem to have a particularly long life span."

She frowned thoughtfully. "I don't know about that. I think Jonah died in an accident when he was only in his early forties, but Josiah Jr., was older. He died of emphysema and lung cancer after years of heavy smoking. Poor Emily had to put her own life on hold for years to take care of him—which wasn't an easy task. Her father was a...difficult man. I remember being very intimidated by his perpetual scowl back when I was a teenager."

Filing that tidbit away, Mac went along with the conversation, looking for other tidbits of information. "Emily is the police chief's wife?"

"Yes. Emily Davenport now."

"No siblings to help her out with her difficult father?"

"She has an older half brother, Lucas, but he had a falling-out with his father—and with most of Honoria, for that matter—and he left town after high school. Fifteen years later, he came back to visit his sister. Their father was already dead then.''

No mention so far of congenital ailments in the McBride family, something Mac needed to know, especially after... "I didn't realize Mrs. Davenport has an older brother. I don't think I've met him."

"No. I've only met him a couple of times myself. He's nine years older than Emily. Lucas and his wife live in California and only come back to visit a couple of times a year. But they'll be here in August for Trent's wedding, I'm sure."

It was increasingly obvious that she didn't share her town's penchant for idle gossip. So far, all Sharon had done was answer his innocuous questions without much embellishment. While Mac admired her discretion, it wasn't getting him very far. He took a calculated risk with a bolder question. "You weren't kidding when you said the folks around here like to gossip. Am I mistaken, or do the McBrides seem to attract more than their share of talk?"

Sharon wrinkled her nose. "You aren't mistaken. It seems as if there's always one scandal or another involving the McBrides. It's unfair for the most part, I might add. They're really a very nice family."

"If you say so."

That noncommittal comment brought her chin up in defense of her friends. "I do say so. I've known them for ages and they've all been very nice to me and my family. I certainly hope you aren't letting a few spiteful locals make you question your decision to hire Trent for your renovation team.''

"I don't base my hiring decisions on idle chatter.''

"Good," she said with a brisk nod. "Any large family in a small town is going to attract its share of gossip, of course. Every big family has its share of scandals—divorces, unwed pregnancies, that sort of thing—and the McBrides are no different. But most of the accusations leveled at the McBrides have later proven to be completely unfounded. Like when Sam Jennings accused Emily of embezzling from his accounts at the bank—he was just trying to stir things up. Sam's also the one who led everyone to believe Lucas killed Roger Jennings, when all along it was Sam himself—and Roger wasn't the first person Sam killed, either."

Mac set down his fork. "I don't think I followed all that."

Sharon made a sound of exasperation, and shook her head. "Sorry. It just makes me so mad that people are telling you these stories about the McBrides. They really don't deserve the treatment they get around here."

"No one mentioned anything about murder to me."

She pushed a strand of hair out of her face, still looking annoyed. "No, of course not. Everyone knows the truth now. I suppose I should tell you the story so you won't go away with a misconception about Lucas."

"I wouldn't want you to betray your friends' trust just to satisfy my curiosity," Mac murmured, feeling vaguely guilty about the lie.

"It's common knowledge around here now," she said with a shrug. "Even though it all happened more than four years ago, it was a huge scandal and people still like to talk about it. It started when Emily was a toddler and her mother—Josiah Jr.'s second wife, Nadine—apparently ran off with a married man, Al Jennings. Josiah was always very bitter after that, and mixed very little with the townspeople. He and Lucas, his son by his first wife, who died of pneumonia, didn't get along well. Actually, Lucas didn't get along well with many people, because he had such a temper as a boy. Probably because his own mother died so young and his father was such an unpleasant man. Especially after Nadine disappeared with Al."

"It sounds like enough to make anyone surly."

Smiling a little in response to Mac's wry comment, Sharon continued, "Anyway, Lucas had a sort of hate/hate relationship with Roger Jennings—the son of the man Nadine supposedly ran away with. Roger blamed all the McBrides for his father's defection, and Lucas took the brunt of it because he and Roger were close in age. One night very soon after Lucas finished high school, they had a particularly bitter public quarrel. Roger died that night."

"How?"

"He fell off a cliff on McBride land, close to Lucas's house. It was all very tragic and very mysterious and, needless to say, the local gossips had a field day. They all decided Lucas killed Roger. They had him tried and convicted even before the funeral. There wasn't enough evidence to arrest Lucas, but the people who never liked him, anyway, didn't care about that. They made life here so unpleasant for him that he felt he had to leave. He took off in the middle of the night, and no one heard from him for years.''

"Which, of course, only made him look more guilty in the eyes of his accusers."

"Exactly. Fifteen years later, Lucas came home to visit his sister, Emily, and the truth came out. Nadine McBride and Al Jennings were murdered by Al's own brother, Sam. It turned out Sam had been a jilted lover of Nadine's, and he killed her and Al in a jealous rage. When Sam's nephew, Roger, came too close to finding out the truth several years later, Sam pushed him over the cliff, making it look as if Lucas was the real murderer."

"You had a triple murderer living right here in Honoria?"

"He was my dentist when I was a teenager. I always thought he was sort of weird, but I never dreamed... Anyway, he even tried to do away with Rachel, Roger's younger sister, when she stumbled onto the truth four years ago. Had it not been for Lucas and Wade rushing to her rescue, he might have killed her. Now Sam is in prison where he belongs and Lucas is married to Rachel and living quite happily in California."

Mac had followed the tale with only a slight effort. "So Lucas married the sister of the man he was accused of murdering?"

"Yes. He owns a successful software company now. He's made loads of money, which might have something to do with why the whole town practically salutes him every time he comes back to visit."

"Success can be the best revenge."

She scowled. "I despise hypocrisy. The same people who were whispering about him now pretend they believed he was innocent all along."

Shifting a bit uncomfortably in his chair, Mac prompted, "So that's when all the gossip about the McBrides began?"

She shrugged. "There were a few other incidents, but that was the most dramatic. The other stuff has been generally exaggerated."

"And I thought nothing exciting ever happened around here."

"We've had our share of scandal. But personally, I prefer a quieter, more peaceful existence. If I'd wanted excitement, I'd have moved to a big city instead of settling down here to be close to my family."

Thinking of some of the "excitement" he'd seen as a vice cop, Mac decided she'd made the right choice.

Sharon nodded toward his glass. "Would you like some more wine?"

"No, I'm fine, thanks."

"I had a couple of thoughts about the renovation project this afternoon—specifically, the little front parlor. Would it be possible to change the doorway to an arch to match the shape of the fanlights in the entryway and dining room?"

He would have liked to ask a few more questions about the McBrides, but there was really no way to pursue it now without arousing Sharon's suspicions. "Actually, that's something I've already discussed with the builder," he said, going along with her for now.

He hadn't forgotten his main purpose in being here this evening. He would find a way to learn more about the McBrides later.

BY CONVINCING HERSELF this was a business dinner, Sharon was able to relax considerably during the remainder of the meal. It was easier to talk about decorating with Mac than to make social small talk. She was still annoyed with herself for babbling on about the McBrides the way she had. She'd let her irritation with the local gossips and her natural inclination to defend her friends carry her away.

Mac had probably been bored by the whole conversation about people he hardly even knew. In all likelihood he considered her as big a gossip as the others he'd encountered around here.

Better, she thought, to stick to business.

Her awkwardness with Mac could be attributed to the fact that it had been a long time since she'd spent an evening with any man other than Jerry, who tended to dominate conversations with talk about himself. An evening with Jerry was usually entertaining—and never made her as nervous and self-conscious as this supposedly simple dinner with Mac. Maybe because Jerry didn't have Mac's habit of studying her across the table as if everything she said or did was inherently interesting.

Seeing that Mac's plate was empty, she asked, "Would you like coffee and dessert? I made a strawberry cake. It's sort of my specialty."

A decidedly odd look crossed his face. "Um...thanks, but strawberries make me break out in hives."

Of course they did. There seemed to be some force at work to cause as many awkward moments as possible between the two of them. "Something else, then? I have ice cream or..."

"Just coffee, thanks. Dinner was so good I've eaten too much already."

"Why don't we have our coffee in the living room. I have a few sketches I'd like to show you in there."

His grin was a brief flash of white, both wicked and disturbing. "Are you offering to show me your etchings?"

"Behave yourself," she said sternly, not sure whether she was talking to him or to her own suddenly activated hormones.

"Yes, ma'am." He stood when she did and reached to move her chair out of the way for her. "Can I help you clear away the dishes first?"

She couldn't help smiling. Mac had the kind of old-fashioned manners that she'd been trying to teach Brad—with only partially satisfying results. "Are your parents still living?" she asked impulsively.

He seemed to go still for a moment. And then he replaced her chair without looking at her. "I was raised by my mother. She died three years ago."

Something in his voice told Sharon he hadn't quite recovered from the loss. Her tone was gentle when she asked, "Was she the one who taught you to be such a gentleman?"

Though the question appeared to disconcert him a bit, he nodded. "My mother was a real stickler for manners. 'Stand up when a lady stands, Miguel.' 'Take your hat off indoors, Miguel.' 'Say please and thank you, Miguel.'"

Intrigued by this fleeting glimpse into his past, she cocked her head. "Miguel? That's your first name?"

He gave her a funny little bow. "Miguel Luis Cordero."

"When did you start answering to Mac?"

He shrugged. "That came from my mother, too. She grew up in San Juan, but she wanted me to have a more mainstream American upbringing. She gave me her father's name, but she thought it would be easier for me to answer to a more common nickname."

He was reaching for his dishes as he spoke. Sharon rested a hand on his arm to stop him. "I'll take care of these later. Why don't you just go on into the living room and I'll bring the coffee.''

He glanced at her hand on his arm, then raised his eyes to hers. And once again she understood what it meant to be held captive by someone's gaze. She wasn't sure she could look away if she tried. She was relieved when Mac broke the contact.

"I take my coffee black," he said.

She deliberately stiffened her knees. "I'll be right in."

She lingered in the kitchen a few minutes longer than was absolutely necessary, giving herself a chance to recover from that moment of connection between them. She was fine with him as long as they stuck to business, but every time she became aware of him as a sexy, single male, she froze. It wasn't that she had anything against sexy, single males, but with Mac she had the feeling things could get complicated—and not only because she would be involved with him professionally for the next few months.

CHAPTER SIX

SHARON ASSEMBLED a tray with two cups of coffee and a plate of chocolate cookies, just in case Mac changed his mind about dessert. When she carried the tray carefully into the living room, she noticed Mac sitting on the couch, examining an antique-reproduction lighting catalog she'd left on the coffee table. "These wall lights you've marked with adhesive strips—are you considering them for the Garrett house?" he asked.

Setting the tray on the coffee table, she settled on the couch next to him to study the photographs. "No, I've ordered those for one of my customers who's redoing her bedroom. She has a house full of Mission and Shaker antiques, and I thought those fixtures would go well with her decor. But there are several others in the catalog you might want to look at for your project."

"I like this one," he said, and pointed to a corner of the page farther from her, so that she had to scoot a little closer to examine the photo he'd indicated.

"That *is* nice," she agreed. "I can envision it in the downstairs hallway, can't you? It would nicely illuminate that dark corner outside the dining room."

He turned a page. "What about something like this in the parlor?"

She leaned a little closer, studying the ad with a thoughtful frown. "Well, it's pretty, of course, but do you really want to go with that look? This fixture is more representative of the 1950s than the 1920s era, but we can certainly mix styles, if that's what you'd like. Some decorators recommend mixing styles and periods for a more complex and eclectic—"

"*You're* the designer on this project," he reminded her. "What I want you to do is decorate the house as if you were going to live in it yourself."

She glanced at him with a smile. "What makes you think I'd want to live in a restored Victorian? How do you know I wouldn't prefer stylized chrome and glass from the 1980s? Or the Danish Modern look of the 1960s?"

"Because I saw your face when you got your first look at the Garrett place. I watched you run your hand over the moldings in the master bedroom. I saw the way you practically melted over the beveled-glass fanlight in the dining room. It was lust, Sharon. Pure, heart-pounding, skin-dampening lust."

It took her a moment to respond coherently to his wholly unexpected side trip into rather erotic fancy. "I, um, love the house, of course—or at least the house I know it can become—but I'm not sure I would describe my feelings as, er—"

"Lust?" He smiled a little. "You don't think the word is appropriate?"

"Well, no, not really. I'll admit I have a certain passion for decorating. I'm excited to be a part of your team. And I certainly might fantasize about owning a place like the Garrett house, myself. But *lust* is perhaps too strong a word to describe my feelings."

He gave a low chuckle. "You've just used the words *passion, excited,* and *fantasize* pretty much in one breath—and you accuse *me* of using too strong a word?"

They were supposed to be talking business, not swapping innuendoes. Somehow this conversation had gotten completely out of hand. She made a weak effort to get it back on track. She looked at the catalog again. "Do you see anything you like?"

"I definitely see something I like," he murmured, bringing her gaze back up to his. He wasn't looking at photographs. His intense dark eyes were focused on her face.

"I, um..." What had she meant to say? The words were gone, having slipped from her suddenly overheated mind like wisps of steam.

She didn't realize he had lifted his hand until she felt his fingertips against the side of her face. What was it about his touch that electrified her, even as it gave her an incredible sense of security? Was it the memory of the way he'd held her the night they'd met? Had that dramatic introduction made her react differently to him—or was it something about the man, himself?

"What did you ask me?" she murmured, trying to clear her thoughts.

"Nothing." His gaze was on her mouth now.

She cleared her throat. "Do you want…?"

His eyes rose to hers again. "Do I want…?"

What was it she'd started to offer? "Coffee."

His smile twisted wryly. "Coffee," he repeated. Neither of them moved.

"This," she said after a moment, still feeling the weight of his fingers against her face, "is what some people might call an awkward moment."

"It doesn't have to be." His thumb moved, tracing across her cheek to her lower lip. "We can go back to talking about fixtures."

Her lip quivered beneath his touch. Talk? She wasn't even sure she could speak coherently.

She could insist on keeping the evening strictly business, and Mac would go along with it. She could move to another chair, away from the feel and heat of him, and he wouldn't try to hold her back. It would be the sensible, practical, *Sharon* thing to do.

Funny, she mused, studying the strong shape of his mouth. She hadn't been quite herself since her car sank beneath the surface of Snake Creek. She hadn't seen things in quite the same light—her job, this town, Jerry. Her life. Maybe because she'd come so close to losing it all. The accident had made her very aware of everything she had—and everything she'd only dreamed of.

She realized abruptly that it would have been a shame if she had died without ever meeting Mac Cordero. Without really knowing what it meant to melt at a touch.

His mouth was very close to hers now. If she reacted so strongly to the feel of his hand, what would it be like to kiss him? Did she really want to miss this chance to find out?

Taking her silence as permission, he covered her mouth with his.

Okay, she thought, somewhat relieved that no fireworks exploded around her, no cymbals crashed in her ears. It was just a kiss, like the kisses she had received before. Just a pleasant, gentle press of lips. Nice, but it certainly wouldn't change her life.

Lulled into relaxing, she closed her eyes and tilted her head for him. Her lips softened, parting just a little. She raised a hand to his shoulder, letting it rest lightly there. Just a simple kiss between two unattached adults, she assured herself. If nothing else, it would satisfy their curiosity, and then they could get on with business.

The tip of his tongue touched her lower lip, eliciting a slight shiver of reaction. Okay, so it was a pretty good kiss. There was no reason to hurry through it. She slipped her other arm around his neck and parted her lips a bit more.

A moment later, her head was spinning, her pulse racing, her toes curling—and she would have sworn there were fireworks going off and cymbals crashing somewhere around her. Every cliché she'd ever heard had just become real for her—and this tricky, unprincipled male had deliberately waited until her guard was down before springing them on her.

Just a kiss? Right—like a tornado was just a stiff breeze.

Somehow his arms had gone around her, and his hands were sneaking into places they shouldn't be, but she didn't want him to move them. Which only proved how good he was at being bad.

His tongue swept her mouth, taunting and teasing until she couldn't resist responding with a few tentative thrusts of her own. Which only seemed to encourage him to take the kiss deeper.

This was why, she thought somewhere in the back of her mind, she had been so jumpy around Mac from the start. Somehow she had known almost from the first time she'd seen him that this would happen—and that it wasn't going to be uncomplicated.

She'd known all along that Mac wasn't like the forgettable men she had dated in the past.

She couldn't think clearly with his arms around her, his mouth on hers, his tongue sparring with hers. It was wonderful. Heady. Exciting. She couldn't seem to care that she had known him only a week. That she still knew very little about him.

All that mattered at the moment was that she'd felt a connection to him from that first dramatic meeting. That she'd been drawn to him every time she had seen him since. That his eyes, his touch, his voice affected her in a way she'd only fantasized about before.

His right hand slid slowly up from her hip, leaving a shivery path behind him. He pressed lightly against the small of her back, urging her closer. She tightened her arm around his neck, letting her fingers burrow into his thick ebony hair.

She didn't know how this had happened, exactly—but she couldn't be sorry it had. It really was a spectacular kiss.

His hand moved again, sliding around her waist to pause perilously close to her breast. Even as she ached to feel him there, she felt herself pulling back.

"Too much?" he murmured against her mouth, moving his hand to a more innocuous position.

"Too soon," she amended candidly.

Very slowly, he drew back. He wasn't smiling, she noted. He didn't look particularly pleased with himself for slipping so neatly behind her defenses. In fact, he looked almost as startled as she felt—and almost as dismayed.

Because he was so very good at masking his emotions, his expression cleared almost immediately. He pulled his hands away from her. "Our coffee's getting cold," he said, his voice only marginally huskier than usual.

Actually, a cold drink sounded pretty good to her just then, considering that she'd been on the verge of overheating. She scooted several inches away from him and reached for her coffee. It annoyed her that her hand wasn't quite steady when she picked up her cup. Just a kiss? Had she really thought it could be that easy with him?

Mac cleared his throat. "I should probably go."

She glanced instinctively at her watch, not certain whether she was relieved or reluctant that he was ready to leave. "It's still early."

"Mmm. More time to get into trouble if I stay," he murmured.

The glint of humor in his eyes made her smile, even as she felt her cheeks warm. He made it clear enough that he would have liked the embrace to go further. And she had to admit that deep down inside, she shared the sentiment. But as she had said, it was entirely too soon to be flirting with that sort of temptation.

She'd known Jerry for ages and hadn't kissed him the way she had just kissed Mac. She hadn't wanted to, for that matter.

"Besides," Mac added, setting his half-emptied coffee cup on the tray, "it's starting to rain."

She hadn't heard the rain until he said that. She hadn't been aware of anything outside this room, actually. For the first time in a while, she remembered her brother. The thought was accompanied by a ripple of guilt that he'd been so far from her mind only moments earlier.

"I hope the fathers on the camp-out made plans for rain," she murmured, looking toward the window in time to see a brief flash of lightning.

"They're idiots if they didn't. The forecasters have been predicting rain for days."

His blunt tone made her smile again as they stood. "Do you always plan for every contingency, Mac?"

"I try." He paused in front of her, reaching out to brush a strand of hair away from her still-tender mouth. His expression was somber. "I didn't plan on you."

Her smile faded. She certainly understood that sentiment. Mac—and her unexpected reaction to him—had certainly thrown *her* for a loop. But some surprises were rather nice ones, she thought as he stroked her cheek lightly again.

Not quite knowing what to say, she walked him to the door. She started to say something about working up design boards for the Garrett house, but it seemed rather foolish to talk business now, to pretend there was nothing else developing between them.

"Thanks for the dinner," he said as they paused at the door. "You were right, it was nice to eat a home-cooked meal for a change."

"I'm glad you enjoyed it. Next time I'll remember about the strawberries." She spoke without thinking, only then realizing that she had just implied there would be more evenings like this.

His mouth quirked into a slight smile. "For another dinner with you, I would even eat strawberries."

Smiling back at him, she quipped, "And risk breaking out in hives? I'm flattered."

"You should be. I hate to itch."

Twisting her hands in front of her, she looked up

at him, suddenly awkward again. "It sounds as if it's starting to rain harder."

A rumble of thunder underscored her words. "You aren't afraid to be alone during thunderstorms, are you?"

"Just the opposite, actually. Would it surprise you to hear that I like thunderstorms?"

"It might have, earlier today. Now—no, it doesn't surprise me at all."

Since they'd kissed, he meant. Since they had created their own storm—and it had been very obvious that she'd liked it.

Another roll of thunder made her glance at the door. "You'll get wet. Let me find you an umbrella."

"I won't melt." He reached for the doorknob. "Good night, Sharon."

"Good night, Mac." It was becoming easier to say his name—perhaps because it would be ridiculous to call him Mr. Cordero now.

He hesitated with one hand still on the doorknob. He placed his free hand behind her head and tugged lightly, bringing her mouth to his for a brief, but still effective kiss. "I'll see you soon," he murmured, the words a promise. And then he was gone, disappearing into the night.

Sharon closed the door behind him, then sagged for a moment against it, her cheek pressed to the cool wood. So much for pretending there was nothing but business between them. Or that she even wanted it that way.

SOME COP HABITS were hard for Mac to break. Keeping detailed notes was one of them. Sitting at the shaky table in his motel room, he studied the yellow legal-pad pages spread in front of him. On one sheet, he had started a rudimentary family tree. At the top, he'd written the names Josiah McBride and Anna Mae Garrett. On the next line were the names of their three sons, Josiah Jr., Jonah and Caleb.

Beneath Josiah Jr., he had written "Lucas, 40," and "Emily McBride Davenport, 31."

He studied those names for a moment, remembering what he'd learned about the eldest McBride brother. Josiah Jr. had apparently been humorless, withdrawn, moody—distant even to his own children. Could Mac's mother have fallen in love with a man like that?

Apparently there had been something about Josiah that some women had been drawn to. He'd married twice, though the second wife had taken a lover soon after. The lover with whom she had been murdered.

According to Sharon's timeline, Josiah had been between wives when Mac was conceived. Which might explain why he would start an affair with a Puerto Rican maid in a Savannah hotel, but it didn't fit with the story Mac's mother had told him. His father had been a married man, she had explained with an old sadness in her musical voice. Although he had talked about leaving his wife for her, his sense of family loyalty had finally drawn him away.

The guy had never known that he left Anita Cordero carrying his child. Anita had refused to use her baby as a marriage trap.

Was it possible that Josiah's marriage had been nothing more than a convenient lie? A coward's way of ending an affair that had lost its novelty for him?

Had Josiah McBride Jr. been Mac's father? If so, it didn't seem as if the man had any reputation left to ruin. Apparently, he'd left little respect or admiration behind when he'd died.

He shoved the unfinished family tree aside in frustration. He had no answers yet, and wouldn't come up with any tonight. Perhaps he would learn more the next time he found an opportunity to discuss the McBride family with Sharon.

Sharon. His mind was suddenly filled with the image of her face. The way she had looked after he kissed her—her skin flushed, her eyes heavy-lidded, her lips damp and reddened. She would never know how hard it had been for him to pull away. It had been too long since he'd held a woman in his arms. Since he had lost himself in a kiss that cleared his mind of questions, plans, memories—leaving nothing there but hunger.

He'd told the truth when he said he hadn't expected to meet her. Even when he'd made the calculated decision to use her knowledge of the McBrides, he hadn't intended to seduce any information out of her. The kiss had been unexpected, unplanned, and had nothing to do with the McBrides or anyone else except Sharon, herself. He had kissed her for no other reason except that he had wanted to. Needed to.

He hadn't planned on that at all.

BRAD WAS HOME early Sunday morning, in a more passive than usual mood after his camp-out. The organizers had planned for rain; the festivities had been moved inside a one-room building at the campground that was usually rented out for parties and family reunions. Though he'd probably had only a couple of hours' sleep, Brad was in a mellow enough mood that he didn't even complain—much—when Sharon insisted he accompany her to church.

Not that it had done much good, she thought ruefully as the service ended. He'd slept through the entire sermon. She poked him discreetly, and he woke with a muffled snort. "Time to go," she said.

He gave her a sheepish smile. "Good. I'm hungry."

She laughed and patted his arm. "Of course you are. You're breathing, aren't you?"

As usual, it took her a while to leave, because so many people detained her. Among the usual casual greetings, there were still a few who wanted to talk about the incident in Snake Creek. Sharon found it hard to believe only eight days had passed since that night. Maybe it seemed longer because she had chosen not to dwell on the experience.

She'd made a special effort not to think about it at all, though she hadn't been able to block the images from her dreams. The only thing that had kept those dreams from becoming nightmares had been the mental echo of Mac's voice, soothing and reassuring her. She'd chosen not to give too much thought to that, either.

Pushing the memories and Mac to the back of her mind, she made her way steadily to the parking lot, where still more members of the congregation waylaid her. Brad waited nearby, shifting from one foot to another, letting out an occasional gusty sigh.

"It's good to see you looking so well, Sharon," Emily Davenport said, smiling over the head of the baby girl in her arms. "I've thought of you often during the past week."

Sharon responded appropriately, then tickled little Claire's dimpled chin. "Hello, sweetie. You get more beautiful every time I see you."

"Say thank you to Miss Sharon, Claire," Emily instructed, though the child was only interested in the activities going on around her.

"Where's Clay?" Sharon looked around for Emily's thirteen-year-old stepson, then spotted him talking to her brother. "Oh, there he is, with Brad. Goodness, that boy seems to have grown six inches since I saw him last, and it's only been a couple of weeks."

"Same with Brad. They're becoming young men, aren't they?"

"I'm afraid so," Sharon agreed pensively. "Is Wade working this morning?"

Emily's smile faded. "Yes. Someone broke into

Discount Motors during the storm last night. They stole a car from the lot and some computer equipment from the office.''

Sharon frowned. It was bad enough that these kinds of crimes were happening in their town, but it especially bothered her that it had occurred so close to where her brother and his friends had been enjoying a wholesome evening of fun. Discount Motors was only half a mile from the campground. That seemed to make the crime even worse, for some reason. ''Does Wade think this break-in is related to the one at the Porter place last weekend?''

''He's certainly pursuing that possibility.'' Emily shifted her daughter into a more comfortable position on her hip. ''We're having a cookout at our place next Saturday. Would you and Brad like to come? Clay would love it. There are never any teenagers for him to talk to at our family gatherings.''

''It sounds like fun. We'd love to come.'' Though Clay was a couple of years younger than Brad, it was a friendship Sharon wanted to encourage. Clay was a good kid—smart, funny, outgoing. Popular with the good crowd, even if being the police chief's son earned him no points in other circles. Sharon worried about Brad getting involved with the wrong crowd. Clay Davenport was exactly the sort of friend she wanted for her brother.

''Great. Then we'll see you around noon on Saturday. Oh, and feel free to bring a friend if you like.''

Sharon suspected Emily was hinting about Jerry.

Matchmaking was the second favorite pastime in this town, right behind gossiping. "Is there anything else I can bring?"

"How about one of your famous strawberry cakes? Wade always goes on about how good they are."

Sharon couldn't help laughing a little. "Not everyone likes strawberries. But I'll make a cake, anyway, just for Wade."

"He'll be your slave."

Sharon laughed again. "I'll keep that in mind."

"Sharon, I'm hungry," Brad complained.

Emily smiled in understanding. "We'll see you Saturday."

"I'm looking forward to it." Sharon turned to her brother. "Okay, Brad. Let's go find something to eat before you collapse."

MAC WAS ON THE ROOF of the Garrett house Sunday morning when someone hailed him from below. He looked curiously over the edge, then masked his surprise. "Well, hello, Chief. Another friendly social visit?"

Wade Davenport grinned lazily up at him. "What you doing up there, Mac?"

"Communing with nature. Hang on, I'll be right down." Abandoning his inspection of the roof, Mac descended the ladder he'd propped against the back of the house. Wade waited for him at the bottom. "I'm beginning to wonder if you're following me around, Chief."

Wade put a hand on the ladder, as if to test its sturdiness. "Just thought I would stop by while I was in the neighborhood."

Mac suspected the chief had a specific reason for being in the neighborhood. And he would bet Wade had stopped by the motel first. "What can I do for you?"

"I wondered if I could talk you into giving me a tour."

"Sure," Mac agreed easily, wondering what, exactly, was behind the request. "Be happy to."

"I'd appreciate it. I've always been curious about this place, but I've never had an excuse to look around. My wife's great-grandfather built this house, you know."

"So I hear. We can go in through this door, which will take us into the kitchen."

Wade didn't move toward the door. His attention was focused on a large, padlocked storage building at the back of the yard. "Actually, I'd like to have a look inside that outbuilding first. If you have no objections, of course."

Mac pushed his hands into the pockets of his jeans, keeping his stance casual. "Any particular reason?"

"Oh, just curiosity."

Yeah, right. "This is just a wild guess, but has there been another break-in recently?"

"Mmm. Last night, out near the campground. Why do you ask?"

Shaking his head, Mac moved toward the outbuilding. "Never mind. Let me show you my storage shed."

Wade followed close at his heels. "You understand, of course, that this is just a request. I don't have a search warrant or anything official like that."

Mac leveled a look at the other man over his shoulder. "Now why would I be concerned about search warrants? This is just a friendly social visit, right?"

"You got it," Wade drawled cheerfully.

Pulling a key from his pocket, Mac opened the heavy padlock and swung the door open. Power lines ran from the outbuilding to a temporary construction utility pole set up nearby, so he was able to reach inside and snap on the bare lightbulb that hung from the rafters. He then stepped back, allowing Wade full access to the building filled with tools and materials. "There you go. Check it out."

A cursory glance seemed to satisfy the police chief. "Yeah, that's pretty much what I expected to see. You've got some expensive tools in there. You might want to step up your security, considering the problems with theft we've had around here lately."

"I'll keep your advice in mind. Thanks." Mac snapped the padlock into place again, tugging at it a couple of times to make sure it was secured. "C'mon, I'll show you around inside. I imagine you'll want to peer into all the nooks and crannies."

"Will I find anything interesting in those nooks and crannies?"

"Only if you're interested in dust and cobwebs."

Wade shrugged. "I'm easily entertained."

Half an hour later, they'd explored the entire house—every nook and cranny. The only questions Wade asked during the tour involved the renovation, itself. He seemed genuinely interested in the project, but Mac was discovering it wasn't always easy to tell what observations were being made behind the chief's expression.

They finished back outside at the ladder. "Thanks," Wade said. "That was very interesting."

"I hope it answered your questions."

"Most of them."

"If you have any others, you know where to find me. I'll be moving into a furnished apartment on West Elm tomorrow afternoon. If I'm not here, I'll most likely be there."

"I'll remember that. Er—I guess I really shouldn't leave without asking one more question. What, exactly, did you do last night?"

"I had a business dinner with Sharon Henderson, my decorator," Mac answered evenly, stressing the professional relationship for Sharon's sake. "I was back in my motel room at just after nine o'clock. I watched a *Star Trek* rerun on cable, caught the late news, then read for an hour or so before going to sleep. Want to know what I dreamed?"

Wade laughed. "Hey, I'm a cop, not a psychiatrist."

"Just checking."

The chief left, saying only that he would be seeing Mac around. One hand squeezing the back of his neck, Mac watched him leave.

Damned if he could figure that guy out. He had the distinct feeling that Wade didn't seriously consider him a suspect in the break-ins, but was generally leery about him, anyway. He would have to be careful not to do anything to further pique the chief's suspicions, especially when it came to the McBrides. He had a feeling Davenport was extremely protective of his wife, and wouldn't allow anyone to bother her. No matter what the family connection turned out to be.

CHAPTER SEVEN

SHARON WAS STILL in her shop ten minutes after closing time on Monday. Tressie had already gone home and Sharon would have followed suit had she not been waiting for her brother. He'd spent the afternoon at a movie with friends who were supposed to have dropped him off twenty minutes ago.

She was beginning to worry. Against her better judgment, she'd given him permission to ride with a sixteen-year-old friend with a driver's license and a car, a decision she'd been second-guessing all day. She'd probably been swayed by Jerry's accusations that she was being overprotective of her brother, that she needed to start treating him like a young man rather than a child. And Brad had been on his best behavior for the past few days, which naturally made her more inclined to indulge him occasionally.

She hoped she hadn't made a mistake.

When the telephone rang, she snatched it up. "Intriguing Interiors."

"I thought I might find you still there."

It hadn't been necessary for Jerry to identify himself, of course. She recognized his voice immediately. "Yes, still here," she said. "I was just about to lock up."

"How was your day?"

"Busy. And yours?"

"The same. You heard about the break-in at Discount Motors, I guess."

"Yes, Emily mentioned it at church yesterday."

"I carry their insurance, and I've spent all morning with Bob Hickey, trying to get a list of everything that was stolen or damaged. Bob's a nice guy, but not the most organized business owner. He..."

Distracted by the sound of the door opening, Sharon looked up paying only marginal attention to what Jerry was saying. She'd expected to see her brother enter the shop. She was surprised when Mac Cordero strolled in, instead. It was even more difficult after that to pay attention to Jerry's play-by-play recitation of his workday. She smiled at Mac and motioned to indicate that she would be right with him.

Jerry was still talking. "And then Martha Godwin called. Boy, was she wound up today. She's decided that she..."

Realizing that Jerry wouldn't be taking a breath anytime soon, Sharon covered the mouthpiece with her hand and spoke softly to Mac, who leaned against the counter nearby. "Hi."

"Want me to wait somewhere else while you finish that?"

Jerry was still going on about Martha's eccentricities. "No, you're fine," she murmured to Mac. "This won't take long."

"Anyway," Jerry said suddenly in her ear,

"we're both too tired to cook this evening. Why don't we go out? We'll take Brad, of course. He'll want pizza, I suppose."

Looking away from Mac, who was thumbing through a wallpaper-sample book to occupy himself while she finished her call, Sharon said, "Thanks, Jerry, but we can't tonight."

There was only a hint of disappointment in his voice. "I guess you already have plans for the evening. I knew it was short notice, but I thought it was worth a try. So...I'll talk to you later, okay?"

She wondered if he was beginning to catch her hints that they should spend less time together. Now that she had forced herself to look objectively at their relationship and had come to the conclusion that it wasn't going anywhere—more importantly, that she didn't really even want it to—she saw no reason to continue. They should both feel free to pursue other...interests, she thought, glancing sideways at Mac. She hoped she wouldn't have to spell it out to Jerry—that would be so awkward and uncomfortable—but she was prepared to do so if necessary. "Sure. We'll talk later."

It had been a brief, unremarkable conversation, on the surface no different from dozens of chats they'd had before. Yet Sharon had the odd feeling that she had just made a significant change in her life as she disconnected Jerry's call and turned to Mac.

He looked up from the wallpaper book, his grave dark eyes searching her face. "Everything okay?"

"I hope so." After putting the telephone away,

Sharon tucked a strand of hair behind her ear, suddenly feeling shy with this man who had kissed her senseless less than forty-eight hours before. "Is there something I can do for you, Mac?"

He hesitated just long enough to make her aware of how many answers there could be to that particular question. And then he smiled. "Actually, I stopped by to give you my new address."

"You aren't staying at the motel now?"

"No. I've moved into an apartment on West Elm."

"Are you pleased with it?"

He shrugged. "It's clean, anyway. Better than a motel room."

"It's furnished?"

"The basics are provided. Enough to satisfy my needs for now."

"What about linens? Cookware? Dishes?"

"I have all that. I carry a couple of boxes of necessities with me from job to job."

She frowned. "It sounds rather bleak when you put it that way. Don't you have a permanent home somewhere?"

"I own a house in Savannah. It's rented out now."

"So you've just been moving from job to job?"

"For the past few years."

"You don't have a family?"

"I'm divorced."

"Oh." She hadn't really considered that he might have once been married. She wondered what had happened to his marriage. Why he lived such a lonely existence now. Had his heart been broken? "No children?"

"No."

She studied his face. There'd been something in that stark single syllable. Something in his voice. A flash of emotion in his eyes. Pain? Regret? A touch of anger? Or was she letting her imagination get completely away from her?

He changed the subject before she could ask any more questions. "Are you finished here for the day?"

"Yes. I'm waiting for my brother. He was supposed to have been here half an hour ago."

"He hasn't called?"

"No. He went to a movie with some friends. They probably stopped by the arcade afterward and let time get away from them."

"That's typical of teenagers, I understand."

"Yes—but Brad knows I expect him to be on time."

"It must be difficult being responsible for a teenage brother. Does he usually follow your rules?"

"He hasn't given me much trouble so far. An incident or two. Some backtalk. No open rebellion yet."

"Still, I bet you'll be glad when your mother comes home."

Mac didn't know her mother, of course. Having Lucy home wouldn't make much difference. She let others take over—usually Sharon. As for Brad—

well, Sharon worried about what would happen when school started again. It had been at school that Brad had hooked up with the wrong crowd in the first place. She wasn't at all sure Lucy could do much if he got into any more trouble. Lucy indulged, she didn't discipline.

"So what's the penalty for being half an hour late?"

"I haven't decided yet. I'll probably take his video game away for the evening. Maybe TV, as well."

"Mmm. That'll show him," Mac murmured.

Sharon shot him a suspicious look. Was that an implied criticism? He was the one who'd said all teenagers did this sort of thing. Did he expect her to ground Brad for life?

The door opened and Brad rushed in, red-faced and panting. "I'm sorry I'm late, sis. Jimbo ran out of gas and we had to—"

The jumbled words came to an abrupt halt when he spotted Mac. He froze practically in midstep. Sharon knew he was startled to find someone else in the shop after closing time, but she couldn't imagine why his cheeks suddenly turned beet red and his face drew into a sullen scowl.

"Brad, this is Mr. Cordero," she said, rushing to fill in the strained silence. "Mac, my brother, Brad Henderson."

"Nice to meet you, Brad."

His gaze on his shoes, Brad muttered something incoherent.

Sharon lifted an eyebrow. Her brother was sometimes awkward, but rarely outright rude. "I'm not sure Mr. Cordero heard that, Brad."

Mac shook his head. "No, it's fine. I'll clear out now. I just wanted to give you my new address."

"Thank you. I'll probably come out to the site tomorrow to take pictures upstairs. It's safe to do that, I presume?"

"As long as you stay clear of the workers. I expect to be there most of the day tomorrow. I'll see you then."

She smiled at him. "See you then."

He looked for a moment at her smile and then raised his eyes to hers again. She had the strangest sensation that she had just been virtually kissed. Her lips actually tingled.

The man really was making her crazy.

Mac turned toward the door then. "See you around, Brad," he said as he passed the teen.

Brad didn't reply.

"You were rude to Mr. Cordero, Brad," Sharon chided when the door closed behind Mac. "I doubt he heard a word you said."

"I don't like him."

She was surprised by the growled response. "What do you mean? You only just met him."

"I don't care. He seems like a jerk to me."

"Honestly, Brad. You shouldn't form judgments about people without even getting to know them. Mr. Cordero is a very nice man." Even as she said it, she was aware of how insipid the word *nice* seemed when applied to Mac.

Brad didn't buy it. "He's a jerk. And I don't like the way he looked at you."

Sharon reached for her purse. "Don't be silly. Let's go home now and get some dinner. And we're going to talk about why you were more than half an hour late."

"I told you, it wasn't my fault."

"We'll talk about it later," she repeated, keys in hand as she moved toward the door.

"Jerry said last Friday night that he was going to try to take us out for pizza or something tonight. Didn't he call?"

"He called, but I turned him down."

"Aw, man! Just because I was a few minutes late?"

"I had several reasons." She let him exit the shop ahead of her.

Brad muttered under his breath as she locked the door. Sharon sighed. It was going to be a long, stressful evening. The only bright spot in the past hour had been Mac's unexpected visit.

CAMERA IN HAND, Sharon stepped through the front door of the Garrett house at just after five Tuesday afternoon. She had passed several vehicles leaving as she arrived, so she assumed work had ended for the day. Mac's truck was still in the parking lot, alongside one other car she recognized as Trevor McBride's.

Wondering why a lawyer was visiting a construction site, she paused just inside the front door at the rack Mac had set up to hold spare hard hats. She couldn't help smiling when she spotted a brand-new, bright yellow hat at the end of the row. Neatly lettered across the front was the word *decorator.*

The hat fit almost perfectly when she settled it on her head. It made her feel very much like a member of the team—a feeling she was starting to enjoy. Somewhat proprietarily, she glanced around the entryway and into the front parlor, imagining how beautiful and welcoming this view would be once she finished her part.

Heavy footsteps on the temporarily reinforced stairs made her look up. Mac and Trevor were on their way down. Neither was wearing a hard hat— probably because the construction work had ended for the day. She studied them as they descended. Two very strong, attractive men, she mused. One dark and sleek, the other golden and slender.

She imagined there would be quite a heated debate among her friends as to which man was the most attractive of the two. As for her—well, she thought as she focused on Mac, there was really no question.

Trevor smiled when he saw Sharon. Mac didn't smile, but there was a sudden gleam in his dark eyes that made her knees quiver for a moment. Because it seemed safer, she concentrated first on his companion. "Hello, Trevor."

"Hi, Sharon. Nice hat."

"Thank you." She glanced at Mac with a quick smile. "It's new."

"Very fetching. Interesting place, hmm?"

"Very. I haven't been upstairs yet, but I'm itching to reveal the potential of the downstairs."

"It's a bit of a maze upstairs, but there's definite potential there, too. Mac just gave me a quick tour. I haven't been in here since I was a kid and I was curious if the place looked anything like I remembered."

"And did it?"

"Not much," Trevor admitted. "But that was a long time ago."

She laughed. "You make it sound as if you're an old man."

He chuckled. "There are days when thirty-two feels pretty old. Especially when I'm trying to keep up with my six-year-old son and three-year-old daughter."

"How is your family?"

"Fine, thank you. I'll give them your regards."

"Do that."

Trevor turned to Mac, who'd been waiting patiently while they exchanged pleasantries. Thanking him again for the tour, Trevor shook Mac's hand, then explained that he had to hurry home to his family. Sharon and Mac were left alone in the house when Trevor closed the front door behind him.

"I was surprised to see Trevor here," Sharon commented, just to fill the sudden silence.

"Trent said something the other day about Trevor

wanting to look around the place before we changed everything. I sent a message for him to stop by anytime.''

''It was nice of you to take the time to walk him through.''

''I had no other plans. And I understood his curiosity.''

''And now I'm the curious one. I can't wait to get upstairs and look around.''

''Then what's keeping you?'' he asked, motioning toward the stairway.

Very aware of Mac following close behind her, she climbed the stairs, wondering what she would find at the top.

As Trevor had commented, the upstairs resembled a maze, with lots of little rooms opening off meandering hallways. To add to the chaos, the workers had started tearing out walls already, leaving gaping holes behind.

Mac guided her through the mess, pointing out features that would remain, describing the changes, even asking her opinion on a couple of options. She took several snapshots, though she knew it would look very different once Mac was finished.

Studying a particularly interesting wall line, she turned and found Mac standing directly in front of her. ''Um…there's not a lot of natural light up here, is there?''

The way he was looking at her, she could tell he wasn't really thinking about the renovation. ''There will be more when we're finished," he said, his eyes never leaving her face.

She moistened her lips, trying to keep her mind on the job. "You're making a lot of changes."

"Yes. But the basic style and structure of the house won't change."

"I know. That's what I find so intriguing about this project."

He lifted a hand to straighten her hard hat, though it already felt straight. He left his hand there when he'd finished, maintaining the contact between them. "Doesn't anything else about this project intrigue you?"

She swallowed. Now, how was she to answer that? "Um..."

"Coward," he murmured just beneath his breath.

Her left eyebrow rose in response to the challenge. "I beg your pardon?"

"Nothing." His attempt at looking innocent was almost laughably ineffective. She didn't think Mac would be trying out for the Honoria Community Theater anytime soon. Innocent was just not an expression he could pull off.

Feeling more at ease with him now, she walked the fingers of her right hand up the front of his denim shirt, holding the camera in her left hand. "If I were a coward," she asked, "would I be here now? Alone in this old house with a guy some people say is involved in organized crime?"

Even though she had spoken lightly, he frowned. "I told you, I am not ... "

She covered his mouth with her fingertips. "I know. I was only teasing."

Moving swiftly, he caught her hand and held it against his lips, planting a kiss in her palm. Funny. She'd never realized there were quite so many nerve endings in her palm. And every one of them sparked to life when Mac's lips brushed her skin.

His head still slightly bent over her hand, he looked at her through his dark lashes. No man had ever looked at her the way Mac did. Others had looked *at* her—Mac seemed to look right into her. And, oh, how it made her feel.

Without releasing her, he slid his other hand behind her neck and gave a gentle tug. She never even considered resisting.

This kiss was as startlingly powerful as the ones they had shared before. She might have thought she would be better prepared this time for the effect his kisses had on her. She'd have been wrong.

She wasn't sure how her arms ended up around his neck. She didn't remember putting them there. She only knew they felt right there. She didn't know what had happened to her camera, though she supposed the slight thud she'd heard at her feet a moment earlier might be a clue. Fortunately, it was an inexpensive and durable model. Not that she cared at the moment.

He twisted so that she rested over his arm, giving him better access to her mouth. His movements were bold. Decisive. There was a hint of wildness in this kiss. A whisper of danger. She wouldn't have expected to be drawn to either. But she was.

From the beginning, Mac had appealed to a part of her she hardly recognized, herself.

He lifted his head, searched her face for a moment, then covered her mouth with his again. The kiss went on for an eternity, and when it ended, there was no doubt left in her mind that he was as affected by the connection between them as she was. His left arm surrounded her, supporting her. His right hand was at the small of her back, pressing lightly, holding her against him. There was no question that he wanted her—and what an experience it was to be wanted by a man like this!

"Did you plan this?" she asked.

"I planned to have you in my arms again since I left your house the other night," he admitted.

"I'm not sure if I should respond by being flattered or insulted."

"Just as long as you respond," he murmured, then kissed her again.

She most definitely responded.

"This is crazy," she murmured between kisses. "We hardly know each other."

He caught her lower lip gently, briefly, between his teeth, causing a current of electricity to race through her. Then he lifted his head. "I'm all for getting to know each other better."

She trailed a fingertip along the strong line of his jaw, realizing that her initial shyness around him was almost gone. "I'd like that."

"Have dinner with me tonight?"

"I have to pick up my brother from baseball practice in half an hour. I was planning to make spaghetti for dinner tonight. Why don't you join us?"

His mouth twisted. "I don't think your brother likes me very much."

She was surprised he'd picked up on that. She still didn't understand Brad's antagonism toward Mac. "He just doesn't know you. Brad's going through an awkwardness stage. I'm sure he'll like you if he spends time with you."

Twisting a strand of her hair around his finger, he gave a slight shrug. "Maybe. Maybe not. Does it matter a great deal to you?"

She felt as if it should. It had always seemed important that Brad liked Jerry. It made things easier when they spent time together. But she wasn't going to let Brad's attitude prevent her from spending more time with the most fascinating man she had met in…well, in her entire life.

"Come for dinner," she said. "Brad will behave."

"What time?"

"Seven."

"I'll be there." He slid his hand into the hair at the back of her head. "You said you have another half hour?"

"Almost."

He smiled as he tossed her hard hat aside and lowered his mouth to hers again. "Sounds like enough time to get to know each other a little better."

CHAPTER EIGHT

"HE'S COMING to our house for dinner? I'm leaving."

Sharon sighed. "I really don't understand your antagonism, Brad. You only met Mac for a couple of minutes."

"I've seen him around town. He's a jerk. Strutting around like he's some hotshot who's better than the hicks around here."

Appalled, Sharon stared at her brother. They stood in their living room—she'd waited until they arrived home before springing the news on him about who was joining them for dinner—and he faced her from the center of the floor, his shaggy hair tumbling into his anger-flushed face. He needed a haircut, she thought inconsequentially. He was beginning to look like someone she didn't know. He certainly sounded like a stranger. "Who's been saying these things to you? I can't believe those are your words."

"Everybody's been talking about him."

"I thought I'd taught you not to listen to the malicious gossip that goes on around this town. You have the intelligence to form your own opinions,

Brad. You have to get to know someone before you decide whether you like him or not.''

"I know all I want to know. He just wants to make some fast money off the old Garrett place and then he'll move on. I don't see why we have to entertain him while he's here."

"How about simple hospitality? He doesn't know many people in town."

"He doesn't belong here. He isn't even our kind."

Sharon felt her eyes narrow. "Would you like to explain that comment?"

Apparently deciding he'd come too close to crossing her personal line, Brad backed down, but not by much. "Nothing," he muttered.

"If I thought you were making a slur against Mr. Cordero's ethnic background, I would send you to your room and make sure you didn't come out again until the school bell rings in the fall. I will not tolerate any form of bigotry in my household, is that clear? But I'm sure that's not what you meant, because our mother did not raise us that way."

His hands shoved in his pockets, Brad stared at the floor, refusing to answer.

"Mr. Cordero will be joining us in about an hour. You will wash up and prepare yourself to be polite, understand?"

"I bet Jerry won't like it that you're spending so much time with this guy."

"I don't consult with Jerry before I invite someone to dinner. Jerry and I are friends, Brad. That's it."

Brad looked suddenly stricken. "You're not going out with this Cordero guy, are you?"

Choosing her words carefully, Sharon answered, "I like Mac. He's an interesting man. He and I are working together on the renovation project, so I will be spending quite a bit of time with him during the next few months. If you would just give him a chance, I'm sure you would like him, too."

"Why can't I just go to Jimbo's for dinner?"

She was tempted to let him, just to avoid any unpleasantness in front of Mac. But it seemed too important to teach her brother about proper behavior—and especially about tolerance. She didn't know which of his friends had been filling his mind with such garbage, but she had no intention of letting it go on. "Because we're having company for dinner and I want you to be here. Now go get cleaned up."

Muttering beneath his breath, Brad stamped upstairs. Sharon watched him worriedly, wondering what was happening to her little brother. Was this typical teenage behavior, or something more? She wished Caleb and Bobbie McBride were in town. Their practical, sometimes blunt advice, along with their experience at raising teenagers, had been valuable to her on many occasions.

Shaking her head, she went into the kitchen to start dinner, hoping she hadn't made a big mistake in inviting Mac to join them.

The telephone rang fifteen minutes before Mac was due to arrive. Sharon answered on the kitchen extension. "Hello?"

"Hi, sweetie."

"Mom." Casting a quick look around the kitchen to make sure nothing needed her attention at the moment, Sharon leaned against the counter for a chat. "How's the Riviera?"

"Oh, darling, it's wonderful. I wish you and Brad were here to enjoy it with me."

Sharon was sure that was true. Lucy had always believed in the more the merrier. Unfortunately, she'd never quite gripped the concept that "more" also involved more money. "I'm glad you're having a nice time."

"I miss my babies, of course. How are you and Brad?"

"We're fine, Mom." She decided against telling her mother about Brad's growing rebelliousness. There was nothing Lucy could do about it long-distance. And little she would do, even if she were here, Sharon admitted to herself.

"I wasn't sure you'd be home. I thought maybe you'd have a date with Jerry."

"No. Not tonight." That was something else she had no intention of discussing just now. The list of safe topics was shrinking rapidly, she thought. "Tell me what you've seen and done since the last time you called," she prompted.

Lucy immediately launched into an eager and colorful monologue that Sharon could only half follow.

Keeping an eye on the clock, she made appropriately interested noises. At five minutes until seven, she broke in to say, "Do you want to talk to Brad before you have to go?"

"Of course I want to talk to my little boy."

Sharon almost sighed. Lucy's "little boy" was five-eight and a hundred forty pounds. Three inches taller than Sharon and twenty pounds heavier. Sharon could only catch glimpses of the sweet-natured child he'd been. And she wished she could better understand the moody young man he'd become. At least if her mother was here, there would be someone to share the worry. "I miss you, Mom. I'll be glad when you're home."

"I know, darling. Just a few more weeks."

"I'll get Brad for you."

Brad took the call on the phone in his room. Sharon had just replaced the receiver in the kitchen when the doorbell rang. She'd asked Brad not to upset his mother with his complaints. She hoped he was complying with her request.

"What's wrong?" Mac asked when she opened the door.

She immediately smoothed her expression. "Nothing. Come in."

Being Mac, he didn't let it go at that. "Something's bothering you," he said as he closed the door behind him. "What is it? Is there anything I can do?"

"Really, Mac. It's okay. I'm just a little concerned about my brother."

"Why?"

She shrugged. "He's a teenager."

His mouth twisted a little as he nodded. "I don't envy you."

She could understand that. Few men would willingly take on the responsibilities Sharon had shouldered. Even though she hoped to have her own place soon, she was realistic enough to know that she wouldn't be able to completely distance herself from her family's problems. Lucy was just too scatterbrained and disorganized to manage well on her own and *definitely* not firm enough to deal with Brad's stubborn moods.

Lucy had indulged Brad too much, and for that matter, so had Sharon. They'd both felt that they had to make it up to him somehow because he'd lost his father so young. Perhaps they'd gone overboard. It was difficult now to suddenly become a disciplinarian.

Mac looked around. "Where is your brother?"

"On the phone with Mom. Probably telling her what an ogre I am," she muttered.

"Every teenager needs an ogre for a guardian."

"You're probably right."

Taking a step closer to her, he reached out to trace her lower lip with a fingertip. "Since I'm *not* a teenager, perhaps you could save this stern frown for your brother?"

Realizing she'd been scowling since he'd arrived, she smiled slightly against his finger. "Sorry."

"That's better."

Brad appeared at the top of the stairs just then. He was obviously displeased to catch them standing so close together, Mac's hand still resting lightly against the side of Sharon's face. The glare he gave them was almost cold enough to cause frostbite.

Mac dropped his hand and moved away, taking his time about it. "Hello, Brad. Nice to see you again," he said casually.

"Hey."

Sharon wasn't exactly pleased with Brad's curt response, but at least it had been audible. He knew better than to be blatantly rude to a guest in their home. At least, she hoped he did.

MAC DIDN'T TRY to push the boy into further conversation during dinner. He and Sharon discussed the anticipated progress of the renovation for the upcoming week, then turned the discussion to national politics, a subject that interested them both. Keeping his head down, Brad concentrated on his food, apparently content to be ignored.

Eventually Sharon seemed to decide it was time for her brother to join in. "How's your food, Brad?" she asked pleasantly. "Do you need anything else?"

"It's fine," the boy replied without looking up from his plate. "Can I have some more bread?"

She passed him the basket of wheat rolls, which he accepted with a muttered, "Thanks."

Because he could tell that Brad's sullenness was disturbing her, Mac said, "This is really good, Sharon. I've always liked spaghetti."

He was rewarded with a smile. "It's my mother's special recipe. She's a very good cook when she pays attention to what she's doing. Remember the time she accidentally used cayenne pepper instead of paprika, Brad? We nearly burned the linings out of our mouths."

The boy didn't share her amusement. "My mom's a great cook," he said, sounding defensive.

Mac shrugged. "Everyone makes mistakes. My mother used to get distracted and burn the plantains. I started thinking of the smoke alarm as a dinner bell."

"Plantains?" Sharon repeated. "I've never had them."

"They look a little like bananas. In Puerto Rico, they're often fried and served as a side dish."

"What other Puerto Rican dishes did your mother make for you?"

He could tell she was relieved that the conversation was moving again, so he decided to expand a bit. "We had arroz con pollo quite often—that's yellow rice with chicken, one of my favorite meals. And asopao, a heavy rice soup, with either chicken or shrimp. Paella. And for dessert, flan. No one made it the way my mother did. I still dream about her flan sometimes," he joked, though it was the truth.

"I like *American* food," Brad muttered.

"Like spaghetti?" his sister asked sarcastically, nodding toward Brad's empty plate.

He flushed and ducked his head again.

A hint of apology in her expression, Sharon turned to Mac again. "Did you ever live in Puerto Rico?"

"No. I visited there once, but I was born and raised in Savannah."

"Which explains the Southern accent," she teased lightly.

"Yes, ma'am."

"Do you speak Spanish?"

"Well enough to make myself understood. I had to learn it pretty much on my own. My mother wanted English to be my primary language."

Sharon tried again to pull her brother into the conversation. "Brad's taking Spanish in school."

"Only because I've got no choice," Brad said immediately. "They won't let us graduate without two years of a foreign language. Don't see the purpose in it, myself. English is the only language I need to know."

Sharon's little brother was in danger of becoming a bigot, Mac mused, remembering some of the slurs he'd heard muttered behind him the evening he'd encountered Brad and his friends outside the arcade. Typical gang mentality. Band together against suspected outsiders. Create an image of superiority by perceiving and treating others as inferiors. Someone needed to get this kid away from that crowd before he got into trouble.

Not that it was any of *his* business, of course.

"I made brownies for dessert," Sharon said,

smoothly changing the subject. "I hope you aren't allergic to chocolate, Mac."

"I have no problems at all with chocolate."

"Can I take mine up to my room? I want to read my new sports magazine."

Sharon gave Brad's request a moment of consideration. "We do have company."

"Don't let me keep you from your magazine," Mac said with a slight shrug.

"Okay, Sharon?"

She gave in. "I suppose it's all right."

The boy practically bolted upstairs.

Sharon looked contritely at Mac. "I'm sorry. I don't know what gets into him when he's around you. I guess you intimidate him, for some reason."

Mac, of course, knew exactly why Brad still resented him. The kid hadn't gotten over being embarrassed in front of his friends. But he was just going to have to get over it. Mac wasn't going to disappear—not until he was good and ready, anyway.

"Let me help you with the dishes," he said, reaching for his empty plate.

"Oh, that's not—"

"Sharon," he cut in firmly. "This is the second time you've fed me. Let me help."

She smiled and caved. "If you insist."

Since Sharon admitted to being the clean-as-she-cooked type, it didn't take long to load the dishwasher and straighten the kitchen. By the time they'd finished, a fresh pot of coffee had brewed.

They carried their cups and plates of pecan brownies into the living room. They'd talked while they worked. Mac was surprised about how easily he conversed with Sharon. He usually found it harder to make small talk. But now he knew it was time to get down to the real reason he was here—or at least that's what he told himself—to find out more about the McBrides.

"Trevor McBride seems like an interesting guy," he said, keeping his tone light as he held his coffee cup and reached for a brownie. "He looks a lot like Trent, but I got the impression when he visited the site this afternoon that they're not much alike on the whole."

"Not a lot," Sharon agreed from the chair she'd chosen near the couch where Mac had settled. "I always thought of Trevor as the more grounded brother. Like their older sister, Tara, he excelled in school—valedictorian, class president, that sort of thing. No one was surprised when he followed in his father's footsteps and went East to law school. He made quite a name for himself in Washington, D.C., before moving back here to raise his children after his wife died so tragically young."

"Had to be tough on him. Being left with two small children to raise, I mean."

"Yes, it was very hard on him. He was lucky to have had his parents here to help him out. They're a very close family. They rally around each other without hesitation when one of them is in need. Then he and Jamie got married, and they seem very happy now. He and the kids are all crazy about Jamie, and she obviously feels the same way about them."

Mac found it hard to identify with a family that unhesitatingly supported each other through every difficulty. It was a luxury he and his mother had been denied. "The McBrides have had their share of troubles, haven't they?"

"Like all big families, I suppose," she said with a shrug.

Not much help there. "I was thinking about Trent's plane crash. I understand he'd been on his way to a career in the air force until the crash grounded him."

She nodded, looking distracted, her eyes on the staircase. Thinking about her brother again? Mac wondered. But at least she was answering his questions.

"Yes, Trent always dreamed of being a pilot. He was as smart as his sister and brother, but grades weren't quite as important to him. He made A's only because he needed them to get him into the Air Force Academy. Tara and Trevor were always rather serious, very focused. Trent was the clown. The daredevil. I suppose that's hard for you to believe now. The crash changed him so much. He's just now learning to enjoy life again. Thanks in no small part to his fiancée, Annie, he's learned that he can be happy doing something other than flying."

"It couldn't have been easy for him to give up the one thing he'd always wanted."

Sharon shook her head. "I'm sure it was the hardest thing he's ever done. His family was so worried about him. Bobbie told me once that she wasn't sure he would make it through—but I always knew he was stronger than that."

"You wouldn't still be carrying a torch for the guy, would you?"

That got her attention. She let out a peal of laughter that was obviously genuine, to his satisfaction. "Good heavens, no. I've always considered Trent a friend. In fact, I probably think of him more like a brother—a cousin, maybe—than anything else."

"Just checking out my competition," he murmured, pleased when she blushed prettily.

"It isn't Trent," she assured him.

"Oh?" He lifted an eyebrow. "Someone else?"

"I've told you, I'm not romantically involved with anyone. I have male friends I see sometimes, but that's all."

He gave her a wicked smile that made her blush deepen. "Good."

She made a pretense of concentrating on her coffee, looking so flustered and vulnerable that it was all Mac could do not to pull her into his arms and make her flush with desire rather than embarrassment. He cleared his throat and forced himself back on topic. "Trevor's several years older than Trent, isn't he?"

She seemed grateful that he'd veered into less personal waters. "Almost six years, I think. Trent's twenty-six, and Trevor is thirty-two."

"And their sister is older?"

"A year older than Trevor," she agreed. "Tara's thirty-three. Um—about your age?" she hazarded, obviously hinting.

"The same," he agreed. "I'm thirty-three." He wondered if the fact that he and Tara McBride had been born only months apart made it more or less likely that they had the same father. He couldn't help wondering how Sharon would react if he made that speculation aloud. She'd proven to be even more helpful than he'd hoped in providing information about the McBrides—but something told him that would stop abruptly if she suspected he had an ax to grind against the family she obviously admired so greatly.

"I'm looking forward to meeting Caleb and Bobbie McBride," he commented, hoping he wasn't pushing his luck. Mac had a pretty strong suspicion that Caleb wasn't the man he was searching for but he might as well find out everything he could. "The way everyone in town talks about them, they sound intriguing."

Sharon smiled. "They are. You'll like them, I'm sure. Caleb's a true Southern gentleman. Jamie says he plays the part of the small-town Southern lawyer to the hilt. She's crazy about him, of course—as I am."

"He's the founder of the McBride Law Firm, right?"

"Right. He opened the practice long before I was born."

"I, um, suppose he has to travel quite a bit in his line of work."

Laughing a little, Sharon shook her head. "Caleb never leaves Honoria. You wouldn't believe what his family went through just to get him to take this vacation. He calls himself the original homebody, someone who is perfectly happy to live his entire life in the town where he was born. I don't remember him ever being gone for more than a day or two at a time, and never without his wife and family to accompany him."

So Caleb never left Honoria. Mac nodded somberly. "He and his wife sound very close. They must be a lot alike."

"I'm sure they are in some ways. But Bobbie—well." She seemed to grope for the most suitable adjectives.

He chuckled. "I've heard she can be…intimidating."

"The people who told you that were probably in her class at one time. She's the terror of Honoria Elementary—and the best teacher in town. Fiercely loyal to her family and friends, a bit gruff but very good-hearted, bossy but well-intentioned. There are some people who are put off by her bluntness, but I'm very fond of her. She and Caleb are a wonderful couple—the perfect foils for each other. They both have something very special to offer. They've been married for almost forty years."

"Are there any McBrides you don't like?" Mac asked, shaking his head.

She laughed. "No, not really. My own family is so small—just Mom and Brad and me, and a few distant relatives we don't see very often. I must admit, I've always been a little fascinated by the McBride clan."

"It shows."

Her mouth twisted. "I suppose that's why you and I always end up discussing them. You must wonder if I ever talk about anything else."

Had she actually convinced herself that she was the one who kept bringing the McBrides into their conversation? If so, Mac had been more subtle than he'd believed—or she was more worried about her brother than she was letting on, which was more likely. Deciding to be content with the progress he'd made for the evening, as well as feeling guilty for manipulating Sharon this way, Mac changed the subject. "Did you get all the photographs you needed today? Will you be out at the site again tomorrow?"

She shook her head. "I'm going car shopping tomorrow afternoon. I can't keep renting."

"Did your insurance come through for you?"

She shrugged ruefully. "To a point. I took a loss, of course, and I'll have to finance a new car."

"It's damn unfair, isn't it? Whoever was driving that van should be the one paying. It wasn't your fault the idiot decided to run you off the road."

"I know. And you're right. It is unfair, and it makes me furious, but I suppose I'll have to live with it until Wade catches the guy. Even then the chances are slim I'll ever be reimbursed, I suppose.''

"I'm afraid so.''

"I try not to think about that night very often,'' she said, looking into her coffee cup. ''It's too disturbing for the most part. But I can't help wondering sometimes…''

"Wondering what?'' he asked gently, sensing she needed to talk.

She looked up at him. "The van seemed to come at me so deliberately. You don't think—you don't think it was deliberate, do you? To keep me from testifying about what I saw, or somehow identifying him, I mean? Am I letting my imagination run away with me when I think along those lines?''

She was asking for reassurance that someone hadn't deliberately tried to kill her. Knowing how horrifying that possibility must be to her, Mac wished he could give her the reassurance she wanted. But in this, at least, he had to be honest with her. "I don't know, Sharon. Maybe it was an accident, but under the circumstances, maybe it wasn't. You can bet it's a question your friend Wade will ask if he ever gets his hands on the guy.''

"When, not if,'' Sharon corrected him automatically. "Wade will catch him.''

From what he was learning about the very thorough police chief, Mac understood why she spoke so confidently. If the driver of that van was still in the area, there was a good chance Wade would catch him. But it was more likely that he was long gone.

Too many crimes like that were never solved, an endless source of frustration to those who worked in law enforcement, and one of the reasons Mac had wanted out.

"Try not to dwell on it," he advised her, knowing that wasn't as easy as it sounded. "You're safe now. It isn't as if you could identify anyone."

"I know. I just can't help remembering every once in a while…" Her voice trailed off as she shivered, and he pictured her reliving the terror during sleepless nights. His fist tightened around his coffee cup. He wished *he* could get his hands on the guy who had almost cost Sharon her life.

She shook her head. "I'm fine, really. And I'll never forget the way you helped me that night."

"I'm just glad I was there. So, is anyone going car shopping with you tomorrow? Or do you prefer to handle that sort of thing on your own?"

"Brad wants to go, but fortunately he has baseball practice. I'm afraid he would try to talk me into buying something completely impractical—like a Corvette or a Viper or something equally out of my price range. I'm quite sure he won't approve of the sensible sedan I intend to buy. My friend Jerry— he's an insurance salesman here in Honoria—offered to go with me, but Jerry's the take-charge type. He'd never let me get a word in edgewise with the car salesperson. He means well, but I'd prefer to handle the purchase myself."

"If you'd like some company, I'd be happy to go

with you. I'd only give my opinion when you ask for it.''

She looked intrigued. ''Are you sure you have the time?''

''I'll make the time—if you want me to go along.''

''Actually, I would appreciate having a second opinion. I thought about asking Trevor or Trent, but I wasn't sure either of them would be available.''

''I'm available.''

Her smile made him glad he'd taken the risk of offering his company. She was obviously pleased—which pleased him in return. ''I'd like that.''

''So would I.'' And he was well aware that it had very little to do with finding out more about the McBrides.

Because it was getting harder with each passing moment to sit so close to her without touching her, he set his coffee cup on the table and stood. ''I'll see you tomorrow.''

She rose with him. ''You're leaving?''

He glanced at the staircase. ''It seems like the wisest choice.''

Following his glance, she nodded. ''Maybe you're right.''

''Where do you want to meet tomorrow?''

''My shop—noon?''

''I'll be there.''

She followed him to the door. Casting one more quick look at the empty staircase, he reached out and pulled her toward him for one long, thorough kiss. It was all he allowed himself—but he simply couldn't leave without it. She returned the embrace with an eagerness that suggested she had needed it as badly as he did—or was that only wishful thinking on his part?

As he drove back to his apartment, Mac tried to analyze exactly what was going on between him and Sharon Henderson. He wanted her—he'd be an idiot to deny that. But he also wanted any background she could give him about the McBrides, especially Caleb and his brothers.

And yet somehow, he had the uncomfortable feeling there was even more between them than that. And he wasn't at all sure what to do about it. His one attempt at commitment had ended in pain and bitterness—he had no intention of going through anything like that again. Especially with a woman who might very well hate him when she found out why he was really here.

CHAPTER NINE

MAC STUDIED the McBride family tree taking shape on the yellow legal pad. Two hours after leaving Sharon's house, he sat at the small round table in the eat-in kitchen of his temporary apartment, his notes spread in front of him. He'd been trying to concentrate on the few new tidbits he'd learned, rather than the way Sharon's mouth had felt beneath his. He'd made an attempt to remember the reason he'd come to Honoria in the first place, rather than the look of reciprocal desire he had seen in Sharon's eyes.

Thinking of Sharon tonight could prove to be far more uncomfortable than brooding on bad memories.

"Caleb and Bobbie McBride," he had written at the top of a fresh sheet of paper. Beneath the names, he'd noted that they'd been married for nearly seven years before Mac's conception—which meant Caleb could have been the married man who'd had an affair with Mac's mother. Although it was possible, Mac was having trouble believing it. There were certain other things that didn't fit at all. Caleb had long been established as an attorney in town, a job that seemed to require no travel. From what everyone said, he and Bobbie were very happily married, almost perfectly suited. So why would he risk everything to have an affair? Especially since Caleb's oldest child, Tara, was Mac's own age, which indicated Caleb and Bobbie had certainly been getting along at least reasonably well thirty-three years ago.

Everything Mac had heard about that branch of the McBride family indicated that they were almost TV-sitcom perfect—a small-town lawyer and a schoolteacher with three attractive, intelligent, popular and successful kids. If scandal really was a McBride legacy, it seemed to have affected that group less dramatically than the others.

Caleb's children seemed to have grown up in the kind of home Mac had secretly fantasized about when he'd been a lonely boy whose single mother worked too long and too hard, leaving him alone too much to daydream about what his life might have been like if things had been different.

He'd watched other boys with their dads and he had wondered what it would be like to have a father of his own. He'd gone through stages of resentment, anger, even rebellion that his father hadn't wanted to be a part of his life. Much like Brad Henderson, he realized. Brad definitely needed a strong male influence in his life, rather than two women who seemed to have gotten into the habit of overindulging him.

Mac had been fortunate to have a mother who had been determined to help him make something of himself, and a few good male role models—a couple of favorite teachers, a coach and a police officer neighbor who'd taken Mac under his wing. He knew Brad was involved in sports, so maybe the boy had a few guys who cared enough to keep him in line, show him what being a real man was all about.

He wondered if Sharon's friend Jerry was one of Brad's role models.

He'd heard about Jerry, even before Sharon had casually mentioned him. Rumor was that Sharon and Jerry had been dating for a while, though no one seemed to think it had gotten serious yet. There'd been a few who felt the need to mention the guy to Mac—as if obliquely warning him that he could be intruding on posted property. Mac had decided to take his cues from Sharon, herself—and she'd certainly given no indication that any other man had a claim on her.

He didn't think she'd appreciate the terms in which he was thinking about her, he thought with a frown. She wasn't property to be claimed by any man, including himself. And yet he was aware that he still didn't like thinking about Jerry. He was sure he wouldn't like him—and he'd never even met the guy. Which meant that what he *really* disliked was the thought of Sharon spending time with any other man.

Slamming his pencil onto the table, he shoved his chair backward and stood. He didn't want to sit here identifying with Sharon's fatherless kid brother, or brooding about her other male friends. And there didn't seem to be any more conclusions he could reach about the McBrides tonight. He still knew almost nothing about Jonah, Josiah Jr. and Caleb's younger brother. He was the remaining piece of the genetic puzzle Mac was trying to assemble.

Mac needed to figure out a way to somehow include Jonah McBride in his next conversation with Sharon. At the moment, that seemed much easier than trying to figure out a way to entice Sharon into his bed.

SHARON HAD KNOWN when she accepted Mac's offer to look for a car with her that the friendship growing between them would no longer be private. She might as well have posted a notice in the *Honoria Gazette* that she was dating him. She knew people would talk. But she didn't really care. She and Mac were single, unattached adults. There was no reason at all why they shouldn't spend time together.

She had such a good time that Wednesday afternoon. She enjoyed being with Mac, valued his advice, appreciated the way he stood back and let her do her own talking and make her own decisions. And she savored the way he looked at her, making her feel feminine and desirable and special in a way no other man had ever made her feel. She was aware that she was becoming majorly infatuated with this man, but she told herself she could handle it.

At least, she hoped she could.

She had hardly parked her new car in the garage that evening when the telephone rang. Tossing her purse aside, she grabbed the kitchen extension. "Hello?"

"Hello, Sharon. It's a pleasant surprise to hear your voice rather than your answering machine."

She grimaced. It was obvious from Jerry's tone that he wasn't happy—and she could guess the reason. "Hi, Jerry."

"I hear you got a new car this afternoon."

"Yes. I was planning to call you first thing in the morning to update my insurance. How did you hear about it?"

"Charlie Hayes came by my office just before closing time to give me the information on his new pickup. He mentioned that he'd seen you at the dealership."

Sharon remembered chatting with the retired school principal who'd once been her mother's boss. She had introduced him to Mac. "Mr. Hayes looks good, doesn't he?" she said. "He seems to have fully recovered from his bout with cancer."

She'd had a faint hope Jerry would allow her to direct the conversation, but she wasn't surprised when he said, instead, "Charlie told me you'd brought a friend with you."

"Yes," she answered evenly. "Mac Cordero volunteered to go with me when I mentioned my plans for the afternoon."

"Perhaps you've forgotten that I also volunteered."

"No, I didn't forget. But I didn't want to take

you away from your office. Mac had some free time this afternoon.''

''Rumor has it you've been spending quite a bit of time with this guy.''

So people *had* been talking. ''I am on his renovation team,'' she said rather lamely.

''And the project isn't anywhere close to where your services are needed. From what I hear, they've just started tearing out walls and old fixtures and wiring. It'll be weeks before they start rebuilding.''

''Mac has asked me to be involved at all stages. He likes my ideas.''

''I'm sure he does,'' Jerry muttered.

Because that comment seemed juvenile, Sharon chose not to respond. ''Would you like to hear about my new car? It isn't fancy, but it's—''

''What I would like to hear,'' he cut in curtly, ''is just what is going on between you and Mac Cordero.''

She wondered why Jerry suddenly sounded so priggish. She'd never really thought of him in those terms before. Of course, she had never really done anything to annoy him this much before. ''I don't owe you any explanations, Jerry. Nor do I have to ask your permission to see other people.''

''Is this why you've been avoiding me lately? You're seeing this Cordero guy?''

''I don't think it's a good time to discuss this.''

''And when *is* a good time, Sharon? Every time I've suggested getting together lately, you've had an excuse.''

That was true, she realized with a grimace. She'd been trying to send gentle hints to Jerry, when it would have been better to tell him outright that she wasn't interested in him romantically. That she valued his friendship and hated to lose it, but she couldn't commit to a relationship that realistically was going nowhere. "Perhaps we could have dinner one night next week?"

There was a taut, lengthy pause. "Don't do me any favors."

"Come on, Jerry. There's no need to..." But Sharon's words were met by a dial tone. He'd hung up on her. She sighed in exasperation.

"He dumped you, didn't he?"

The voice from behind her made her start, the phone still clutched in her hand. "Brad, you startled me," she said, shaking her head as she replaced the receiver. "I nearly jumped out of my shoes. Do you want to see my new—"

"Did you let Jerry break up with you?" her brother interrupted.

She realized only then that Brad looked furious.

She spoke calmly. "Jerry and I didn't 'break up.' We weren't involved in that way. You make us sound like your high-school friends who go steady."

"He's mad at you because you've been hanging out with Cordero, isn't he?"

Sharon was beginning to resent this line of interrogation from her brother, especially so soon after Jerry's cross-examination. "This really isn't any of your business."

"I heard you took him with you when you went looking at cars today."

"How in the world—"

"Why did you do that? Didn't you know everyone would talk about it?"

"I don't see anything wrong with taking a friend shopping with me."

"It makes you look like you're chasing the guy."

"Brad!"

"Jimbo says you can't trust a guy like that. Traveling from place to place, never sticking around. Hitting on women wherever he goes, looking for an easy—"

"Jimbo doesn't know what he's talking about," she snapped. "And, frankly, neither do you."

"I know the guys are all making fun of you. They think you're stupid to fall for a jerk like that. They told me if I don't talk some sense into you, he's going to make a fool of you. You'll end up like Connie Moser if somebody doesn't stop you."

Sharon had to roll her eyes at that. Connie Moser was a sixteen-year-old single mother who'd become pregnant after a summer fling with a boy her own age who'd come to Honoria from Saint Louis to visit his grandparents. She hardly saw a correlation. "Give me credit for a little more sense than that, will you, Brad? You're being ridiculous. Mac and I are both adults. Why shouldn't we go out if we want?"

"You already have a boyfriend. Jerry."

"Jerry is *not* my boyfriend." She found herself

raising her voice in frustration, and realized she was coming close to getting into an undignified shouting match with her maddening younger brother. She took a deep breath to steady herself. "I'm not asking your permission to date Mac."

"So how come I have to ask *your* permission to do anything?"

"Because, whether you like it or not, I'm the adult in charge in this household, at least until Mom comes home. I've tried to be fair and I've tried to cut you a great deal of slack, but when it comes down to it, the final decisions—and the responsibility—are mine. Frankly, I don't consider it an ideal situation, either, but Mom asked us this favor and we both agreed to it, so we're going to uphold our end of the deal."

"But—"

"You have neither the right nor the responsibility to 'talk sense into me' about anything I do. I don't have to seek your approval, and I have no interest whatever in Jimbo's opinion. Have I made myself very clear?"

Sullenly refusing to answer, Brad only nodded, looking down at his feet.

"Go upstairs and wash up. Dinner will be ready in half an hour, and then we'll need to leave for church. I'm sure you remember that you have youth group tonight."

He looked as though he wanted to argue, but he didn't. For one thing, he probably knew he'd pushed her too far. And for another, she knew he enjoyed

his youth group meetings, though he wasn't in the
mood to admit that—or anything else—to her now.
He swiveled and left the room, his steps much heavier than they needed to be.

She waited until he was out of sight and then
sagged against the counter, her anger dissipating and
leaving her shaky. How on earth had she ended up
in this situation? What had made her think she could
handle this? Her mother had made it sound so simple—just keep an eye out for Brad for a few weeks,
make sure he didn't get into trouble and take care
of the house until Lucy returned. No problem, right?

Wrong. Sharon could feel the whole arrangement
beginning to crumble around her and she wasn't at
all sure what to do about it. Brad was changing.
Openly challenging her in a way he'd never done
before. Maybe it was only natural for a boy his age,
or maybe it was something more serious than that—
how was she to know?

She wished again that Bobbie and Caleb McBride
were in town.

Maybe she could talk to Wade Davenport. His son
was a teenager and seemed so well adjusted. Maybe
the police chief could offer some suggestion. Or
what about one of the other men in Brad's life? His
baseball coach. His tennis instructor. Officer Dodson, who seemed to have the boys' respect even
though he kept a close eye on them. Would any of
them know what to do?

For some reason, she found herself wanting to
talk to Mac, though he didn't have a teenager and

didn't even know Brad, really. She thought just hearing his voice would make her feel better—and that realization worried her almost as much as Brad's tantrum had.

MAC WAS GETTING into the habit of eating dinner at Cora's Café. He wasn't the only regular, and it wasn't hard to understand why the place was so popular. The food was good. There was a different blue plate special every day, so he didn't get bored with the menu. And then there were Cora's pies...

Loneliness wasn't a problem during his meals, either. Cora's longtime employee, Mindy Hooper, was jovial, dry-witted and naturally talkative. She made a point to stop by his table and visit whenever she had a few moments. Her manner toward him wasn't flirtatious. Though she couldn't have been more than forty, she treated him in an almost maternal fashion—the same way she behaved toward most of the other customers.

Although Mac had only been in town for a couple of weeks, she already seemed to consider him a local, having learned his choice of dinner beverage, his favorite salad dressing, the way he drank his coffee, and that he liked every flavor of pie except strawberry. It was nice to be so easily accepted by someone who took what she knew about him at face value without being overwhelmed by curiosity to learn more.

Other diners occasionally stopped by Mac's table to greet him—people he'd met through the renovation project, some he'd encountered in other places such as the post office and hardware store, and a few friendly folks who just wanted to stop and introduce themselves. Although he wasn't particularly interested in making friends in Honoria—he had no plan to return once he'd accomplished his personal and professional goals—he made a point to respond to the greetings pleasantly enough. There was no reason to be impolite, he figured.

Pleasantly full and in a pretty good mood Thursday evening, he left the café and headed for his truck, which he had parked nearby. He would rather have spent the evening with Sharon, of course, but he figured they both needed some time apart. The hours they'd spent car shopping the day before had been very pleasant—almost *too* nice, as far as he was concerned. He hadn't learned anything new about the McBrides—in fact, he'd hardly given them a passing thought. And it bothered him that his growing desire for Sharon was beginning to interfere with his purpose for being in this town.

He'd come too far in this quest to let it go now. He couldn't allow Sharon—or anyone else—to get in his way of finding the truth. Once he had his answers, it would be entirely up to him to decide what to do with them. He had told himself he didn't really care who got hurt when the truth came out. As badly as he'd been hurt during his lifetime, he deserved to have his payback.

But being around Sharon made him question his

actions and his motives. Made him begin to wonder if some things were more important than revenge.

He definitely needed some time away from her.

Lost in his thoughts of Sharon, it took him a moment to notice the deep gouge that ran down the driver's side of his truck. It was a long, ugly scratch that ran from fender to fender, cutting through the black paint to reveal the gray metal beneath. Deliberately inflicted—most likely with a nail, a knife or some equally sharp object. It had not been there when he'd parked the truck barely forty-five minutes earlier.

Whoever had done this had known exactly what sort of damage he was doing. And who he was doing it to. Mac had no doubt that nearly everyone in this nosy little town recognized his truck by now.

Last time he'd been in Honoria, he'd rented two different dark, nondescript cars, hoping he could learn something about the McBrides without calling attention to himself. Of course, he hadn't realized then just how little actually went by without notice in this town, how the slightest change from the ordinary was cause for suspicion. He'd almost been accused of stalking Annie Stewart, when it had actually been Trent McBride he'd been observing. It had taken some glib talking on his part to get him out of that one, having to convince Trent that he had been looking to hire him for the renovation team, not keeping an eye on him or his girlfriend.

On this trip, he'd driven his own functional black pickup with its distinctive markings and chrome accessories. And now it had been deliberately targeted...

Hearing running footsteps, he whirled just in time to see someone disappear around a corner down the street. Someone who'd probably been hiding in an alley or behind another vehicle when Mac went past.

Someone who very strongly resembled Brad Henderson.

"Dammit," he muttered and whipped his cell phone out of his pocket. He punched in Sharon's number. She answered on the second ring.

"Where's your brother?" he asked without bothering to identify himself.

She sounded puzzled. "He has a ball game this evening, but he's having dinner first with the rest of his team. Why?"

"Where are they having dinner?"

"Probably at the new soda shop on Maple Street. They all like the burgers and shakes there. What's this all about, Mac?"

The soda shop was only a few blocks away from Cora's Café. There was no doubt that Brad could easily have walked the distance. He might even have had someone with him; just because Mac had seen only one boy didn't mean there hadn't been more who'd slipped away unnoticed. "My mistake," he said to Sharon. "I thought I saw Brad, but I must have been wrong."

She didn't buy his glib explanation. "Mac?"

"Don't worry about it, okay? Sorry I disturbed you."

"But—"

"I'll talk to you tomorrow. G'night, Sharon." He closed the phone and slipped it back into his pocket, trying to determine his next move.

"What happened here?"

Mac turned, and recognized the man who had spoken as one of the police officers he'd met the night Sharon had been run off the road. Dolan? Dobbins? Dodson, he remembered. "Evening, Officer."

The other man, who looked to be about Mac's age, closed the door of the aging SUV he'd just climbed out of. "I'm on my way to dinner at Cora's, but I see you've got a problem here. Anything I can do?"

Mac glanced at the gouge and shook his head, irritated all over again. "No, thanks."

"You'll be wanting to make a police report, I imagine. That scratch looks like it was put there on purpose. Have you already made yourself some enemies in town, Mr. Cordero?"

"Not as far as I know. There's no need for you to make a report, Officer. I can handle this."

"Now, don't you go trying to handle trouble like this on your own. I know you were once a big-city detective, but me and Wade are the law around here."

It was all Mac could do not to grimace. Was the guy *trying* to sound like a bad movie stereotype of a Southern-hick cop? If so, he was doing a hell of a good job. "I said I'll take care of it, Officer. But thanks for the advice."

Dodson shrugged. "Suit yourself. Guess I'll go have my dinner, then."

"The coconut pie is especially good this evening," Mac said genially.

"I'll keep that in mind. See you around."

Mac nodded and opened the driver's door of his truck. Whoever had inflicted the damage was long gone now, of course, probably safely among the rest of the ball team and ready to swear he—or they—had never left the group. But Mac had no intention of letting it go that easily. He wanted to have a few words with Sharon Henderson's kid brother. And the boy had better listen, if he knew what was good for him.

"I'M TELLING YOU, Chief, I don't like that guy. He gives me the creeps."

Wade studied Gilbert Dodson over steepled fingers. "What is it, exactly, that you find so creepy about him?"

"That attitude of his. All cool and superior. Like he knows something everyone else doesn't. I'm telling you, Chief, I'd keep looking at him in regard to those break-ins. I'd bet he has something to do with them."

"You've been trying to convince me of that for more than a week now, Gil, but you haven't brought me any proof." Wade leaned farther back in his chair, making the springs squeak. "Bring me something I can work with, and I'll do something about it. But until then…"

He left the rest of the sentence hanging.

Dodson sighed with his usual pessimism. "I'm doing my best, Chief."

"I'm sure you are, Gil. So go out and do some more of it."

Nodding heavily, Dodson shuffled out of Wade's office.

Gilbert seemed convinced Mac Cordero was up to something nefarious, Wade mused, still staring at the empty doorway. His officer's dislike of the other man was curious—Gilbert usually got along just fine with everyone.

Wade was starting to have more questions than answers—about many things. And it was really getting on his nerves.

Looked as if it was time to pay Mac Cordero another call.

CHAPTER TEN

SHARON LEFT her shop as soon as Tressie returned from her lunch break Friday afternoon. "I'll be back later," she said on her way out.

"Enjoy your lunch," Tressie called after her. "I hope you'll be sharing it with someone...interesting."

Since Tressie had been teasing her mercilessly all week about Mac, Sharon let the barb sail by unchallenged. For one thing, she *did* plan to see Mac while she was gone. She wanted to ask him exactly what he'd meant by that strange phone call last night.

Knowing it would only set Brad off again, she hadn't mentioned the call to him, but she'd questioned him closely about what he'd done before she'd arrived at the ballpark to watch his game. He'd shrugged carelessly and told her he and the rest of the guys had eaten dinner at the soda shop and then headed for the park to change into their uniforms and warm up. Nothing special, he assured her. Just ask any of his friends.

It bothered her that he hadn't quite been able to meet her eyes during the conversation.

Mac's truck was parked outside the Garrett house,

along with a few others. She was glad she'd caught him before he left. Now if she could catch him in private for a few minutes to ask him…

She saw the scrape on his truck almost as soon as she got out of her car. Walking slowly toward it, she winced as she studied the long slash of metal, bared where the black paint had been scraped away. While she knew it was possible the damage had been caused by accident, deep inside she knew what had happened. Someone had done this on purpose. A malicious act of vandalism—or an ugly message.

"If you're here to see me, you almost missed out," she heard Mac say from behind her. "I was just about to leave for lunch."

She turned to look at him, motioning toward the truck behind her. "When did this happen?"

"Yesterday evening—while I was having dinner at Cora's Café."

"You discovered it just before you called me?"

"Not long before."

"You thought Brad did this."

"The possibility crossed my mind," he said, and there was something in his expression she couldn't quite interpret.

"Mac, you can't possibly believe—"

Talking and laughing loudly, two workers Sharon knew emerged from the front door of the house and headed toward the outbuilding where the supplies were kept. On their way past, they called out greetings to her, which she returned with forced patience before looking at Mac again. "You really don't think..."

"Have you eaten?" he asked.

She frowned. "No."

"I haven't, either, and I'm starved. Let's talk about this over lunch, okay?"

"Well, I..."

He opened the driver's-side door to his pickup. "Let me help you in."

Since the vehicle was rather high off the ground, she silently accepted his hand for assistance, climbing into the truck and sliding across the bench seat to the passenger's side. She was glad she'd worn a functional gray pantsuit today rather than the long, straight black skirt she'd almost put on that morning.

She waited only until Mac was behind the wheel with the engine running. "I hope you don't really think Brad would do something like that to your truck. Or to anyone else's, for that matter."

"Do you like barbecue?"

It was obvious he wasn't going to discuss his truck or his suspicions. Since she couldn't actually force him to talk about it, she fastened her seat belt and sat back. "Yes, I like barbecue."

"Someone told me Bud's Place makes a great pulled-pork sandwich. Sound good to you?"

"The food is fine, but Bud's Place is strictly a drive-through. There are no dining facilities."

"So we'll take the food to my apartment. It isn't far, and we can talk in private there."

His apartment. Sharon moistened her lips and

twined her fingers together in her lap. It *would* be best to discuss this in private, she thought. She certainly wouldn't want anyone to overhear Mac say he suspected her brother of vandalizing his truck. There was no telling how fast *that* rumor would get around—or how it might be embellished along the way. "All right. We'll talk at your place."

If he was particularly pleased or surprised by her agreement, she certainly couldn't tell.

BUD'S PLACE WAS popular for take-out lunches, so the line of vehicles at the order window was long, even though the lunch rush had passed. Mac ordered two pulled-pork sandwiches with coleslaw, a large order of seasoned fries, two fried peach pies and two large iced teas. The only choice Sharon was given was whether she wanted mild or spicy sauce on her sandwich. She chose mild. Mac ordered spicy.

His apartment complex was aging but relatively well maintained. It catered to contractors and work crews and others who were in town only temporarily. People who were only passing through—like Mac, she thought with an odd, hollow feeling.

He escorted her into a ground-floor apartment on one end of the main building. The furnishings, she noted, made the place seem more like a motel suite than an apartment, but at least it wasn't cramped. The decent-size living room held a couch, two armchairs, a coffee table, an end table and a TV on a rolling stand. An efficiently compact eat-in kitchen opened off to one side of the main room, and a bed-

and-bath combination off to the other. Set into the back wall of the living room was a door that led out to a tiny brick patio that held two plastic lawn chairs and looked over a neatly groomed grassy compound.

"Not bad," she said.

Mac shrugged. "It suits my needs for now."

For now. Again, a reminder that he wasn't here to stay. Could Sharon see him off with a smile, grateful to have known him even for that brief time, or would she be left brokenhearted when he moved on to the next project?

She decided she wouldn't think about that right now. One problem at a time, she told herself as she and Mac spread their lunches on his table. She'd noticed that Mac had cleared away a stack of legal papers to give them room; she assumed they were notes about the renovation project.

"About the damage to your truck," she said as soon as they'd taken their seats.

"Did *you* do it?" he asked with one of his disconcertingly inscrutable half smiles.

She blinked. "No. Of course not."

"Then don't worry about it. I'll take care of it."

"So you *don't* think Brad had anything to do with it?"

He took a bite of his sandwich, neatly avoiding an answer.

"I know Brad has been unfriendly to you, but that's only because he doesn't adjust to strangers very quickly. He really isn't a bad boy. He's gotten into mischief a time or two, but he's never vandalized anything before. He wouldn't do anything that destructive or malicious.''

''Mmm.'' Mac bit into a French fry without elaborating.

''You do believe me, don't you? You have to admit, I know my brother better than you do.''

''Of course.'' He finished his sandwich and eyed the peach pies while she seethed in frustration on the other side of the table. ''Everyone was right,'' he commented after a moment. ''This really is good food. Want a fried pie?''

''You aren't going to talk about this with me, are you?''

''I'm perfectly willing to discuss this good food with you.''

''That isn't what I meant and you know it. I'm trying to talk to you about Brad.''

''I see no purpose in discussing your brother just now. I have no proof that he damaged my truck, and you're convinced he didn't. That's really all there is to say about it at the moment.''

''It bothers me that you still seem to believe Brad is capable of doing something like this.''

''You pointed out, yourself, that I don't know the boy as well as you do. It will probably take a little more time for me to form my own opinions about what he is or is not capable of doing. All I know for certain at this point is that he dislikes me, for reasons of his own. That doesn't bother me, particularly, unless it comes between you and me. And then I suppose I would have to do something about it.''

He'd spoken so dispassionately. Did it really not bother him that Brad disliked him so intensely? It would trouble her if a member of Mac's family took an immediate and unwarranted objection to her. Maybe that only further illustrated how different she and Mac were. Or maybe her family and friends didn't matter all that much to him because he didn't expect to be a part of her life for very long.

"Here," he said, pushing a paper-wrapped pastry toward her. "Have some pie. Guaranteed to put you in a better mood."

She sighed and accepted the dessert. "You are an infuriating man, Mac Cordero."

He chuckled softly. "Now there's something I've never heard before," he murmured, obviously lying.

Shaking her head, she unwrapped the pie and bit into it. It was good—packed with sweetened dried peaches in a cinnamony filling, the flaky, half moon–shaped pastry crust deep-fried to just the right crispness. He was right; it was hard to be in a bad mood while eating a fried peach pie, but her worry about the conflict between Brad and Mac had only been suppressed, not eradicated.

"WOULD YOU LIKE me to make some coffee or anything?" Mac asked when they'd washed down the last of the pie with their iced tea.

"No, thank you."

He stood and gathered up the leftover garbage,

tossing it into a wastebasket. "When do you have to be back at work?"

"No specific time. Tressie's quite capable of running the store while I'm out. If she needs me, she knows I always have my cell phone nearby."

He reached out with the swiftness of the jungle cat she'd often mentally compared him to and pulled her toward him. "Well?" he challenged. "Are you going to let your kid brother's tantrums come between us?"

It sounded so foolish the way he said it. Letting a teenager set the rules for her. It was long past time for her to make her own rules. Her own choices. Her own decisions.

It seemed easier to show Mac her answer than to tell him. Pushing all her worries to the back of her mind, she focused solely on the moment. What she wanted now.

She wanted Mac.

Resting her hands on his shoulders, she rose on tiptoe to offer her mouth to him. She didn't have to offer twice.

He didn't even try to lull her into a sense of security this time. He went straight for the explosions and the fireworks, stunning her senses, shattering her defenses, clearing her mind of anything but him. All she could do was to hold on—and try to set off a few fireworks of her own. Apparently, she succeeded. She heard Mac's breath catch in the back of his throat, and felt his whole body grow taut.

He locked his arms around her and deepened the

kiss, invading and staking every inch of her mouth. She thought it only fair that she should have the same privilege. He seemed to agree, since he put up no resistance when she claimed her right to explore.

His skillful hands were as bold as his clever mouth. He traced her curves with his fingers, as meticulously as a blind art lover studying a famous statue, seemingly intent on exploring and memorizing by feel alone. Yet Sharon wasn't made of marble. Every nerve ending reacted to his touch, leaving her feeling as though tiny electric charges were sparking all over her body. She had the fanciful sensation that she would almost glow if someone turned out the lights.

She hadn't been fanciful before she'd met Mac.

Dragging his mouth across her cheek, he nibbled his way to the soft hollow behind her ear, where her pulse pounded wildly against his lips. Even if she had wanted to, she couldn't have hidden her reaction to him. She had been vulnerable to Mac from the beginning, and she suspected he knew it. She had to trust that he would not use that knowledge against her.

It wasn't easy for her to put that much faith in a man who was still very much a stranger. There was so much about Mac she still didn't know—deeply hidden aspects of him she sensed but didn't quite understand. She could only hope that her trust in him would prove justified.

He lifted his right hand to the back of her head, buried his fingers in her hair, and tightened them until she was held gently, but securely, in place, gazing up at him. The move was an almost aggressive one on his part, but she had no fear as she stood in his grasp. Oddly enough, she felt safe there—the way she always felt when Mac held her.

His voice was rough when he said, "This is between you and me, Sharon. No one else."

She could hardly think of anyone *but* him at the moment. "I know."

"You aren't what I expected to find here," he muttered, his lips hovering only a breath above hers.

Her fingers flexed against the firm muscles of his upper arms. "What did you expect to find, Mac?"

"Myself," he answered after the slightest hesitation. And then covered her mouth with his before she could ask him to elaborate.

This kiss was different, somehow. There was a new hint of masculine arrogance in his attitude—as if he'd won some sort of victory. She really should call him on it, remind him that nothing had been decided, no irreversible steps had been taken. She might even have convinced him of it—had she completely believed it, herself.

She slid both arms around his neck, allowing herself to sink against him. His right hand fell to the small of her back, pressing her more snugly against him, giving her unmistakable evidence of where he wanted the next step to take them. It had been building toward this from the start, the urgency intensifying with every kiss, every touch, almost every glance that passed between them.

As cautious as she had been during the past few years, every action deliberate and carefully considered, every potential consequence studied and weighed, she found it hard to believe that she was even considering a reckless fling with this man. She wouldn't be acting on impulse, exactly. She knew precisely what she would be putting at stake—her heart, her reputation, her relationship with her brother. Even her professional status, since she would be getting involved with a client, which was never a prudent choice.

Yet when Mac held her this way, when he kissed her with a hunger that seemed at times to border on desperation, she found herself believing that no risk was too great. Being with Mac could well be reward enough for whatever price she might have to pay.

He slid his hand beneath her fitted top. His fingertips brushed against the frivolous scrap of black lace she wore underneath. A slight shudder went through her at the thought of having his hand against her sensitive bare skin.

Attuned to her reactions, he murmured against her mouth, "Am I frightening you?"

"No," she managed to say candidly, though her mouth was dry and her heart seemed to be tap-dancing in her throat. "You're seducing me."

He gave a low groan and crushed her mouth beneath his again, pulling her so tightly against him that she was quite graphically convinced that she wasn't the only one being seduced.

Long, heated moments later, he broke off the kiss

with a gasp. "This wasn't why I brought you here," he groaned.

Distracted by the firm line of his jaw, she traced it with a fingertip. "Why *did* you bring me here?"

"To, uh…" He caught her wandering hand and pressed a kiss against it. "To talk."

It occurred to her that she hadn't seen him without a shirt. She didn't know if his chest was smooth or furry. She would bet on smooth. Curious to discover if the bet would have paid off, she unfastened a button of his shirt. "What did you want to talk about?"

He seemed to hold a silent debate between several options, then apparently rejected them all. "Never mind," he growled as she undid two more buttons.

She slid one hand slowly into the opening she'd made. *Smooth,* she thought. *I win.*

She rewarded herself by lifting her mouth to his again. As eagerly as he responded, he seemed to be under the impression that *he* had won something.

"Mac," she murmured into his mouth, sensing a slight hesitation.

He caught her lower lip gently between his teeth. "Mmm?"

"I need to be back at work in another hour or so."

His lips moved against her flushed cheek. "That doesn't give us much time."

"No," she whispered, surprisingly bold. "So let's not waste any of it."

Moving with a speed that made her a bit dizzy, he swung her into his arms and began to move to-

ward the bedroom. She laughed breathlessly, clinging to him as excitement and anticipation mingled
with shivery trepidation. She knew this wasn't a safe
or sensible choice, but the woman Mac had dragged
out of Snake Creek was much more adventurous
than the old Sharon had been. She didn't believe in
wasting opportunities.

Mac had left his bed neatly made that morning.
He tumbled with her onto the top of the covers,
pushing pillows to the floor with a sweep of one
arm. Sharon's heart was beating so hard in her chest
she was surprised it wasn't shaking the bed. This
was *not* what she'd expected when she'd dressed for
work that morning. This wasn't at all the sort of
thing that ever happened in the middle of her workday.

Not that she was complaining, she decided as
Mac's mouth closed over hers again.

She felt a tremor in his hand when he fumbled
with the buttons of her jacket. Muttering a curse
beneath his breath, he tried again, having more success this time. She felt cool air on bare skin when
he gave her an endearingly sheepish smile. "Sorry.
I really wasn't prepared for this."

She had expected him to be smoother, more polished. It delighted her that he wasn't. This glimpse
of vulnerability made her even more certain that
Mac Cordero was as special as she had come to
believe.

"Changing your mind?" she asked, sliding her
hands inside his open shirt.

His response was half laugh, half groan, making his chest vibrate against her fingertips. "Hardly."

"Good." She pushed his shirt off his shoulders, baring him from the waist up. She felt her insides turn to jelly as she looked at him. *Beautiful* was all she could think as she gazed at his taut brown skin, sleekly defined musculature and flat, firm stomach. There were scars, as well, evidence of a hard life. But, overall—perfection.

She couldn't wait to see the rest of him.

He'd gotten his momentary, uncharacteristic lack of composure under control. His fingers were skillful when he returned to the task of removing her clothes. And when the trim gray pantsuit lay on the floor, along with the lacy garments she'd worn beneath, he revealed a talent that left her dazed.

Demonstrating the attention to detail she'd observed in his work, he concentrated on exploring every inch of her, his hands and mouth moving over her slowly and painstakingly. Leaving her breasts damp and heaving with her gasping breaths, he moved lower, tracing her ribs, nibbling her belly, making her squirm with a pleasure so intense it almost hurt. She wanted to reciprocate, to do some exploring of her own, but he had somehow drained all her energy. She wasn't even sure she could lift her head from the pillow. The only movements she seemed capable of making were completely involuntary.

She tried to focus on the physical, rather than the emotional, elements of their lovemaking. The heat of Mac's skin against hers. The roughness of his work-callused fingers. The sound of his uneven breathing in her ear. The feel of his heart pounding against his chest. The hardness of the erection straining against the zipper of his jeans. Her own reactions—racing pulse, tightened throat, oversensitized skin. A deep, wet ache in her lower abdomen.

It was safer concentrating on those sensations than on the feelings bubbling inside her. The heart-swelling emotions threatened to overcome her, bringing a hint of tears to her eyes and a certainty that nothing would ever be the same for her after this.

She couldn't think about that now. She had other things to concentrate on—like what Mac was doing with his right hand at that moment. And, oh, was he doing it well!

He laughed softly when she tugged at him with impatient hands. "In a hurry to get back to work?" he asked in her ear.

She was in no mood to be teased. "Mac—"

"What do you want, Sharon?"

"You," she whispered, moving against him in a way that made it very clear what she wanted.

"Happy to oblige, ma'am," he murmured, reaching for the snap of his jeans.

He kept condoms in the nightstand. Sharon didn't want to think just then about whether he stored them there as a general precaution or because he found himself in frequent need of them. She decided, instead, to be grateful he had them available now.

It didn't take him very long to return to her, but it felt like forever. She wanted him so badly, she ached. Desperately needed him to appease the hunger he'd created in her. "Now," she demanded, reaching for him.

Amusement mixed with desire in his voice. "You really are the take-charge type, aren't you?"

She cupped his gorgeous face in her hands. "I've had to be," she answered simply. "Does that worry you?"

"*You* worry me," he said, and the amusement was gone now. "But that doesn't seem to make any difference."

She didn't always understand this man, but that didn't seem to make any difference, either. She brought his mouth to hers. "*Now,* Mac," she said against his lips.

He settled between her raised knees. The muscles of his back bunched beneath her hands as he prepared to thrust forward—like a sleek cat getting ready to spring, she thought, still enamored with the imagery.

Holding himself very still, he looked at her, his dark eyes burning with roiling emotions she couldn't begin to interpret. She only knew that she trusted him. "Sharon," he growled, "whatever happens— don't regret this."

"No," she whispered, utterly certain that she was telling the truth. "No regrets."

His muscles rippled, and he moved again—and the mental image of a wild, dangerous animal dissolved into shards of pure sensation. She was no longer able to maintain coherent thought.

Her fingers curled into his shoulders, as if clinging to sanity. A choked cry lodged in the back of her throat, trapped there by the press of his lips against hers. She could do nothing more than whimper as he pushed her higher and farther, toward a conclusion they both desperately craved.

He tore his mouth from hers with a harsh groan, and the cry he had imprisoned escaped her. Thin and quivery, it seemed to echo in the small room as shudders of release coursed through her, again and again.

Even as the echoes died away and the shudders subsided, Sharon realized that she'd been right to be wary of this. She'd been afraid her life would never be the same. Now she knew for certain she'd been right. Everything had changed.

Now that she had been with Mac Cordero, she would never again be content with ordinary.

CHAPTER ELEVEN

MAC FELT as though dozens of people were watching when he climbed out of his truck at the Garrett house. As if there was someone standing in every window, gaping and speculating. He hadn't felt that way when they'd left the site together, but he did now. Things had changed.

His concern was for Sharon, not himself. Knowing the way rumors circulated in this town, and the pleasure the locals took in embellishment, he hated to think of Sharon being the subject of those tales. He hadn't given much thought to it before, never having cared particularly what people said about him, but it was different now. He found himself suddenly feeling protective and possessive, two emotions he hadn't intended to feel.

He'd told himself all he wanted from Sharon was some information, not sex. Now he didn't know what the hell he wanted. He only knew he couldn't let Sharon be hurt by his personal vendetta. For the first time since his world had fallen apart two years ago, he cared about someone else's feelings besides his own.

He helped her out of his truck. She smiled up at him, her eyes glowing, her cheeks flushed, her hand resting so trustingly in his, and it made his stomach tighten.

He wouldn't hurt her, he promised himself.

"I have to go back to the shop," she said, making little effort to hide her reluctance.

He didn't want to let go of her hand, but he did. "I know. I have to get back to work."

"Mac?"

She'd learned to say his name so beautifully. The single syllable sounded almost musical from her lips. And he was starting to feel like a foolish sap standing here mooning over her. "Yeah?" he asked, more gruffly than he had intended.

"I had a great lunch."

Damn, he wanted to kiss her. It was only the thought of those watching eyes that held him back. "So did I," he said, instead.

Proving she wasn't oblivious to possible onlookers, either, she glanced quickly at the house before reaching out to touch his hand. "No regrets," she reminded him.

Damning to hell anybody watching, he lifted her hand to his mouth, pressing a quick, hard kiss against it. "I'll call you later," he promised as he released her and stepped back.

She smiled, and turned toward her car. Something stopped her just as she reached for the door handle. "Emily Davenport invited me to a party at her house tomorrow afternoon," she said, looking at him over the top of her car. "She encouraged me to bring a friend. Would you like to go as my guest?"

A party at the Davenport house. He was sure every McBride in Honoria would be in attendance, maybe a few from out of town. A great chance to get a good look at them, maybe pick up a bit more information, he realized. This was the reason he'd cultivated Sharon's friendship from the beginning, wasn't it? Because she gave him better access to the McBrides. So why was he suddenly feeling like a snake?

"I'd really like you to come," she added when he hesitated.

"Is your brother going to be there?"

She bit her lip, and he could tell that she'd forgotten her brother temporarily—and that she was flooded with sudden guilt because of it. "Yes," she said after a moment. "He'll be there. But he'll behave himself, I guarantee that. And maybe after you spend a little more time with him, you'll realize that he couldn't possibly have...well, you know."

Mac glanced at the scrape on his truck, and remembered that fleeting glimpse of Brad Henderson disappearing around the corner of a building. Because he'd made a vow to himself that Sharon wouldn't be hurt, he chose to keep that memory to himself. He could handle a punk kid with an attitude problem. "If you're sure I wouldn't be out of place, I'd like to come with you tomorrow."

She smiled. "Great. Do you want to ride with us or meet us there?"

"I'll meet you," he decided, choosing to forgo the car ride with her brother.

"Okay. See you there. One o'clock. Do you know where they live?"

Wade and Emily Davenport lived in a house that had been built by Josiah McBride Jr., who had a one-in-three chance of being Mac's father. "Yeah. I know where they live."

"Great. Um—call me tonight?"

"I will." He watched her get into her car and drive away, giving him a little wave as she disappeared down the driveway. It took him back for a moment—his wife used to wave to him like that when she drove away.

She hadn't waved when she'd left the last time. Her shoulders had been slumped with grief and defeat as she had driven away. And, knowing when it was time to let go, Mac hadn't tried to stop her.

He'd decided his course that day—that he would find the answers to the questions that had haunted him all his life. That he would make someone pay for the pain he and his mother had suffered. Pain that had carried over to destroy his marriage. And now another woman was in a position to be hurt by him.

If there was a curse involved with being born a bastard McBride, then the most generous thing for him to do would be to stay far away from Sharon Henderson. Unfortunately, he was afraid it was already too late to protect her.

"Hey, boss," a jovial carpenter called out on his way to the supply building. "Didya' have a nice lunch?"

Mac's first instinct was to belt the guy. And then he realized the question had been asked without any ulterior meaning, that he was the one who was making too much of it. "Yeah, it was fine," he said, trying to keep his tone pleasant. "How's it going in there?"

"Moving along at a good pace. This house is going to be spiffed up and ready to sell in no time."

As far as Mac was concerned, it couldn't be too soon.

He was beginning to think he'd made a terrible mistake by coming to Honoria.

SHARON MADE SURE her hair was neat, her lipstick was fresh, her clothes were straight and her expression was unrevealing before she entered her shop. Finally confident that there were no clues to be found in her expression about how she'd spent her lunch hour, she walked in with her head high and a cheery smile on her face.

"Oh, my," Tressie said after taking one look at her. "You must have had an interesting lunch."

Sharon's jaw nearly dropped. "Why did you say that?"

"You were with Mac Cordero, weren't you?"

"How do you know?"

"I can tell by the glow in your eyes."

Sharon scowled.

Tressie laughed again. "I'm only teasing you, Sharon. Kyle McAllister stopped by for his wife's wallpaper borders, and he said he saw you and Mac picking up barbecue at Bud's.''

"Dammit, can't someone even eat a sandwich in this town without everyone talking about it?'' Sharon felt like stamping her feet in frustration. It was hard enough trying to figure out for herself what was developing between her and Mac. It made it even more stressful when she knew everything they did was being watched and whispered about.

Tressie merely shrugged. ''You know this town, Sharon. It's infuriating at times, but that's just the way things are. How do you think I found out my weasel of an ex-husband was running around with that health-club bimbo, hmm? I always suspected he had some emotional problems, but I never knew he was completely stupid. He seemed shocked that I heard about his affair—he thought he'd been so very clever. He should have remembered that secrets have a way of coming out in this town.''

For some reason, Tressie's words made a funny prickle of apprehension course down Sharon's spine. She didn't know why. While she was trying to keep her relationship with Mac private for now, it wasn't as though they were trying to conceal any great secret. They weren't doing anything wrong. They were falling in love, and they didn't want to do that in the public eye.

She felt the blood drain suddenly out of her face. Falling in love? Was *that* what they were doing? She didn't know about Mac, but the words felt all too right to her.

Tressie was looking at her in concern now. "Sharon? You okay?"

Forcing a smile, Sharon pressed a hand to her stomach. "Barbecue in the middle of a workday. I'll spend the rest of the afternoon popping antacids."

"You're sure you don't want to talk about anything? I'm a pretty good listener, you know. And, believe it or not, I can keep my mouth shut when I'm asked to."

Knowing the offer was sincere, and that Tressie really would respect her privacy, Sharon was tempted. It might make her feel better to share what she was going through with another woman—her excitement, her worries, her hopes, her fears, the roller-coaster of emotions that went along with falling in love.

While Sharon had a lot of women friends, there was no one she felt comfortable confiding her most private emotions to, especially since her closest friend from high school had married and moved away a year or so ago. Her mother and Bobbie McBride, two confidantes she'd always counted on, wouldn't be back for a while yet. She'd been keeping so much to herself lately—her dissatisfaction with the rut she and Jerry had fallen into, her developing attraction to Mac, her growing concerns about Brad. She would certainly value any advice she could get.

Still, she heard herself saying, "Thanks, Tressie, but everything's fine. Just busy, as usual. Did you hear anything yet about that order we placed for Mabel Watson?''

Tressie was obviously reluctant to change the subject, but a long look at Sharon's expression must have convinced her that she really had no choice. She sighed and shook her head. ''I'll go call about it right now.''

''Thank you. I have some paperwork to do, so I'll be at the computer if you need me.''

''And you know where to find me if you need me,'' Tressie countered.

''Yes, I do. Thank you.''

Sharon spent the rest of the afternoon trying to concentrate on work and failing abysmally. The heady euphoria of lovemaking had faded, leaving only a deep, warm glow inside her. An occasional flash of memory made her catch her breath and close her eyes, instantly transported back to the bed in Mac's apartment. But for the most part she found herself spending more time worrying than savoring.

She kept picturing that ugly scrape on the side of Mac's truck. Whoever had inflicted it had wanted to cause damage. It had been malicious and calculated. A random act of vandalism or a personal attack against Mac? Who in town disliked him that much?

Other than Brad, of course.

She didn't want to believe her brother capable of something like that, even though it was obvious Mac didn't share her faith. Brad was her little brother. He went to church with her. His raggedy old teddy bear still sat on a shelf in his closet. He wouldn't have deliberately caused hundreds of dollars' worth of damage just because he'd taken an irrational dislike to Mac, would he? Of course not.

But what if…?

The telephone rang. Knowing Tressie was busy with a customer, she reached for it, grateful for the distraction. "Intriguing Interiors. May I help you?"

"Hey, sis. Tommy's having a pool party next Friday and he wants to know if me and Jimbo can spend the night. His mom will be there and everything. Is it okay?"

Thinking of Mac's truck again, she wondered if she should ask Brad about it. If there was any chance he'd been involved…

"Tommy's mom said you can call her if you want to ask her anything, but she'd like to know as soon as possible so they can make plans. Is it okay?"

She gave his request another moment's thought. She was beginning to have doubts about Brad spending so much time with Jimbo, but Tommy seemed like a decent kid. She'd met his mother, a PTA officer and soccer mom who, while spreading herself a bit thin with all her volunteer activities, seemed involved in her two sons' lives. "I suppose there's no harm in it."

"Cool. Thanks, Sharon."

He sounded so genuinely pleased and grateful that she couldn't help softening. "You're welcome, Brad. Promise me you'll be good."

"Sure. No problem."

The guarantee was given so glibly that she

couldn't take much reassurance from it. "Brad," she began impulsively, suddenly needing an answer about Mac's truck.

"Mmm? I've got to go. Jimbo's waiting for me. We've got baseball practice."

She swallowed the words she'd almost blurted. This wasn't the time to question him, not about something so important. Not over the phone. And not while Jimbo was waiting for him.

Besides, she reminded herself, she didn't really believe Brad had done it. More likely Joe Wimble had gotten drunk again and felt like causing trouble. Until someone had decided to try his hand at larceny recently, Joe's drunken shenanigans had been the worst crimes Honoria had seen since Sam Jennings had been hauled off for murder more than four years ago.

Her little brother wasn't a criminal. She was sure Mac would see that for himself soon.

They only needed time.

WORK FINISHED for the day, Mac locked the Garrett house and headed for his truck. He found Wade Davenport leaning casually against the driver's side.

His first instinct was to curse. He was tired and confused, and he needed some time alone. He was in no mood to be interrogated by the police chief. His nod was curt. "'Afternoon, Chief."

"Hey, Mac, how's it going?"

"Can't complain."

"Nasty scratch on your truck here. Get too close to something?"

"Apparently."

"Do you know who did this, Mac?"

"Not for certain, no."

"But you have suspicions?"

Mac only shrugged.

"Officer Dodson's concerned that you've got a feud going with someone. He said he got the feeling you were planning to handle this yourself."

"Now comes the part where you tell me you don't want any trouble around here, right? I know the speech, Chief. Your officer already gave it to me."

"Yeah, but did you listen?"

Mac let silence be his answer.

Wade shook his head, glanced at the scarred truck again, then changed the subject. "We found the van that was used in the Porter robbery."

That brought Mac's head up. He was most definitely interested in any progress that had been made in apprehending the bastard who'd almost killed Sharon. "Just the van? Or did you find out who was driving it?"

"No, it was abandoned. And wiped clean. It doesn't appear we're going to learn much from it."

"Registration?"

"It was stolen from a used-car lot in Carollton a couple of days before the Porter break-in. No witnesses to that theft."

Hardly encouraging news. "Where did you find the van?"

"Officer Dodson found it in the garage of a vacant house a couple of streets back from the motel where you were staying."

Mac sighed. "You don't suppose I was driving the van *and* following Sharon in my truck, do you?"

Wade chuckled. "I doubt you're that talented. You asked where the van was found. I told you. That's all."

"Still have your suspicions about me, Chief?"

Wade's lazy grin never wavered. "Let's just say you aren't a man I would make the mistake of underestimating."

"I've been invited to a party at your house tomorrow. Do you feel safe having me around your family, or would you rather I decline?"

If Wade was surprised, he didn't let it show. "We'd be delighted to have you. Did Trent ask you?"

"Actually, it was Sharon."

"I see. Well, any friend of Sharon's—" He didn't bother finishing the cliché, but straightened away from the truck and stuck his hands in his pockets. "I guess I'll be seeing you tomorrow, then. My wife will be delighted to meet you. She's heard about you, of course, and she's been curious."

Mac had decidedly mixed feelings about meeting Emily McBride Davenport, the woman who was either his cousin or his sister. "I'll look forward to meeting her."

"I guess I'd better get home for dinner. If you change your mind about making a report on your truck, let me know."

Without responding, Mac watched the chief climb into his Jeep and drive away.

Being among the McBrides tomorrow could be very interesting—or prove to be a huge mistake, he thought. One of many he'd made since coming to Honoria.

He hoped that making love to Sharon Henderson didn't turn out to be the biggest mistake he'd made yet.

MAC DECIDED to eat at Cora's again that evening. Because it was a Friday and many locals tended to eat out on weekends, there was more of a crowd than usual. He had to park down the street, close to the arcade. There was no group of boys on the sidewalk outside the place this time, he noted in satisfaction. He wasn't really in the mood for another confrontation.

He had just reached the arcade when Brad stepped out the door, accompanied by the tall boy who'd egged him on the last time. Brad's first reaction at seeing Mac was surprise. The surprise changed quickly to what Mac interpreted as half-guilty defiance. "Hello, Brad," he said, meeting the boy's eyes.

Brad looked down at his shoes and nodded stiffly.

Another couple of steps brought Mac closer. "How have you been? Keeping yourself busy?"

Brad shrugged.

"Oddly enough, I spotted a boy who looked very much like you in this same area just yesterday evening. He was running down the street. Like he'd done something wrong and was trying to get away before anyone saw him."

"I don't know what you're talking about," Brad muttered, his eyes shifting away.

"Hey, man, leave my friend alone," the bigger boy said, stepping closer. "He ain't done nothing."

Mac answered without looking away from Brad. "If that's true, he has no reason to be concerned."

"Are you concerned about this guy, Brad?" the bigger boy asked mockingly.

"Be quiet, Jimbo," Brad muttered. "I can handle this."

Mac glanced dismissively at Jimbo before speaking again to Brad. "Looks to me like your buddy here is just itching to get you in trouble, Brad. Maybe you need to ask yourself if he's really a pal."

Brad straightened his shoulders. "I pick my own friends."

"Yeah—so do yourself a favor and choose wisely."

"You going to take advice from the player who's been doing your sister, Brad?" Jimbo jeered.

"Shut *up,* Jimbo!"

Even as Brad rounded on his companion, Mac was moving. A moment later, Jimbo was pinned against the brick wall behind him, Mac's hands fisted in the boy's designer-label shirt. Caught completely by surprise, Jimbo had gone pale, his eyes wide, his mouth hanging open. He was perhaps an inch taller than Mac, but there was no doubt who was the dominant male in this confrontation.

"One more word out of your mouth about Brad's sister, and you'll be sorry you were ever born," Mac said very quietly, his nose only inches from the kid's. "Is that very clear?"

"Let him go." Brad sounded both furious and terrified. "He didn't mean anything."

Keeping his eyes on Jimbo, Mac asked, "You let your friends talk about your sister that way, Brad? Does she really deserve that?"

"He was just trying to make you mad."

"It worked." Mac tightened his hands on Jimbo's shirt. He wouldn't really hurt the kid, of course— but he'd make him think he would.

"Hey! Let him go, Cordero." The order came from just behind them.

Maintaining his grip, Mac glanced over his shoulder. Officer Dodson was approaching at a half run, his gloomy face creased with a frown. "What's going on here?"

"Just having a chat with the boys, Officer," Mac replied affably.

"He's—he's crazy, Dodson. Arrest him or something," Jimbo stuttered.

"I think we've heard enough of your opinions, Jimbo," Mac suggested.

"Okay, Cordero, let him go. You can't go around

town assaulting our kids—not unless you want to end up in jail.''

"Okay, Jimbo, I'm letting you go," Mac said. "I'm assuming you've gotten my message. Watch your mouth from now on."

The boy stumbled when Mac abruptly released him. "Well?" he demanded, turning to the hovering officer. "Aren't you going to cuff him?"

Mac smiled faintly. "I think Officer Dodson understands that I wasn't assaulting you. Just giving you a little demonstration. If you're going to act like a tough guy, you better be tough enough to deal with the trouble you stir up."

Dodson didn't look as if he knew what to do. His first choice would probably be to lock Mac up just for causing trouble. Another part of him seemed to want to just walk on and have his dinner, forgetting he'd seen anything at all.

Taking pity on the guy, Mac stuck his hands in his pockets and stepped away from the boys. "Trouble's over, Officer. I'll behave."

Looking relieved, Dodson nodded curtly. "Good. Don't you boys have somewhere to go? Brad, ain't your sister waiting for you at her shop?"

Shaken, and keeping his gaze averted from Mac, Brad nodded and took a few steps away.

Jimbo was still staring at Dodson in disbelief. "You're not going to do *anything?* You're just going to let him strut away like he's some kind of big shot or something?"

"Give it a rest, Jimbo," Dodson said wearily. "Quit while you're ahead."

The boy gritted out a curse that was even uglier because of his age, and spun on one heel. "C'mon, Brad."

"Brad," Mac said as the boy scuttled past him.

Brad gave him a nervous, angry look. "What?"

"For your sister's sake, I'm letting you off the hook about my truck. I won't be so generous a second time."

The boy's eyes were so hot with emotion it was a wonder Mac's skin didn't blister. But then he turned and stamped off in the wake of his obnoxious pal.

Dodson gave a heavy sigh. "Do you go looking for trouble, Cordero, or does it just follow you around?"

"Let's just say I deal with it when I find it."

"You're starting to worry me, Cordero. I don't think you fit in around here."

Mac chose not to comment.

The officer shook his head, his expression morose again. "I'm hungry. I'm going to eat. Stay away from the kids, okay? I can't let you get away with something like that a second time."

"There shouldn't be a second time. Enjoy your dinner, Officer." Mac turned and headed back toward his truck. He was no longer hungry.

CHAPTER TWELVE

"YOU HAVEN'T TOUCHED your dinner, Brad. Aren't you hungry?"

Brad looked up from playing with his food. Something in his eyes made Sharon's throat tighten. He looked so troubled. "Brad? Honey, is something wrong? You've been so quiet all evening. Aren't you feeling well?"

He shrugged. "I feel okay."

"Didn't you and Jimbo have a good time at the arcade?"

"Jimbo can be a real jerk sometimes," he muttered.

So that was the problem. Brad had quarreled with his friend. She relaxed a little. That wasn't so bad. Teenagers squabbled all the time. And she'd been wanting him to spend less time with Jimbo, anyway. "Do you want to talk about it?"

"No."

"Are you sure? I can be a good listener."

"I don't want to talk about it, okay?"

"Fine. There's no need to snap."

Brad muttered something incomprehensible and went back to toying with his dinner.

"I talked to Emily Davenport this afternoon," she

said, trying again to make conversation. "She said Clay is really glad you're coming to his house tomorrow. He likes you, you know."

"He's a kid."

"He's a nice kid."

"He's okay."

Sharon considered telling Brad that Mac would be attending the cookout too. She rejected the idea because he was already in such a bad mood. He was likely to refuse to go altogether if he knew Mac would be there. She had to trust that he wouldn't be terribly rude in front of their friends. And that spending more time with Mac would help her brother accept him better.

Brad shoved his plate away. "I'm really not very hungry. I think I'll go read or something."

She started to remind him about the dishes, but decided she would just as soon do them herself tonight. It seemed easier in the long run than dealing with Brad in this disposition. "All right. Let me know if you need anything."

Rubbing her aching temples, she started cleaning up when he left. She was so tired. She looked forward to being alone in her bedroom where she could think about the events of the day and prepare herself for tomorrow.

The telephone rang just as she finished cleaning the kitchen. She sensed who was calling even before she answered. Her hunch was confirmed when Mac spoke. "How's it going?" he asked.

"It's a little strained around here this evening,"

she answered candidly. "Brad's in one of his moods."

"Did he mention his encounter with me earlier this evening?"

She frowned. "You talked to Brad today?"

"I ran into him and his friend when they were coming out of the arcade. I don't blame him for not wanting to tell you about it, but I imagine you'll hear soon enough. I'm sure there were witnesses."

She closed her eyes and leaned against the counter, her head starting to pound harder. She just knew she wasn't going to like this. "What happened?"

"Not a lot. Brad's buddy Jimbo shot off his mouth and I politely informed him that his attitude could use some adjustment."

"Brad seems angry at Jimbo tonight."

"He should be. The guy's a certifiable jerk. Why do you let your brother hang out with him?"

"They've been friends for years. Jimbo has some family problems. His parents are divorced and his father's out of the picture, which gives the boys something in common. He's living with his grandparents now while his mother tries to get her life back together. He's not a bad boy, really—just angry and hurt."

"Excuses only go so far, Sharon. He's old enough to make his own choices now. Someone needs to make it clear to him that his choices have consequences."

Sharon wondered if they were talking about Jimbo now—or Brad. "What did you say to them?"

"Not much. I just made it clear that I won't tolerate much from either of them. And I told them to stay away from my truck."

"You still think Brad did that?"

"If he did, I'm sure he had help and encouragement from his buddy. Your brother seems to be more of a follower than a leader. He's going to have to watch that he doesn't follow someone straight to jail."

Growing defensive now, Sharon lifted her chin and tightened her grip on the telephone. "Thank you for the advice, Mac, but I know my brother. He isn't quite as weak-minded as you believe."

"I never said he was weak-minded. I just pointed out that he's walking a thin line."

"Then I'll help guide him. It's support he needs, not threats."

"When it comes to teenagers, it sometimes takes both."

"I'm sure you mean well, Mac, but—as people often say—it's easy to tell other people how to raise their kids when you don't have any, yourself."

The silence that followed her words was so heavy and so fraught with tension that she realized she must have unwittingly hit a nerve. Always overprotective of her family, she'd allowed his criticism of Brad to make her angry, and she'd struck back. She drew a deep breath. "Mac, I—"

"Don't apologize," he cut in. "You say anything

you feel like saying to me, okay? I'm not interested in tiptoeing around in carefully polite conversations with you. That's not what I want from you.''

"What *do* you want from me, Mac?'' she risked asking.

After another momentary hesitation, he replied, "That's not a question I can answer right now.''

"Fair enough,'' she murmured, telling herself it was foolish to be disappointed.

His short, dry chuckle was barely audible through the phone lines. "You're going to be satisfied with that? You don't want me to start spouting poetry or promising you the moon and stars?''

"I don't want poetry or promises. I just need you to be honest with me.''

There was another pause. And then Mac cleared his throat. "I'm trying.''

Something in his voice made her sense deeper meaning to his words. She knew there were things about Mac he hadn't told her. Parts of himself he hadn't yet allowed her to see. But they'd only known each other a matter of weeks. The explosive connection between them had developed so rapidly. The rest would come with time, she hoped. For now, they had to rely on trust.

She was painfully aware that she had already taken a huge risk of trusting Mac with her heart.

"Maybe it would be better if I skip the cookout tomorrow,'' he suggested after a moment. "You know everyone's going to be watching us. And your brother would certainly enjoy the party more if I'm not there."

Her first reaction was to adamantly shake her head, even though he couldn't see her. "No. I really want you to be there. You'll meet my friends—the ones you haven't already met, of course. As for Brad, he needs to spend more time with you to get over his initial antagonism. And frankly, I think you need to be around him for the same reason."

"You think we've got a testosterone tussle going on, do you?" he asked, sounding amused now.

She smiled. "I hadn't thought of it quite that way, but it's possible, isn't it?"

"Actually, that's exactly what it is," he surprised her by admitting. "A new male has moved into the area and the young studs are peeing all over the place to mark their territory."

She was startled into a quick laugh. "I definitely wouldn't have phrased it in those terms."

"That's because you're not a guy." He sounded almost cheerful all of a sudden.

Bemused by his rapidly changing moods, Sharon decided to encourage this one. "I'm glad you've noticed."

"I noticed that right off."

"So you'll be there tomorrow?"

"If you're sure you know what you're doing."

"I'm very sure. I want you there."

"And I want you—anywhere I can get you."

The murmured comment made her blush. "Mac—"

"Weren't you the one who said you want me to be honest?" Without giving her a chance to respond, he added, "See you tomorrow, Sharon."

He hung up without further comment.

Sharon replaced her own receiver slowly. She thought about going straight up to Brad's room to talk to him about this irksome feud he had going with Mac, and to confront him once and for all about whether he'd damaged Mac's truck. But something held her back, just as it had during dinner. She found herself oddly afraid to challenge him—maybe because she wasn't sure she wanted to hear his answer.

Just the possibility that Brad had been involved was overwhelming to her. She felt totally unqualified to deal with anything of this magnitude. Property damage that extensive was a matter for the police to handle, not an older sister. It should more likely result in someone being sent to jail, not sent to his room. Maybe she didn't want to admit the culprit could be Brad because she just didn't know what she would do if it had been.

Mac had assured her he'd taken care of the problem. Was she being totally cowardly and irresponsible to leave it at that?

She just couldn't handle this tonight. Too much had happened today. She couldn't process any more. Her whole life had changed that afternoon and she needed some quiet time alone to deal with that. There would be time tomorrow to figure out what to do with Brad.

She had fallen in love. Surely she deserved at

least a few hours to savor the feeling before dealing with the inevitable ramifications.

EVEN AS HE PARKED his truck in the Davenports' crowded driveway, Mac was half convinced he was making a mistake. His relationship with Sharon was complex enough in private; taking it public this way could only complicate everything. Add to that his secret connection to the McBride family and this afternoon was likely to prove very awkward for him. He wasn't crazy about parties, anyway—and he definitely had no experience with family gatherings. So what the hell was he doing here?

Okay, so he already knew the answer to that question. He was here partly to discover more about the McBrides—but mostly because Sharon was here.

An aging pickup Mac recognized as Trent McBride's pulled into the long driveway and parked behind Mac's truck. Trent climbed out of the driver's-side door, then turned to assist his fiancée out. "Hey, Mac," Trent said, showing no surprise at seeing him there.

"Hello, Trent."

"You remember my fiancée, Annie Stewart?"

"Of course. It's nice to see you again, Ms. Stewart."

Petite and deceptively delicate-looking, she smiled up at him. "Please call me Annie."

"Only if you'll call me Mac."

"Of course. Trent's been keeping me informed about the progress of your renovation project. He said the house is going to be spectacular when it's finished. I know the cabinetwork will be beautiful," she added with a proud look at Trent. "Have you seen any of the furniture Trent makes, Mac? He's very talented. He's made some of the most beautiful rocking chairs I've ever seen."

"Annie," Trent murmured, looking abashed by her bragging.

Mac looked from one to the other. "I'd like to see the rockers. I've always got an eye out for quality furniture."

"I'll show you sometime. Right now, I'm more interested in lunch." Trent reached into his truck and pulled out a small cooler. "C'mon, Mac, we'll show you around."

"Can I help you carry that?" The cooler looked heavy, and Mac knew that Trent had sustained a back injury in the plane crash.

Trent scowled. "Thanks, but I've got it."

Annie rolled her eyes in response to her fiancé's curt tone. "He *never* admits that he needs help, whether he does or not," she murmured.

"I said I've got it. Now, do you two want to eat or stand here running your mouths?"

Mac chuckled and held out his arm to Annie. "Shall we?"

She slipped her hand beneath his elbow and dimpled up at him. "Why, thank you, sir."

Trent glanced over his shoulder. "Careful, Mac. I'm the jealous type."

Aware of the dry humor in Trent's voice, Mac

responded in kind. "Don't worry. I think of her almost like family."

It was a sick joke, of course, and at the McBrides' expense. But Mac had to entertain himself somehow.

Following Trent around the side of the big old white-frame, black-shuttered house with its wraparound porch, Mac steeled himself for what was to come.

The backyard was large and nicely landscaped, shaded by big, spreading trees and decorated with masses of colorful flowers. It was a warm, cloudless day, and the adults and children mingling around a large, smoking barbecue grill and several picnic tables were dressed in lightweight, brightly colored clothing. Quite a welcoming and domestic sight, Mac thought wryly. Like a scene from a Disney movie.

Probably because he was looking for her, he spotted Sharon immediately. She was standing beside one of the picnic tables talking with three other women. He identified the striking redhead as Trevor's wife, Jamie. Though he hadn't been introduced to her, he'd seen her entering the law firm enough times to know who she was. The fresh-faced blonde was Emily Davenport. He had seen her from a distance, though he'd made no effort to meet her before now. He didn't recognize the cool-looking woman with dark auburn hair standing next to Sharon. He'd never seen her around town.

They were all very attractive, but the only one

who made Mac's pulse rate increase was Sharon. She wore her hair down in a smooth, glossy curtain to her collar. The bright sunlight brought out rich, warm highlights, and he could almost feel the silken strands in his hands again, almost smell the clean, fresh scent of her shampoo. She wore a sleeveless, scoop-neck white blouse that closed down the front with tiny buttons, and khaki shorts that revealed a modest, but delectable stretch of legs.

He found himself fantasizing about releasing the buttons of her blouse, stripping away her shorts to expose the parts of her he had so painstakingly explored in his bedroom only twenty-four hours earlier. He forced himself to clear his mind of those thoughts before he embarrassed himself.

She smiled when she saw him. He remembered the first time she'd visited the Garrett house, when she'd been surprised to find Trent McBride waiting in the kitchen. Mac had wondered then how it would feel to be on the receiving end of one of her bright, warm, generous smiles. Now he knew. It felt great.

Wade, Trevor and another man were gathered around the barbecue grill, holding beers and frowning intently at the sizzling meat. Trent glanced at Mac and chuckled. "They look like they're performing brain surgery, don't they?"

Spotting them, Wade handed his beer to Trevor and ambled their way. "Hey, guys. Annie, you look lovely as always."

She smiled. "And you are as charming as always."

"How's that dumb mutt of yours?"

"Bozo is just fine, thank you. And he isn't dumb," she added firmly. "Just—unconventional."

Trent snorted. "The mutt's got the IQ of a bowl of oatmeal," he muttered.

Annie pretended to be offended, but she was smiling. "Admit it, Trent, you like my dog."

Trent shrugged ironically. "He and I have come to an arrangement. We'll each share Annie—to a point."

Wade turned to greet Mac. "Good to see you, Mac. Trent, give me that cooler and show Mac where we keep the beer."

Having made his point by carrying the cooler this far, Trent relinquished it without argument. He led Mac to a large, ice-filled metal tub that held a variety of canned beverages. Sharon and her companions joined them there.

"Hi, Mac."

He accepted a dripping can of cold beer from Trent, then turned to acknowledge Sharon's greeting. "Hi, yourself."

"It's a beautiful day for a cookout, isn't it?"

The words were merely polite trivialities, but her eyes said so much more. She was glad to see him. And it shook him to realize how much that meant to him. "Yes, it's very nice."

He pulled his gaze from her and glanced around the lawn, noting that the only children in evidence were three blond little girls, not much more than toddlers, playing with some plastic toys on the grass near the picnic table where the women had just been sitting. "Did your brother decide not to join you today?" he asked Sharon, wondering if Brad had chosen to stay away rather than chance another meeting with him.

"Brad's inside playing video games with Wade's son, Clay, and Trevor's son, Sam."

"A day like this and they're playing inside?"

Having overheard Mac's question, Wade grimaced. "I told them they could stay in there until lunch is ready, but then they're joining us out here in the fresh air. The problem is that Lucas just sent Clay a new game and of course they couldn't wait to try it out."

"Remember I told you about Lucas, Wade's brother-in-law who owns a software-design company in California," Sharon said. "Brad thinks it's just about the coolest thing in the world that Clay's uncle has a company that creates video games and that Clay gets to try them out before they even hit the market."

"Let me introduce you to our other guests, Mac," Wade offered, playing the gracious host. "You know Trent and Trevor, of course, but you haven't met their brother-in-law, Blake Fox. He and Tara live in Atlanta with their daughter, Alison—the littlest one over there. Blake, this is Mac Cordero, the contractor we told you about."

Shaking Blake's hand, Mac noted that the other man was golden-haired, blue-eyed and built in a way that some might have described as elegantly slender.

He had the look of a 1940s film star—probably deliberately enhanced by his choice of loose, perfectly tailored clothing. But there was a sharp gleam of streetwise intelligence in his bright blue eyes that was entirely modern.

The guy fit in well with the fair-skinned, light-haired McBrides, Mac thought, aware again of the dramatic contrast between them and himself.

"Good to meet you, Mac," Blake said, and though his manner was quite casual, Mac had the sensation he'd just been studied, memorized and categorized. Blake had the look of a hustler, or a particularly slick con man. Mac had encountered several of them over the years. He knew Tara was a lawyer—maybe she'd married one, as well, he thought as he returned the greeting.

Blake turned to the auburn-haired woman who'd approached as the introductions were made. "Mac, this is my wife, Tara."

Extending her hand, Tara smiled warmly, dispelling his initial impression of coolness. "It's very nice to meet you, Mr. Cordero. My brothers have told me you're remodeling the Garrett house. I've always thought it was a fascinating old place. I'm glad someone else recognized its potential."

"Okay, I've waited long enough." The woman Mac had identified as Jamie McBride pushed good-naturedly forward, multiple earrings dangling, numerous bracelets jingling. Her flame-red hair was chopped in a stylishly haphazard fashion and her willowy figure was boldly displayed in a brightly colored, spaghetti-strap top and brief denim shorts. Her lips, fingernails and toenails were all painted a bright fuchsia. "I want to meet this fascinating man who has the whole town talking."

Trevor sighed. "Mac, allow me to introduce my wife, Jamie. If your first impression is that she's basically a fruitcake—well, you'd be right."

Jamie laughed and punched her husband's arm. "I just want to meet him, Trev. It isn't often we get a dashing stranger in this town."

It was obvious to Mac that this stage-actress-turned-high-school-drama teacher loved attracting attention with her unconventional behavior. Happy to oblige, he took her outstretched hand and bent to press his lips to it. "It's a great honor to make your acquaintance, Mrs. McBride."

She giggled. "I know a rogue when I see one—and I adore them. You can stay."

"Very considerate of you. Especially since this is my house." After making the dry comment to her cousin's wife, Emily Davenport stepped forward to be included in the introductions. "I'm Emily, Mr. Cordero. I'm so glad you could join us today."

"I appreciate your hospitality. And I answer to Mac."

Jamie nodded firmly. "That's good. This is a cookout, not a business meeting."

"Mommy. Claire's eating grass again," the eldest of the three little girls playing by the picnic table announced, causing all the adults to spin around.

Mac watched as Jamie immediately abandoned

her outrageous behavior and responded maternally to her stepdaughter, Abbie, who had loudly tattled on her little cousin. Emily diverted little Claire's attention from snacking on the grass, and the men went back to their cooking.

For a moment, Mac couldn't look away from the children. His son would have been about their age now, he thought. He could easily picture dark-haired, dark-eyed Emilio toddling on the grass with these pretty little girls. The image made him almost flinch with an old, long-suppressed pain.

Sharon placed a hand on his arm. "Mac? Is everything okay?"

He forced a faint smile. "Everything's fine. I was just watching the kids."

"Cute, aren't they? I wish Caleb and Bobbie were here, so you could meet them, too. They're such a wonderful couple."

"Yeah, I'd like to meet them." Caleb McBride might prove to be the only man still living who could provide the answers Mac was looking for. He sure as hell didn't seem to be making much headway on his own.

During the next few hours, Mac couldn't quite understand why his mood grew steadily darker and heavier. The company was entertaining, the food delicious, the weather perfect. With the exception of Brad Henderson, who had almost turned purple when he saw Mac, everyone had been very friendly. But it seemed the more pleasantly the afternoon progressed, the grimmer Mac felt.

The McBride relatives chattered spiritedly all through the meal, catching up on recent events in each other's lives, sharing tidbits of innocuous gossip from around town, bragging about their children. And then they lapsed into reminiscing, sharing embarrassing tales about each other, teasing mercilessly, finishing each other's sentences as they tried to explain to the spouses and guests who didn't already know the stories. The anecdotes were amusing. Mac chuckled at the appropriate times and made the right comments, but he couldn't say he was actually enjoying them.

"Remember the time Trent got locked in Grandma McBride's root cellar?" Tara shook her head with a smile as she addressed her brothers and cousin. "He was just a toddler, not much older than our Alison is now. Savannah got hysterical. She'd just read a book about the Lindbergh baby and she was convinced Trent had been kidnapped. She didn't calm down until half an hour or so after Trent was found."

"I can't say I remember that," Trent murmured, looking uncomfortable when his fiancée smiled quizzically at him.

"Savannah?" Mac asked, playing his part.

"Our cousin," Trevor explained. "She's a year older than Tara. Her father, Jonah, was our dad's youngest brother. Uncle Jonah died when Savannah was only ten. Trent and I don't even remember him."

"Neither do I," Emily said, "but I wish I did. Everyone who knew him loved him."

"I remember him a little," Tara said. "He was a lot like our dad—very good-natured, always cutting up. He had a deep laugh and carried butterscotch candies in his pocket. He was a salesman and he often brought gifts for everyone when he came back from a trip. And he absolutely adored Savannah."

"He spoiled her rotten," Trent commented. "She grew up thinking she was a princess because her daddy always told her she was."

"Yes, well, she had to get over that when she became the mother of twins," Tara said matter-of-factly.

So everyone had loved Jonah McBride, the salesman who'd often been away on trips. Had Anita Cordero loved him, as well? Wouldn't it be ironic if the man she'd spent her life missing and hoping to someday see again had died less than ten years after he'd deserted her?

How would Jonah's little princess react to finding out she had a younger brother she'd never known? A brother who had been denied the camaraderie and memories she shared with her cousins. A brother who had never known what it was like to be spoiled by a doting father.

"Is everyone ready for dessert?" Emily asked, standing. "We have several types. Wade and Clay, Sharon brought her strawberry cake that you both love so much."

Wade and his teenage son immediately wore identical looks of greed. "Sharon makes the best strawberry cake I've ever tasted," Wade told Mac. "Wait'll you try it—pure heaven."

Sharon laughed softly. "Mac's allergic to strawberries. He'd be better off having some of Emily's famous German-chocolate cake."

"I like German chocolate," he assured her, aware that some of the others were looking at them speculatively now—probably because Sharon had spoken about him in such an indulgently familiar tone. If they hadn't already suspected something was going on between him and Sharon, they probably did now.

Somehow during dessert the conversation turned to the rash of break-ins lately, and the near-tragic accident through which Mac and Sharon had met. It was during that discussion that Mac learned Blake Fox was a private investigator in Atlanta; Wade seemed to value his advice about tracking down the culprits. Aware that Mac was listening closely, Wade turned to him at one point and said, "Do you have anything you'd like to add, Mac?"

"Sounds to me as if you've got it covered," Mac answered with a slight shrug.

"What would *he* know about police work?" Brad muttered across the table, his tone jeering. "He just fixes up houses."

"Tell that to some of the crooks he put behind bars in Savannah," Wade answered, implicitly rebuking Brad for his rudeness.

Mac swallowed a groan. He hadn't meant for this to come up today. He should have known better. Even among this relatively discreet group, secrets seemed to have a way of coming out.

CHAPTER THIRTEEN

"YOU WERE A COP, Mac?" Blake asked, apparently the first to understand the reference.

He nodded, almost feeling Sharon's startled gaze on his face. "For ten years. I retired a few years ago to become a restoration contractor, something I'd always been interested in trying."

"I don't suppose you want me to mention your citations? Or the fact that you retired after being shot in the line of duty, saving a group of innocent bystanders from a lunatic with an assault rifle?"

Wade's expression was so bland Mac was half tempted to punch him, just to see if it ruffled him. The chief really had investigated him thoroughly. Hell, he'd probably even talked to Mac's superior officers in Savannah. He'd been right when he'd assumed that there wasn't much that slipped past Wade Davenport.

"You were *shot?*" Sharon whispered, looking pale.

He shook his head reassuringly. "Just grazed. Hardly a scratch."

It was a lie, of course. He'd been hospitalized for ten days. But he saw no need to go into that now.

Jamie McBride was the one who broke the startled silence, and of course she did it with an outrageous comment. "Cordero-the-hero," she murmured, tongue in cheek. "That's what they call you around town, you know, because you saved Sharon's life that night. Just imagine the name you'd pick up if they heard about *this*."

Mac felt his cheeks darken, the closest he'd come to a blush in years. Wade laughed. Trevor rolled his eyes in resignation at his wife's impudence. Brad Henderson made a sound of disgust and pushed away from the table. "C'mon, Clay, let's go check out your new game. I'm starting to get nauseous."

"That boy really doesn't like you, Mac," Wade said when the teens had left, with Trevor's almost-seven-year-old son tagging eagerly along.

"It's just taking him longer than most people to respond to my natural charm," Mac drawled in return, making Wade chuckle.

"Mac thinks Brad is a bit threatened because Mac and I have become friends," Sharon said, looking concerned about her brother's behavior.

Trent shrugged. "Makes sense. Teenagers don't like change."

"That's what I told Mac," Sharon agreed quickly. "All Brad needs is some time and understanding—"

"And a good swift kick to the butt," Trent murmured.

Mac chuckled at Sharon's expression. "That's what I told *her*."

"Sympathy and understanding only go so far with

teenagers,'' Wade advised Sharon. "Sometimes it takes a tougher approach.''

Sharon sighed and lifted a hand to her temple. "Okay, I'll try.''

"Brad's a good boy,'' Emily said firmly. "Don't let them upset you, Sharon.''

Sharon looked only marginally reassured.

One of the younger children—either Emily's Claire or Tara's Alison, Mac tended to mix them up—toddled up to him and set a stuffed toy on his knee. She looked up at him with enormous blue eyes, apparently waiting for him to make a comment. "That's, uh, real nice. Claire,'' he added, figuring the odds were pretty good that he was right.

"That's Alison,'' Abbie informed him with a haughtiness that was rather pronounced considering she wasn't even four yet. "Claire's over there.''

He really wasn't faring very well with the younger set here today, Mac thought resignedly as the little girl he'd misidentified bustled happily away.

The child looked healthy, he mused, watching her chubby little legs pumping along. All the McBride descendants looked downright robust. He fervently hoped the same would prove true of any future offspring. No parent deserved the kind of heartbreak he had been through.

He glanced at his watch. The afternoon was well advanced. Shadows were lengthening in the yard. The kids were starting to look tired. And so was he, he imagined. He needed to get away.

Sitting next to him, Sharon leaned closer, masking her voice beneath the lively chatter of the others. "You look as though you're getting ready to bolt."

"I need to run by the house," he said. "The electricians were there this morning and I like to make sure everything's locked up after the crews leave."

Sharon stood as he did. "I'll walk you to your truck."

Looking only at her, he smiled a little. It calmed him to focus on her at the moment. Helped him concentrate on the present rather than the past.

Mac took his leave of the others, all of whom assured him they'd been delighted to have him there.

"I'm so glad you could come, Mac," Emily said, her hand in his. "Please visit us again."

He looked into her friendly blue eyes, seeing nothing but warm sincerity in her expression. A very nice woman, he thought. Would he ruin her comfortable life if he pursued his private investigation, if he made it publicly known that her father could be his, as well? He hadn't really cared when he came here who might be hurt or embarrassed if the truth was revealed, but that was before he'd met the McBrides. Before he'd been welcomed so graciously among them.

Whether they knew it or not, they were his family—and he didn't know how much, if anything, he owed them because of that coincidence of genetics.

Sharon was still thinking of her brother as she accompanied Mac around the side of the house.

"Brad really will come around, Mac. He just needs time."

Time. He considered that a moment. It would be several months before the renovation was finished. While it wasn't absolutely necessary for him to oversee every day of the work, it was his practice to be very actively involved in his projects from beginning to end. He enjoyed the work, and took great satisfaction in watching the daily progress.

It was *not* his practice to get involved with a woman in town during his jobs. There had been the occasional encounter since his divorce; he hadn't quite lived a monk's life since his divorce. But not far from it. And none of the few other women had made him question what he wanted or where he was headed the way Sharon did.

They paused together beside his truck. Sharon reached out to touch the deep scratch across the door. "You're going to have this repaired, aren't you?"

"Eventually."

She drew a deep breath, the action pushing her breasts against the thin fabric of her summery blouse. Again, his fingers itched to have a go at that row of tiny, flirty buttons. Her next comment brought his attention abruptly away from her cleavage.

"I want you to bill the repairs to me," she said firmly.

He studied her determined expression. "Forget it."

"I'm serious, Mac."

"So am I. You aren't paying for my repairs."

"Look, I know you still think Brad had something to do with this. And even though I really hope you're wrong, I believe in taking care of my responsibilities. If there's even a possibility that he's the guilty party, then I should pay for—"

"I said forget it." He wasn't about to let her take this any further. "Regardless of what I believe about the person who did this, I know for certain that it wasn't you. You aren't going to pay for it."

"But if Brad really did—"

"If Brad's guilty, then it should be up to him to make restitution, not you. I won't take your money, Sharon."

"But—"

"Have you even asked Brad if he had anything to do with it?" he asked gently.

Her stricken expression was answer enough.

"You haven't," he interpreted. "You're afraid of what he might say."

She sighed and rubbed her temples. "I'm such a coward."

Catching her wrists, he pulled her hands away from her head. "You," he said, "are the least cowardly person I've ever met. I can't imagine many other women your age who would have accepted the amount of responsibility you've taken on this summer. You're the one who deserves a vacation, but it seems like everyone's taking one except you. No one could expect more of you than what you've already given.''

Her hands cradled in his, she shook her head. "I don't mind watching out for my brother while my mother takes a trip that was the chance of a lifetime for her. It's just—well, not quite as easy as I'd expected."

"So don't take on more stress than you've already got. I'll take care of my problems, even if they involve your brother. Neither Brad nor I need you to handle this for us."

She bit her lip, seeming to contemplate his words for a moment. And then she gazed up at him again. "Mac? Why didn't you tell me you were a police officer?"

He winced. "It didn't come up?" he offered lamely.

She only looked at him.

He sighed. "I don't know. It just never seemed like the right time to mention it."

"Or maybe you thought it was something I had no need to know about you?"

He wasn't sure how to answer that.

She let him off the hook with a slight smile and a shake of her head. "It's okay. I'm not trying to learn all your secrets. I just wondered."

All his secrets. He glanced toward the house where so many of the McBrides were still gathered. "Sharon—"

"I guess I'm just a little stressed today."

"I don't want to cause you any more."

She squeezed his hands. "Don't worry about it. I can handle it."

He remembered the vow he'd made to himself that he wouldn't hurt her. He devoutly hoped it was a promise he would be able to keep. Taking a chance that they wouldn't be seen—and not really caring at that moment if they were—he leaned over to brush his lips across hers. Her mouth was warm and soft and clung to his for a moment before he straightened away from her. It wasn't easy for him to release her hands and step back. What he really wanted to do was toss her into his truck, take her to his apartment and spend the next twenty-four hours making love to her.

At least twenty-four hours.

"I want to see you again," he said, his voice gruff. "When can you get away?"

He didn't think he needed to clarify that he wanted to see her alone. She smiled at him in a way that let him know she understood. "Soon," she said. "I want to be with you, too."

He almost kissed her again. Instead, he reached for the door handle of the truck. "I'll call you later."

"You do that," she said, then turned to rejoin her friends.

So what, exactly, had he accomplished? he asked himself as he turned out of the Davenports' driveway and onto the road that would take him to the Garrett house. He'd learned that there was a good chance Jonah McBride had been his father—something he'd already figured. He'd caused Sharon to be embarrassed by her brother's behavior—and they'd both known it was a possibility. And, even though he knew the McBrides weren't prone to gossip, he'd made the relationship between Sharon and himself the focus of attention at least briefly that afternoon.

What *had* he accomplished? Damned if he knew.

But it was becoming harder and harder for him to think of the McBrides as just a group of people who owed him answers and apologies.

JAMIE WAS POISED to pounce almost the moment Sharon returned. "Well?" she said while the others were busy taking care of the little ones and putting away cookout supplies. "Anything you want to share with me?"

"What do you mean?" Sharon asked, though she knew very well what had piqued Jamie's curiosity.

"You're seeing Mac Cordero, aren't you? I'd heard around town that you are, and now that I've seen you together, I think the rumors might have some merit for a change."

Sharon still wasn't sure who'd started that rumor. She and Mac had been very discreet. They'd hardly been seen in public together. She could only assume that some of the construction workers had reached certain conclusions from watching them together—which only proved that men were just as bad as women to spread gossip, she thought with a shake of her head.

"Mac and I have been spending some time together. But it's still very early, Jamie. Much too soon to make any predictions."

Jamie laughed and patted Sharon's arm. "Don't worry, I'm not starting a betting pool. I just thought it was sweet the way he looked at you. It feels great to have a guy walking into walls when you're around, doesn't it?"

Flustered, Sharon laughed. "He doesn't actually—"

Jamie waved her hand dismissively. "I was speaking metaphorically, of course. Mac could hardly take his eyes off you all afternoon, even though he was very discreet about it. He's like Trevor, I think. It isn't easy for him to express his emotions, but he feels them very deeply."

Sharon remembered the afternoon when she had watched Mac and Trevor descending the stairs of the Garrett house side by side. Even though they were very different physically, she'd had the feeling that they were quite a bit alike in other ways.

"I guess you've heard Jerry's been telling everyone in town that you dumped him for Mac."

Sharon frowned. "No, I hadn't heard that. Has he really been saying those things?"

"I'm afraid so. He's really quite bitter about it."

Sharon put a hand to her head. "I wish he wouldn't do that. It isn't as if Jerry and I were ever really a couple. There was never any talk of a future between us."

"Men." Jamie heaved a dramatic sigh. "There's no understanding them."

Sharon heartily agreed.

Abruptly turning serious, Jamie touched Sharon's arm again. "I know your mom's away and you have a lot on your plate now, with your brother and everything. I remember how terrifying it was starting a new relationship. I know how it feels to fall for a complex, exasperating man with emotional baggage—which I would bet big money describes your Mac as well as my Trevor. If you ever need to talk, you know where to find me."

"Is it that obvious?" Sharon heard the touch of wistfulness in her own voice. "That I'm falling for him, I mean."

Her eyes ruefully sympathetic, Jamie smiled. "Sweetie, you might as well be wearing a sign."

Sharon groaned.

"Maybe I'm just particularly sensitive to it because it hasn't been that long since it happened to me," Jamie encouraged her. "Maybe no one else noticed."

Glancing automatically at the others, Sharon decided that every other woman there seemed to be surreptitiously watching her and Jamie. Oh, yes, she thought. They had noticed.

She might as well have been wearing a sign.

MAC WAS SITTING at his kitchen table again, brooding. His notes were spread in front of him, but it was the photograph in his hand that held his attention. A bottle of bourbon sat on the table, a half-empty glass near his elbow. He didn't drink often, but tonight there had seemed to be no reason to stay completely sober. He had nothing better to do and no one to do it with.

From the snapshot, his ex-wife and infant son gazed up at him. The picture had been taken in a hospital. Karla sat in a wooden rocker with four-week-old Emilio in her arms. Several tubes were attached to the baby, leading to equipment outside the boundaries of the shot. Emilio had never known a day without tubes or needles. Two weeks after this photo had been taken, the child had died, as quietly and unassumingly as he had lived.

Mac was in the photograph, too, kneeling beside Karla's chair. He hadn't wanted to have this picture taken, but Karla had insisted, and it had seemed like little enough to do for her during that nightmarish ordeal. It was ironic that she hadn't wanted to take the photograph with her when she left him.

The doctors had told them that Emilio's birth defect was genetic, something passed down through generations. Having been adopted as a baby, Karla knew nothing of her own genetic history. Mac, of course, knew only that there had been no history of the disease on his mother's side. There had been tests available to find out which of them carried the gene that had caused Emilio's death, but Mac hadn't bothered to take them. It had been too easy for him to shoulder the blame, himself.

Perhaps Karla had been tested during the past two

years. Mac wouldn't know. He hadn't talked to her since they'd drifted apart in the weeks after they'd lost their child.

It had been Karla who had filed for divorce, even though Mac had tried to talk her into giving their marriage another try. He'd even offered to go to counseling with her—and he hated that sort of thing. But she hadn't been interested. Whatever love she'd had for him in the beginning had been lost in grief and anger and bitterness. And his own distance.

Mac accepted his share of the blame for the end of the marriage. He'd lost his mother only six months before Emilio's birth, and he'd still been reeling from that devastating loss. He and his mother had been very close. They'd had to be. They were all the family each of them had.

Still grieving for his mother and trying to deal with the facts he'd learned after her death about his own parentage, he hadn't been adequately prepared for the second blow of losing his son. Maybe he hadn't been supportive enough of Karla during the difficult six weeks that Emilio had lived. Or maybe what they'd had simply wasn't strong enough to survive that kind of hardship.

He'd thought attraction, passion and affection were enough. Apparently, he'd been wrong.

What he was starting to feel for Sharon was entirely different than what he'd shared with Karla. But how was he to know whether this was any more real? Any more lasting?

The doorbell rang, drawing him out of his painful

reverie. He wasn't expecting anyone, which meant there was a good chance this wasn't something he wanted to hear. He sighed heavily, took another sip of his bourbon and rose.

A few moments later, he opened the front door to find Sharon Henderson standing on the other side.

"I probably should have called," she said, eyeing him uncertainly.

Aware that his hair was tousled, his shirt half unbuttoned and his feet bare, he cleared his throat. "No. I was just relaxing. Come in."

He moved aside to hold the door open for her. After only a momentary hesitation, she entered his apartment.

He closed the door behind her.

SHARON COULDN'T TAKE her eyes off Mac's face as she stepped inside his living room. As usual, his expression gave away little of his thoughts, but she had become strangely attuned to his emotions. She sensed that he had been feeling sad this evening. "What's wrong?" she asked.

"Nothing. You just caught me by surprise."

She really should have called. She had never been the type to act on impulse, but she'd done a lot of things that were out of character for her since Mac had come into her life. "I found myself on my own for the evening and I wondered if you would be interested in keeping me company for a few hours. But if you have other plans..."

"On your own, huh?"

"Yes. Clay and Brad talked me into letting Brad spend the night there. They'll probably play video games until dawn."

"And you thought maybe you and I could play a few games of our own?"

She loved the way his mouth quirked when he sort of smiled. "Only if you're interested, of course."

He reached out to tug her into his arms. "I am most definitely interested," he assured her, his mouth close enough to hers that she could feel the warmth of his breath on her face.

"You've been drinking," she murmured, noting the faint scent of alcohol and the slight flush on his cheeks.

"Yeah. Are you worried that I'm a closet drunk?"

She thought about it only a moment before shaking her head. "No. I think you've had a drink tonight because you were upset about something."

"Something like that."

"Did it help?"

His mouth twisted. "No."

She raised a hand to his jaw. "Is there something I can do?"

Catching her hand, he planted a kiss in the palm. "Oh, yeah."

The fervency of his reply made her smile. "Why don't you tell me what you need?"

He slid his hands down her sides, gripped her hips

and pulled her closer. "Why don't I show you, instead?"

Wrapping her arms around his neck, she murmured into his mouth, "That would work."

He didn't carry her to bed this time. They walked side by side, their bodies close together, their steps slow. They both knew there was no reason to hurry.

They left the overhead light off, turning on the small, dim lamp beside the bed for illumination. Sharon pushed Mac's shirt off his shoulders and then reached for the snap of his jeans. She intended to take a much more active role this time.

Because she was looking, she found the white scar low on his back, just above his left hip. Her fingertips brushed the puckered flesh. "This is where you were shot?"

"It wasn't that bad. My injuries were never life-threatening."

Kneeling beside him, she pressed her lips to the scar. "It must have been very painful."

The way he flinched when her lips touched him, she'd have thought he was in pain now. And perhaps he was, she mused with a secret smile. But it was a good pain this time—an ache only she could soothe.

Standing unselfconsciously nude in front of her, he lifted her up and reached for the first tiny pearlized button on her white summer top. "I wanted to do this all afternoon."

"I know." She smiled wickedly at him, remembering Jamie's comment about how good it felt to have a man "walking into walls." "I could tell by the way you looked at me."

Brushing his lips across her forehead, he murmured, "Sometimes I worry that you see too much when you look at me."

She didn't know how to answer that, so she didn't try. Instead, she placed a hand on either side of his face and brought his mouth to hers.

By the time the kiss ended, her blouse and bra were on the floor and her shorts were puddled around her feet. Mac lifted her out of them and fell to the bed with her. "You are so perfect," he half groaned, running his hands over her.

"Not perfect. I have a scar, too."

"Where?"

Feeling deliciously mischievous, she smiled and ran a finger across his lower lip. "Why don't you try to find it?"

It was a challenge he accepted with enthusiasm. There wasn't an inch of her he missed in his search—not an inch he didn't touch or kiss. Even after he found the small scar from her childhood appendectomy, he kept looking—just in case, he informed her gravely, there was a flaw he had missed. Not until he'd kissed his way to her toes did he pronounce her as perfect as he had believed her to be.

By then, she could hardly think clearly enough to remember what he'd been looking for.

He was doing it again, she thought weakly. Clouding her mind with passion and pleasure, keeping her so dazed and befuddled she could only lie against the pillows and gasp. Calling on all her strength, she pushed herself off the pillows and pressed him onto his back. "My turn," she said firmly.

He spread his arms. "Knock yourself out."

Her breath catching on a giggle, she bent over him. It wasn't the most romantic invitation she'd ever had, but it was sincerely offered, and that was what mattered. By the time this night ended, she promised herself, she would know his body as well as he knew hers.

It wasn't easy keeping him still while she explored him. He kept wanting to roll her beneath him. Sharon had to hold him in place with a firm hand. He could easily have overpowered her, of course. He wouldn't even have had to put much effort into flipping her onto her back and pinning her there with his own body. But he let her set the pace, even though he almost quivered with impatience.

He jerked violently when she took him into her hand. Groaned deep in his chest when she placed her mouth on him. And a few long, emotion-filled moments later, he did something she hadn't expected from this strong, hard man. He begged. "Sharon—please..."

The request affected her in a way no amount of machismo could have. She melted. "Mac—"

They moved together, a fluid, silent duet of desire. It took only a heartbeat for him to don protection, and then another for him to bury himself so deeply inside her she felt as if he had become a part of her.

She couldn't have begun to guess how much time passed—minutes...hours...days. There were no words, no coherent thoughts. Only ragged breathing and broken cries. And so much raw, honest emotion that her heart seemed to swell almost to bursting with it.

She was so desperately in love with this man. It didn't seem to matter that they'd known each other such a short time, or that there were still secrets between them, at least on his part. She loved him. Whether that love would lead to a happy ending— well, that remained to be seen.

CHAPTER FOURTEEN

HIS CHEEK on her breast, his arm across her, Mac lay on his stomach next to her as they very slowly recovered their breath. Their sanity.

"Tell me this isn't a fantastic dream," he muttered after a while, without lifting his head.

She laughed. "I don't think you had *that* much to drink before I arrived."

"Half a glass."

"So which was more effective at making you feel better? The booze? Or me?"

He lifted his head to give her a faintly reproachful look. "Fishing?"

Unabashed, she touched his face. "Yes."

"You are infinitely better than bourbon."

She grinned. "I'll take any compliment I can get."

Propping himself on one elbow, Mac smoothed her tangled hair away from her face. "You're in a feisty mood tonight."

"I guess being bold and bad does that to me."

"'Bold and bad'? Is that what you're feeling?"

"Of course. I don't do things like this. Ever. I'm always sensible and responsible. I don't take chances, I don't have flings and I don't act on impulse. Not usually. Not until you came along.''

He considered her words, and he didn't look entirely pleased by them. "A fling," he repeated in a murmur.

"For want of a better term."

"I don't care for that one."

"Do you have a better word to offer?" she challenged, still in that oddly daring mood.

"No," he said after a brief pause. "But it isn't a fling."

It wasn't much—but it was something. She decided to be satisfied with that for now.

Her hand rested on his side, just inches from the scar on his back. "Why did you quit the police force? Was it because you were shot?"

"Not entirely. I was just tired of giving everything I had to a job and not seeing any real results for my efforts. I'd put one drug dealer behind bars and three more would take his place. For every at-risk teenager we set straight, we lost a dozen more. I started dreading going in to work in the mornings. I felt more and more like I was trying to put out a forest fire with a squirt gun.''

It pleased her that he'd answered her so candidly, giving her another glimpse into his character. She didn't think less of Mac for walking away from a job that had grown frustrating for him; she knew it was because he had cared so deeply that he couldn't stay. "So you went into the restoration business, where you could see definite results. You take something old and neglected and you make it useful and beautiful again.''

"Something like that," he said with a slight shrug. Despite his offhand tone, she could tell her assessment had been on track.

Because he seemed in a mood to talk, she risked another personal question. "How did your wife feel about your change of profession? Was she relieved?"

"Actually, she rather liked being married to a cop. A contractor wasn't nearly as exciting to her."

That couldn't have been the only reason the marriage ended, she mused. "How long were you married after you quit police work?"

"About a year."

It must have been a difficult year, she decided, studying his expression. But maybe she didn't want to talk about his marriage right now, after all. "Tell me about your mother," she said, instead.

His eyebrows lifted. "You really *are* feeling chatty, aren't you?"

"I'm sorry. Would you rather I be quiet?"

"No. Ask anything you like. What do you want to know about my mother?"

"From what little you've told me about her, I can tell you were close to her. She must have been very special."

"She was." His voice held a mixture of pride and wistfulness, making it clear he still missed her very much.

"She was born in Puerto Rico?"

"Yes. She was married in San Juan when she was seventeen. She followed her husband to Savannah, where he went to work on the docks and she found work as a hotel maid. A year later, he was killed in a job accident, leaving her a widow before her nineteenth birthday."

"And pregnant with you—how terrible for her."

"No. Her husband wasn't my father." There was no emotion in his voice. "My mother fell in love with another man almost ten years later. He was married to someone else. I was conceived from that relationship. Her very Catholic family turned against her because she had a child out of wedlock. She raised me on her own, without any help from anyone."

"Your father?" she murmured, studying his impassive face.

He shrugged. "I never met him. He had no interest in staying behind to deal with the devastation he had caused in my mother's life."

"She must have been a very strong woman."

"She was. She never accepted any assistance from anyone. She raised me on what she earned as a hotel maid. By the time I was five, she was the head housekeeper. She never made a lot of money, but what she had went to my health care and education. I started working to help her out when I was just a kid, but it was always a struggle to convince her to take money from me."

"She named you Miguel, but she called you Mac. And she made sure you could speak English."

"As I said, she wanted me to fit in. She hoped I would become a doctor or a lawyer. But when I chose to enter the police academy, instead—following in the footsteps of a neighbor I admired and who had always taken an interest in mentoring me—she couldn't have acted more proud of me."

"You loved her very much, didn't you?"

"I adored her."

His simply and sincerely worded reply made her throat tighten. She would like to think that if she ever had a son, he would speak of her with the same respect and devotion with which Mac remembered his mother.

"After my mother died," he said, looking into the distance over Sharon's head as if gazing into his past, "I found out that she had put every extra dollar she made into life insurance policies naming me as the beneficiary. Even after I was grown and supporting myself, she felt she needed to provide for me."

"It sounds as though she adored you in return."

"She did. I used the insurance money to establish my new business. I think she would have approved."

"She gave you the ability to pursue a dream, even if it might have been different from her dreams for you. Yes, I'm sure she would have approved."

"You'd have liked her, I think."

"I'm sure I would have loved her." How could she not have loved the woman who had raised this very special man?

Mac gave a little shake of his head, as if shaking off the memories, and moved a hand over her bare body. "Have we talked enough now?"

She reached up to brush back a lock of silky black hair that had fallen onto his forehead. "Do you have something else in mind?"

Lowering his head to her breast, he murmured, "Something's bound to come up."

She giggled, and then gasped when his tongue swept over her nipple. "Okay," she said breathlessly, her fingers tightening in his hair. "That's enough talk for now."

He gathered her closer. "Good."

SHARON WOKE at 2:00 a.m., thirsty and disoriented. After taking a moment to gather her bearings, she turned her head on the pillow to look at Mac. He was soundly asleep, his limbs sprawled, his mouth just slightly parted. Sleep didn't soften his features much, she mused. Even now he looked powerful and strong. Still slightly dangerous.

She knew now that there was a soft side hidden behind that stern exterior. A side he would allow few people to see. She felt fortunate to be one of them.

She lay there for a moment, just watching him. Fantasizing and hoping...

Her thirst finally pulled her from the bed. She snatched Mac's denim shirt from the floor where she'd thrown it earlier and slipped her arms into the sleeves. It was long enough on her to serve as a short robe, covering her enough for modesty's sake. Wrapping it around her, she headed for the kitchen.

Mac had left the light on. The kitchen table was cluttered with papers. An open bottle of bourbon sat next to a half-empty tumbler. The cap lay beside the bottle.

Automatically reaching to replace the cap, she paused when her gaze fell on a photograph lying on top of the scattered papers. In it, a dark-haired woman held a tiny, black-haired, black-eyed baby. The setting was obviously a hospital. In the picture, Mac knelt beside the chair, his right hand resting protectively on the baby's head, as if to protect the child.

He looked very much like a worried father.

Her fingers shook a little as she reached out to touch the photo. She could picture Mac sitting here alone, sipping his drink and staring at this photograph. Only one explanation occurred to her. Had this child been Mac's? He had told her he and his wife had no children. Could their baby have died?

No wonder she had sensed such sadness in him when she'd first arrived. Did it still hurt him to talk about it? Was that why he hadn't told her?

He deserved his privacy. Prepared to step away from the table, she moved her hand from the photograph. It was then that the name McBride caught her attention. It was written in block letters at the top of one of the legal-pad pages. *All* of the pages, she corrected herself, looking slowly from one sheet to another.

Why was Mac compiling a comprehensive file about the McBride family?

They were all there—parents noted at the tops of the pages and offspring listed beneath. He'd even recorded the ages of each of the cousins.

She had given him much of this information herself, she realized, remembering several conversations in which the McBrides had been discussed fairly extensively. She'd actually been embarrassed by her babbling, worried that Mac had been bored. But now she wondered if she had been manipulated by an expert.

But why?

A pen lay on the pad, as if recently abandoned. Only a few lines had been written on the top page. "Jonah McBride. Wife, Ernestine. Daughter, Savannah, 34. Traveling salesman. Unhappy marriage."

He'd learned this information only a few hours earlier, she thought, pressing a hand to her stomach.

"Would you like to go through my wallet, too?"

She jumped when he spoke from the doorway behind him. Whirling on him, she scowled. "Don't you dare go on the offensive with me! Why are you spying on my friends?"

Leaning against the doorjamb, wearing only a pair of unsnapped jeans, he didn't change his expression. "Is that what you think I'm doing?"

That stoic, inscrutable look on his face only made her madder. "And don't play word games. It's obvious what you're doing. You have everything but their shoe sizes written here."

He only continued to look at her.

"Mac, I want answers."

"So do I. But we don't always get what we want."

Clenching the back of a chair so tightly her knuckles whitened, she glared at him. "Were the McBrides the reason you came to Honoria?"

He didn't respond.

"Were they the reason you were so friendly to me? Because of my friendship with them? Were you using me to get to them?"

Mac sighed and shoved a hand through his hair. "Sharon, calm down. We need to talk."

"I'm perfectly calm. And the only words I want to hear from you are an explanation of what these pages mean."

"Can't you just believe me when I tell you I don't mean the McBrides any harm?"

"You're asking me to trust you?"

"Yes." His eyes bored into hers. "That's exactly what I'm asking you to do."

Releasing the chair, she twirled her fingers in the front of his oversize shirt, abruptly aware of how little it covered. Strangely enough, she felt more naked now than she had in his bed wearing nothing at all. "Before I make that decision, will you answer just one question for me? Honestly?"

"That depends on what you ask," he said guardedly.

"*Did* you first ask me out because of my friendship with the McBrides?"

"Yes."

His starkly honest answer made her heart sink. "Damn," she whispered.

Mac had used her. He'd just admitted it. It seemed that Brad had been right. She would try to remember to apologize to him—after she'd had a good cry.

"I want to get dressed now," she said, moving toward the doorway in which he stood.

He didn't move, but continued to block her passage. "Maybe it started out that way, but that isn't why I'm here with you now."

"I'd like to believe that," she murmured, unable to meet his eyes. "But I saw what you've written on these pages. I don't know what you're doing, or why, but I know you got part of that information from me. You used me."

"In some ways, that's true. And I'm sorry. But—"

"Please let me get dressed, Mac," she begged miserably. "I can't think clearly like this."

He hesitated for one tense moment, then moved aside.

She almost dashed to the bedroom.

She couldn't look at the rumpled bed while she gathered her clothes and took them into the bathroom to dress. Her thoughts were whirling, her stomach clenching. She had plunged so swiftly from euphoria to despair that she could hardly process what had happened to her. She still didn't have a clue what Mac was up to, but it didn't really matter just then. She knew she wasn't going to like it. If there was a simple, innocuous explanation, he would have told her already. And he had already admitted that he'd first been interested in her because of her connection to the McBrides.

Foolishly enough, she'd thought it was her personality he'd been drawn to. Her talent, perhaps. Hell, she wouldn't have been this upset if he'd confessed that he'd only wanted her for her body. But to use her against her friends, to pump her for information about the people she liked so much, and who had been so good to her...well, that really hurt.

Whatever he was up to, there was no excuse.

Dressed again in her blouse and shorts, she wished she had worn something more formal that evening. It wasn't easy to be cool, clipped and intimidating in shorts. But she intended to try. She took several deep breaths before she stepped out of the bathroom. She wasn't eager to face Mac again.

He was still in the kitchen. The photograph had been put away, she noted. So had his notes. The bourbon bottle still sat on the table, capped now. The tumbler was empty.

Mac leaned against the counter, his arms crossed over his bare chest. "Do you feel better now?"

"No." She wasn't sure she would ever feel better again, not as badly as he had hurt her tonight. "Will you tell me now why you're gathering information about my friends?"

"I can't, Sharon. Not yet."

"Do you ever plan to tell me?"

He hesitated for a long time before answering. "I don't know. I haven't decided."

"Does it have something to do with your police work? Are you undercover for some reason? Do you think any of the McBrides are involved in something illegal?"

He was shaking his head even before she paused for a breath. "I'm not a cop, Sharon. Not anymore. My reasons for being here are strictly personal."

"And you won't tell me what they are."

"There are people who might be hurt. I don't know yet if I want to be responsible for that."

"You must have known when you came here that someone could be hurt. Didn't it bother you then?"

"I didn't know them then."

That made her pause to study him. He sounded as if he had begun to like the McBrides. As if he was having second thoughts about whatever had brought him here.

She thought of what she had seen on those pages. The names of Caleb and his brothers, their wives and children. Notes about their jobs and their marriages.

My mother fell in love with another man. He was married to someone else. I was conceived from that relationship.

And his mother had called him Mac.

The insight came to her in a stunning flash. "You're looking for your father."

A muscle in his jaw was the only part of him that moved.

"Is that it, Mac? Do you think Caleb or one of his brothers was the married man who had an affair with your mother?"

He ground out a curse through clenched teeth, and then sighed. "I know one of them was. I just don't know which one."

"*How* do you know?"

"I found the name in my mother's papers after she died. Just the last name. She probably never expected me to find it, or to make anything of it. I contacted her sister in Puerto Rico, who confirmed that she knew the man's name was McBride and that he was from a place called Honoria, Georgia. She knew that because my mother told her. Mother expected to live in Honoria someday, when her lover divorced his wife and married her."

Aware of the bitterness in his voice, she asked gently, "Your aunt didn't know his first name?"

"Only the last name—and only because my mother told her that she called me Mac because my father's name was McBride. A tribute to the man who abandoned her."

"So you came here to find out for yourself."

"I figured he owed me some answers. I didn't know when I started this that most of the suspects were dead."

Imitating him, she folded her arms and tried to speak unemotionally. "Have you decided which one it was?"

He shrugged. "I figure Jonah is the most likely suspect."

She remembered what he'd written about Jonah. "Traveling salesman. Unhappy marriage." He was probably right. "Jonah's been dead for years."

"I know."

"His widow and his daughter are still living, of course. Ernestine is a very proud and snobbish woman. It would humiliate her to learn that her husband had an affair and fathered a child while they were married."

"I didn't come here to humiliate an innocent bystander. His wife wasn't to blame for what he did. Mother knew he was married when they started their affair. She foolishly fell in love anyway. And she believed his lies that he loved her enough to marry her."

"What about Savannah? If Jonah was your father, that makes her your sister. Don't you want to get to know her?"

His face hardened. "I came here to find answers, not a new family. If Jonah had been alive, I might have tried to hurt him as much as he hurt my mother. I wouldn't have cared much about who got hurt along with him. But he's dead. It's too late for me to do anything to him. His widow and his daughter have nothing to do with me. I have no reason to have anything to do with either of them."

The hardness in his voice shocked her. This wasn't the man she had fallen in love with. This was a stranger. Angry, bitter, cold.

This was the man who had callously used her for

his own purposes. She wasn't even sure this man was capable of love.

Was this only another side of the Mac she'd thought she knew? Or had she completely deluded herself while falling in love with a stranger?

"There is still one McBride brother living. Caleb," she said quietly. "Is there any chance…?"

Mac shrugged again. "He's been happily married for nearly forty years. He rarely leaves Honoria. I'd say it's far more likely that Jonah was the sperm donor in my case. From what I've heard about him, I can understand why he fell in love with my mother. I just can't understand why he left her."

"Caleb will be home in a week. Are you going to ask him if he knows anything about this?"

"Don't you think I have that right?"

"The right to cause an uproar in a very happy family?" She shook her head. "I don't know."

Mac's voice turned even colder than it had been before. "My mother died still loving the man who'd broken her heart. She never got over him, never stopped hoping he would come back to her. She named me after him, dammit. I have a right to know who did that to her. The duty to seek retribution on my mother's behalf."

"Retribution?"

His eyes glittered like black stones. "Whichever McBride seduced my mother, he would not have wanted his gutless actions widely known by his children, his grandchildren, his neighbors and friends. And the way gossip travels around this town, it wouldn't take long for everyone to know if I choose to drop a few well-placed words.''

The thought of Mac deliberately causing that kind of pain to so many people made her sick. She could understand his anger. She could even understand his desire for revenge. But to know that so many innocents would be hurt in the process—and that in the long run, nothing would really be accomplished... She just couldn't approve of that.

She didn't know what to say. She only knew that the entire situation broke her heart. But what hurt her the most was the fact that Mac had used her for his own purposes.

Though he didn't move, he seemed to physically withdraw from her. ''It's obvious whose side you're on.''

That brought her chin up again. ''I'm not on anyone's side. I won't be put in the middle of your private war, Mac. You've used me to this point, but I won't let you use me any longer.''

''It was more than that,'' he muttered.

''Was it?'' She kept her voice steady with an effort. ''Earlier tonight, I asked if you had a word to describe our relationship. You didn't. Do you have one now?''

Placing a hand on the back of his neck, he started to speak, then fell silent.

''I didn't think so.'' She turned on one heel toward the doorway.

''You're leaving?''

''Yes.'' She didn't look back. She didn't want

him to see the tears forming in her eyes. "Don't worry, Mac, I won't say anything about what I've learned here tonight. I won't interfere with your vendetta, but I won't help you, either. Whatever information you dig up now, you won't be getting it from me. And whatever you do with that information is entirely your decision. I only hope you make the right choice."

"What about the job?"

She couldn't believe he'd brought that up now. It was wounded pride that made her square her shoulders, turn, and face him without expression. "I'd recommend that you bring in a professional decorator from Atlanta. This time you'll probably want to hire someone on the basis of their training and experience, rather than their friendship with a family you want to destroy."

"That wasn't the reason I hired you," he said flatly. "When it comes to my jobs, I choose the best people—and you're the best. I'm holding you to your professional obligation."

"Fine," she snapped. "This assignment will look good on my résumé. I suppose it's only fair if I use you in this."

He inclined his head in an almost royal gesture. "Just do a good job."

"I always do." She turned and left, before she ruined her cool performance by bursting into tears.

BRAD FOUND Sharon crying Sunday evening. She had been proud of herself for not giving in to tears since she'd left Mac's house in the wee hours of the morning. But something made her think of him Sunday evening, after she thought Brad was in bed, and the floodgates opened despite her efforts.

She was sitting in the kitchen, an untouched cup of herbal tea in front of her. Her elbows resting on the table, she buried her face in her hands and sobbed quietly. It hurt so badly to think that she had risked so much and had been given so little in return. She hadn't been naive enough to think that he'd fallen in love with her at first sight, but she'd thought there was something real between them. Something that had a chance of lasting forever.

She'd obviously been more naive than she'd thought.

She'd been nothing more to him than a pawn in a calculated quest for revenge. Because of his manipulation, she had unwittingly aided his assault on her friends. It hurt so much she wasn't sure she could bear it.

"Sharon? What's wrong? What's happened?" There was a note of panic in Brad's voice as he spoke from the doorway behind her. He had seen her cry so rarely that he must have assumed something terrible had happened.

She caught her breath and mopped at her face with her hands. "It's okay, Brad," she said, trying to speak reassuringly. "Nothing's wrong."

"You're crying."

"I'm just feeling sad this evening. Women do that sometimes."

He didn't buy it. "Something's happened. Someone's hurt you. It's Cordero, isn't it? What did he do?"

She sighed. "Brad, please. Let it go."

"Did he say something about me?"

"It wasn't about you. It had nothing to do with you."

"But he said *something*."

"We had a disagreement. My feelings were hurt, but I'll recover, okay? Things like this just happen sometimes."

"So you won't be seeing him anymore?" Brad asked hopefully.

"I'm still working for him on the Garrett house renovation. But our relationship is strictly professional from now on."

"Why don't you just tell him to stuff his renovation job?"

"Because I have a business to run. And a professional reputation to uphold. I can't just walk away from a business commitment in a huff because the client hurt my feelings."

"I told you about that guy. I told you he wasn't as cool as you and everyone else thought he was."

Funny that her first instinct was still to defend Mac. He and his mother had suffered a great deal because of his father's callous abandonment. His mother certainly wasn't blameless in the affair, but Mac had admittedly adored her. He had owed her everything. It was only natural that he would want to defend her. And if he'd also lost a child not long after his mother passed away, then it made sense, knowing him, that he would turn that grief to anger.

She couldn't blame him for wanting to lash out at his absentee father. But she wouldn't excuse him for being willing to hurt so many other people in the process. She hadn't deserved to be one of his casualties.

"There are some things about Mac you don't understand," she told her brother quietly. "He isn't as bad as you think."

Brad snorted in disgust. "You've still got a thing for him, don't you? Even after he made you cry."

Wearily, she rubbed her aching temples. "Brad, please. I don't want to talk about this tonight. You're supposed to be in bed."

"I was thirsty."

It was a late-night foray for water that had caused Sharon such pain in the first place, she couldn't help remembering. "Get a drink and then go back to bed. We'll talk again tomorrow," she said.

"But—"

"Brad. Please."

He grumbled, but poured himself a glass of water. Downing it quickly, he set the glass aside, then paused by her chair to awkwardly pat her shoulder. "The guy ain't worth crying over, sis. He'll get his, don't you worry."

"Just stay away from him, Brad. Please. For my sake."

He muttered something she didn't quite catch and moved on toward the doorway.

Sharon watched him leave with a worried frown. She really hadn't handled that well, she thought. He had caught her off guard, at a time when she wasn't thinking clearly enough to deal with him. She had messed everything up today, she thought with a dispirited sigh.

She didn't know what it was going to take to get her life back on the comfortable track she had established before Mac Cordero came to town.

CHAPTER FIFTEEN

THERE WAS ALWAYS a lot of time to think during a stakeout. Mac had gotten some of his best ideas while sitting in a car or at a window, waiting for something that might or might not happen.

On this particular Friday night, he was sitting in a deeply shadowed hollow beneath a huge oak tree on the outskirts of the property surrounding the Garrett house. It was almost midnight and he'd been sitting there an hour, so he'd had plenty of time to think. Not that he hadn't already done far too much thinking in the six days that had passed since Sharon stormed out of his kitchen.

It was a clear, fragrant evening, the light breeze just slightly cool against his face. Only a slice of moon floated in the inky sky, so the shadows were deep, hiding their secrets in darkness. Mac knew he was just as well concealed in his black shirt and jeans. A part of the summer night, with secrets of his own to hide. Somewhere above him, an owl hooted, sounding as if it was mocking him as the fool he knew himself to be.

He hadn't seen Sharon since she'd walked out of his apartment. He knew she'd been avoiding him— and, to be honest, he'd been doing the same. He still couldn't remember the hurt in her eyes without flinching. He hadn't been able to tell her that he hadn't used her—because, truth was, he had. And, worse, he had done it intentionally.

He hadn't meant to fall in love with her in the process.

She'd wanted him to put a name to what he felt for her, to convince her that it was more than sex, more than convenience. He hadn't spoken because he hadn't known what to say. His track record with commitment was lousy. He'd already hurt her once, he didn't want to risk doing so again. Her brother hated him, and so would her friends if they found out why he was here. It was a hopeless relationship—and Sharon deserved better.

In a way, it had been very unselfish on his part to let her go before he hurt her again, he told himself. So why did he still feel like such a slug? Like someone who belonged in the shadows, hidden away from the sunlight?

Why did it still hurt so badly to think of her walking away from him?

A sound behind him made him tense. Sitting absolutely still, he listened as the voices grew closer. He recognized one as Brad Henderson's.

"I'm not sure about this, Jimbo. I think maybe we'd better—"

"Come on, Brad, you're not chickening out, are you? Not now."

"It's just—well, what if we get caught? What if Tommy's mom finds out we snuck out?"

"We won't get caught. Trust me. Me and Tommy know what we're doing. His mom sleeps like the dead when she takes one of her pills, and Tommy watched her take one tonight. And we've got Gil on our side."

"I don't know—"

Another boy spoke this time, his voice gruff with impatience. "C'mon, Brad, you hate this guy. You said he deserved this."

"It's going to be a piece of cake, Brad." Jimbo, again. "We use these bolt cutters to cut the locks on the storage building, help ourselves to the best tools, and then we'll have a little fun in the house. Gil said that fancy glass is leaded. Original. *Real* hard to replace. That'll show Cordero what happens when he pushes us around."

"I don't have a problem with breaking his windows," Brad muttered. "He deserves that for being such a jerk. But the stealing...I didn't know you guys were involved with that."

"Don't get preachy on us, Brad," Jimbo warned. "We haven't taken anything from anybody who didn't have insurance to cover it. And you sure have liked it that we've had extra money to spend on food and arcade games and movies and stuff. You didn't worry about where the money came from when we were spending it, did you?"

"Well, maybe—but the Porter place, guys. I didn't know it was you driving that van. My sister could've been killed."

"I told you—I didn't mean for that to happen. I

panicked, okay? I'd never driven a van like that before. But she's okay now. And you're making up for it tonight. You said this bastard made her cry. Here's your chance to make *him* pay.''

Mac felt like the bastard they had called him—the bastard he was—when he thought of Sharon crying over him. She hadn't deserved that. She didn't deserve this, either. His anger with her brother grew.

''I don't know,'' Brad said again, and there was temptation as well as fear in his voice.

''I'm tired of this,'' the third boy announced flatly. ''Let's do it, guys. Brad, are you with us or not?''

''He's with us. Ain't you, Brad?''

''Yeah. I—I guess so. Just give me a minute, okay? You guys go on and I'll meet up with you.''

''He's backing out,'' the other boy announced scornfully.

''No, I'm not. Really. I just—I just need to pee, okay? I'll be there in a minute.''

''You better. Come on, Jimbo. Let's do it.''

''Right with you, man. Don't let us down, Brad.''

Mac listened while the other boys moved toward the house. Brad stayed where he was, cursing frantically beneath his breath, obviously torn between joining his friends and making a run for it. Feeling as if fate had stepped in to give him a break, Mac decided it was time for him to assist the boy in his decision making.

Brad never had a warning. Mac had an arm around him and a hand over his mouth before the kid knew he wasn't alone. It wasn't hard for Mac to overpower the skinny, panic-stricken teenager. "Be still before you get hurt," he said quietly into Brad's ear. "You know who I am, don't you?"

Brad nodded stiffly.

"Your friends are walking straight into Chief Davenport's arms. He's waiting for them behind my storage building. He'll probably let them cut the lock before he moves in, just to make sure of what they're up to. And then he'll put them behind locks they won't be able to cut."

Brad groaned.

"I'm giving you a break, kid. Not because I think you deserve it. To be honest, I think it would do you a world of good to spend some time in juvenile detention. But you see, I know that would devastate your sister. And unlike you, that matters very much to me."

Brad moved sharply, forcing Mac to tighten his grip. "Don't argue with me, boy. If you really cared about your sister, you wouldn't be here doing something that you know would break her heart. You wouldn't be hanging out with a guy who trashes her reputation. The same guy who almost killed her less than a month ago. What kind of man chooses a jerk like that over his own family? You're damn lucky to have a sister like Sharon. You should be her defender, not one of the people who hurts her."

Brad jerked his mouth free of Mac's hand. "*You* hurt her. You made her cry."

"You're right," Mac said evenly. "And I deserve

every name you want to call me. But you're her brother.''

Brad couldn't answer that.

''We're too far out of town for you to walk safely back at this hour. My truck is parked a hundred yards up the road from here. Go wait in it for me. The keys are in my pocket, but I left the doors unlocked. You should recognize the truck. It's the one with the big, ugly scratch down one side.''

Brad muttered something Mac didn't even try to catch.

''Unless you want to join your friends with Chief Davenport, of course. But I wouldn't recommend it. From what I heard, they deserve what they're going to get. You just squeaked by. Now, I can take you home to your sister or I can turn you over to the cops. Your call.''

''I'll wait in your truck,'' Brad conceded grudgingly.

''That's the first smart choice I've seen you make yet, boy.'' Cautiously, Mac released him, half prepared for him to run. But Brad only stood there, his head down, his shoulders slumped, looking suddenly younger than his fifteen years.

''Get in the truck,'' Mac urged. ''I'm going to make sure everything's taken care of at the house. I'll drive you home when I'm finished.''

''Are Jimbo and Tommy really going to jail?''

Mac hardened his voice. ''If you're tempted to feel sorry for them, spend the time while you're waiting for me thinking about how easily your sister could have drowned in Snake Creek.''

Without comment, Brad shuffled off toward Mac's truck.

Mac found Wade and two of his officers beside the storage building, Jimbo and Tommy handcuffed between them. Jimbo was sniveling, Tommy looked sullen and defiant.

Mac spoke to Wade. ''Looks like you got your perps.''

''Yeah. Got 'em just as they were about to help themselves to your tools.''

Clicking his tongue, Mac shook his head at the boys. ''Now, is that any way to treat a guest in your hometown?''

They both glared at him.

Turning his back to them, Mac looked at Wade again. ''Thanks for tipping me off, Chief. I am, most definitely, pressing charges.''

''No kidding. Uh—we rather expected to catch more than two of them.''

Keeping his expression impassive, Mac shrugged. ''I guess their friends had enough sense not to get involved in this.''

''I'm glad to hear it.''

Mac was aware that Officer Gilbert Dodson was notably absent from the crime scene. ''I'm sorry about your man, Wade. It always gets you when a cop goes bad, doesn't it?''

His face strained, Wade nodded. ''Yeah. It does.''

''If you don't need me for anything else right

now, I've got an errand to run. I'll see you sometime tomorrow."

"Yeah. See ya', Mac."

Brad was waiting in the truck, slumped down on the seat, the most miserable kid Mac had seen in a long time. He climbed behind the wheel and slammed his door. "Your buddies are in cuffs. Be glad you aren't."

"I am." The admission was made grudgingly. "I guess I should thank you for what you did for me."

Mac started the engine. "I didn't do it for you, remember?"

"I know. You did it for Sharon."

"Fasten your seat belt." He drove the truck onto the road and headed for town.

"Are you going to tell her?" Brad asked after a tense pause.

"Don't you think I should?"

The boy looked down at his tightly entwined hands.

Mac gave him another minute to worry, then said, "I'm not going to tell her. The whole point of this is to keep her from finding out what a moron you almost were."

Though he obviously resented Mac's blunt words, Brad was hardly in a position to protest. "What about when she hears about Jimbo and Tommy? If they're going to jail, everyone will be talking about it."

"And she knows you started the evening in their company. You're just going to have to tell her you found out what they were planning and chose to go home rather than get involved with something you knew was wrong. Don't lie to her, just stick to that story.''

Brad looked out the passenger window as Mac turned onto the street where he lived. He waited until Mac parked in the driveway before saying, ''If you hadn't stopped me, I'd have been in jail right now.''

''Are you just figuring that out?''

''No. I just—well, thanks, okay? I really didn't want to go to jail. I didn't have anything to do with those other break-ins, I swear. I didn't even know Jimbo was involved until he told me tonight. He didn't think I'd go along with them before, but he thought I might tonight.''

''Because it was my place they were hitting this time.''

''Yeah.''

''They thought you hated me enough to help them. Then once they had you involved, it would have been easy enough for them to continue to control you by threatening to turn you in for this one.''

''I guess.''

''Trust me, that's how it works. I've seen it a hundred times. That's how Gilbert Dodson was able to get the kids to steal for him. He got them involved, strung them along with money and gifts, then coerced them into staying with him. Not that your buddies tonight seemed to need much coercion.''

"I didn't know Officer Dodson was crooked. I thought he was a straight-up cop. I knew a lot of the guys liked to hang out with him, but I thought he was just…you know, mentoring them or something."

Sensing that the boy was still badly shaken from his near brush with the law, Mac kept his voice calm and steady. "He 'mentored' them straight into jail. Even cops can go bad when they let greed and stupidity take over. They start feeling superior to everyone else, for one reason or another, and they begin to think the rules that apply to ordinary folks don't apply to them."

"Jimbo told me tonight that they only stole from people who were jerks. And everyone had insurance, so nobody really lost anything."

"Do you agree with that line of reasoning?"

After only a moment, Brad shook his head.

"The insurance companies lose—and so do the people who have to pay higher rates. The crime victims who have to pay deductibles and then scramble to replace their belongings lose. You saw what your sister had to go through to replace her car and the things in it. It cost her quite a bit—and it wasn't her fault."

"I don't need the lecture. I didn't steal anything. I wouldn't have gone through with it tonight. Even against you. I've been raised better than that. But I probably would have gotten into trouble, anyway, because I'd have run after them and tried to stop them. Nobody would've believed me."

"Probably not."

Brad sighed wearily. "Jimbo said you wanted me out of the way so I wouldn't interfere with you chasing after my sister. He said you would do anything you could to come between us. He said if I hassled you enough, you'd decide she wasn't worth it and you would leave us alone."

"If I wanted you out of the way, I'd have let Chief Davenport haul you off tonight, now, wouldn't I?"

"Yeah. I guess."

"Yeah. Go on in now. It's late. And don't scare your sister. Ring the bell and let her know who you are."

"I will." Brad didn't seem to know quite what to say at that point. Mac knew the kid still had major issues with him. He was obviously torn between his previous dislike and his gratitude that he'd been spared a traumatic ordeal.

"Go on in, Brad," Mac repeated quietly.

Brad apparently decided they'd said enough. He opened the door and slid out of the truck.

"Brad?" Mac spoke before the boy closed the door.

"Yeah?"

"This is two strikes against you now. Three strikes and you're out. Is that clear?"

"There won't be another one."

"Make sure of that."

Showing he wasn't entirely cowed by the events

of the evening, Brad shut the door with somewhat more force than necessary.

Mac backed out of the driveway, then stopped a few yards down the deserted street until he saw Sharon open the front door to her brother. Then he drove off quickly, hoping she hadn't spotted him. It would be difficult for Brad to explain how he'd ended up riding home in Mac's truck without telling her exactly where they'd met up.

Maybe he'd done something good tonight, he mused as he headed for his apartment. Maybe he'd put a confused kid on the right path. Or maybe by letting Brad off the hook tonight, he'd only contributed to the development of a juvenile delinquent.

All he knew for certain was that, whatever the results of his actions, he had done it all for Sharon.

He owed her that much, at least.

BY SATURDAY AFTERNOON, Mac had decided to leave town.

Though it wasn't the way he preferred to do business, he could oversee the renovation project from a distance, leaving a foreman in charge of the day-to-day supervision. Maybe the job wouldn't be handled with his usual, almost obsessive attention to detail, but it would be adequately completed. He could then put the place up for sale and forget he'd ever started this futile quest.

That would probably be the best move for everyone, he thought with the memory of Sharon's smile haunting the shadowy back corners of his mind.

He stood in the master bedroom of the Garrett house. The workers had all left for the afternoon and the house was still, the silence as heavy as Mac's mood. Since most of the work to this point had been upstairs and in the kitchen, this room had hardly been touched. It still looked almost exactly the same as it had the first time he'd seen it.

Sharon loved this room. The big fireplace. The high ceiling. The wide, detailed moldings. The wooden floor that would soon gleam with a satiny sheen again. She'd confided to him that she saw this room decorated in lace and antiques. A decorative white-iron bed. Old stained-glass shades on bedside lamps. A thick, handmade rug on the floor.

She wouldn't actually be choosing the furniture for the house, of course—that would be up to the future owner. But she'd already talked about the wallpaper and lights she would select, as well as the fixtures for the attached bath. She'd made him see it all so clearly.

He could picture it now as he stood there alone in the dust and the shadows. The soft lights. The fire. The big bed, rumpled from lovemaking. The mental image made him yearn for things he couldn't quite identify—or perhaps he just didn't have the nerve to try.

A sound from behind him brought him out of his lonely thoughts. Someone was in the house with him. Though he wasn't expecting anyone in particular, Trent McBride had said he might stop by with a sample cabinet door for his approval.

Yet somehow he knew it wasn't Trent. He turned very slowly to face the door and wait for her.

Sharon looked a bit uncertain as she stepped into the room, her gaze locking immediately with his. She wore a sleeveless, scoop-neck, pale yellow knit dress. That particular shade of yellow was her favorite color. He knew that small detail about her— along with so many other tidbits he'd filed into his memory. Like the faintly floral scent of her shampoo. The way her pulse fluttered in her throat when he kissed her there. The way her fingers twined in his hair when he made love to her, and twined together in front of her when she was nervous.

They were entwined that way now, her knuckles almost white with the pressure she exerted on them.

"How did you know where to find me?" he asked, realizing she had walked directly to this room.

The question seemed to confuse her a little. "I don't know."

It wasn't important, of course. "Why are you here?"

"I need to talk to you."

"What about?"

He watched her take a deep breath, the movement stretching her thin knit dress across the breasts he had kissed until she sighed with pleasure. He raised his gaze from them with an effort.

"Brad told me what you did for him. I don't quite know how to thank you."

"Er—what did he tell you?" he asked cautiously, uncertain of what he should say.

"Everything," she answered simply. "Starting with keying the side of your truck and ending with you stopping him before he broke into your place last night."

He was frankly surprised. "Did he now?"

"Yes. If it wasn't for you, Brad would be in jail today. Maybe he deserved to be—but I'm so very glad he didn't have to go through that. We owe you so much—"

"You owe me nothing," he said flatly. "I heard the boys talking. I knew Brad had not been involved in any of the previous break-ins. I could tell he was being led into something that deep down he wanted no part of. I just helped him make the right choice. I'm surprised he told you, though."

"He said he needed to. He was so shaken by what almost happened that I don't think he slept a wink last night. He cried when he told me about it. He was so disappointed in Jimbo and Tommy and Mike—another boy who'd been involved in the previous break-ins. So disillusioned by Officer Dodson's involvement. And so stunned and grateful for what you did for him, even after the way he had treated you."

"I told him I didn't do it for him."

"I know." She took a couple of steps toward him, her eyes holding his. "He told me that, too. He said you did it for me. But I think you did it for both of us."

Even though she stood close enough for him to catch a faint scent of her floral shampoo, he didn't reach out to touch her. He had to fist his hands in his pockets to stop himself from trying. Gratitude and indebtedness were not what he wanted from Sharon—even though he still didn't know what, exactly, he did want.

She seemed perplexed by his silence. She cleared her throat. "Brad didn't know how you and Wade learned of the boys' plans last night."

"Wade got a tip. One of the kids spouted off to a friend, who got a conscience and told his father the whole story. Wade had already been following his own hunch on Dodson and he found a storage-warehouse in Carollton with a unit full of stuff taken in area break-ins. The unit had been rented under an assumed name, but the storage warehouse owner identified Dodson from a photograph. As for last night—the kid with the big mouth had been bragging about what they were going to do to the 'cocky Latino' who'd come to town and stirred up so much trouble. So Wade was ready for them last night."

"And Wade told you?"

"He heard they might try to pull Brad in because of his antagonism toward me. Because of my friendship with you—and his own—he gave me a chance to intercede. Had Brad gotten all the way to the storage building with the other kids, there would have been nothing Wade could do. He was already skirting the ethical line to bring me in."

"I'll have to thank him—"

"No. As far as Wade knows officially, Brad was never there. I've never confirmed that he was, nor will I. The other boys won't say anything, and even if they do, they have nothing on him. Brad was never involved. Let's leave it at that."

Her eyes were so sad and troubled, it made his chest ache to look at her. He wanted very badly to reach out to her. He contented himself with smoothing a strand of hair away from her face. His fingertips brushed her warm, flushed skin, and the temptation was strong to press his lips to hers, but he restrained himself.

If he kissed her now, and she responded, he couldn't know if it was only gratitude motivating her actions. He couldn't accept that.

He dropped his hand, shoving it back into his pocket.

Sharon moistened her lips, as if she sensed how close he had come to kissing them. And then she spoke again, her voice firmer this time. "Brad *was* involved in damaging your truck. He said he let Jimbo goad him into it because of a confrontation they had with you. One they felt they lost."

"I've always known it was Brad. I saw him."

"But you didn't pursue it. Again, for my sake."

He merely shrugged.

Her chin lifted in a show of pride. "I'm sorry I didn't listen to you. And I *am* going to pay for your repairs."

"You are not paying for anything and that's the end of it. If Brad makes the offer, I'll let him work it off doing cleanup around the site. I won't take money from him that he would probably get from you, anyway.''

She didn't look entirely satisfied, but she let it drop. Wrapping her arms at her waist, she chewed her lower lip, looking as though she couldn't decide what to say next. The distance between them seemed suddenly more pronounced than the three feet or so that separated them physically.

He hated it.

"Caleb and Bobbie McBride got back in town this morning. I don't know if you heard."

"No. But I knew they were due soon." He wished she hadn't brought up the McBrides, reminding him of the biggest area of contention between them. It still stung that she'd so quickly taken their side, that she had seemed so judgmental of him for pursuing a goal she didn't approve of. It appeared that the McBrides had everything—including Sharon's loyalty and affection.

And if he kept thinking along those lines, he would digress into maudlin self-pity, he thought with a touch of disgust.

Her head lowered now, she looked up at him through her lashes. "Have you decided what you're going to do? Are you going to ask Caleb if he's your father?"

"I'm leaving town," he said abruptly. "I'll probably be gone by the middle of next week."

Sharon looked to be in shock. "You're leaving?" she repeated, staring at him.

He nodded. "I'll pick a foreman to be in charge of the project. I thought I'd ask Trent if he's interested in the job. Then I'll check in with him every day or two for reports, and make a personal visit every few weeks. Any decorating problems you encounter or questions that come up, you'd talk to him, and he'll relay them to me. The same with the other subcontractors."

"But, Mac, why? Why do you have to leave?"

"Because of the nature of this town," he answered bluntly. "If I stay here, renovating my grandparents' house, working side by side with my cousins or siblings or whatever the hell they are to me, something's liable to get out. You figured out why I came here, there's a chance others might do the same. Maybe I wanted to hurt someone when I came here, but that doesn't matter now. There are too many innocents in the line of fire. Too little to be gained by continuing. You win. The McBrides win. It's time for me to retreat."

Looking distressed, she reached out to him, laying a hand on his arm, her fingers curling into the thin fabric of his shirt. "I can't agree with you," she said. "There's no reason anyone should ever find out the truth, unless you want them to. All you have to do is put away your notes and be discreet. You have so much invested in this project. You know you want to see it through."

He looked at her hand on his arm, thinking how easy it would be to pull her against him and crush her mouth beneath his. His voice was just a bit hoarse when he said, "I'm not leaving entirely because of the McBrides. It's also because of you."

Her fingers clenched spasmodically. "Why because of me?" she whispered.

"I've caused you enough trouble. I don't want to make you feel awkward around your friends. Or around me."

Her eyes suddenly swam beneath a sheen of moisture. His heart twisted as she leaned toward him, her lips slightly parted, her gaze beseeching. "Mac, I—"

From the front of the house came a sudden heavy pounding on the door. Drawn so abruptly out of their tense exchange, both of them jumped and turned instinctively in that direction.

"That's probably Trent," Mac said, raising a hand to the back of his neck, which had tightened almost painfully. "He said he might stop by."

Her head down, Sharon took a step back from him. "I guess I'd better go. I just...I just wanted to thank you."

"It wasn't necessary. But it's good to see you," he added, thinking again how pretty she looked. She brightened the dark, gloomy room just by standing in it in her pale yellow dress. The only drawback was knowing she would soon be gone again.

Without speaking, she walked with him to the front door. Mac couldn't think of anything to say. He assumed the same was true for Sharon.

They were both struck truly speechless when he opened the door to find Caleb McBride standing on the other side.

CHAPTER SIXTEEN

SHARON FELT her heart stop when she recognized the man on Mac's doorstep. What was Caleb doing here? Had he somehow found out why Mac was in Honoria?

"Sharon," he said, spotting her with a bright smile. "This is a nice surprise."

"It's good to see you, too, Caleb," she said, presenting her cheek for his kiss of greeting. "How was your vacation?"

"Bobbie enjoyed it," he said, his expression wry. "I found it very pleasant, but I was ready to come home about a week ago."

"I'm sure you couldn't wait to get back to work," Sharon teased lightly, though from the corner of her eye she watched Mac watching them.

Mac had to be asking himself the same question that kept repeating in her mind. Why was Caleb here? She had no doubt that Mac recognized the older man; he'd done his homework quite thoroughly. How did it feel, she couldn't help wondering, for Mac to meet his uncle for the first time this way?

Caleb turned to Mac and extended his hand. "I'm

sorry. I was distracted by your lovely guest. I'm Caleb McBride.''

Sharon thought Mac hesitated for a fraction of a moment before taking Caleb's hand. "Mac Cordero," he said. "It's nice to meet you."

"I hope you'll forgive the surprise visit. My curiosity made me impatient. My mother grew up in this house, which is why I was very intrigued when I heard you planned to restore it. And especially since my son is a member of your renovation team."

"A valued member," Mac said graciously. "Your son does beautiful woodwork. It's hard to find anyone these days who puts so much time and effort into his work."

"Yes, he's very talented. We're quite proud of him."

Standing to one side of them, Sharon thought Caleb appeared to be watching Mac very closely, studying his face as if something there intrigued him. Or was she letting her imagination run away with her?

"Is your contracting business based here in Georgia, Mac?" Caleb asked.

Mac nodded. "I was born and raised in Savannah. I still maintain a home there."

For some reason, Sharon found herself holding her breath as she watched Caleb's expression change. The genial, country-lawyer smile he always wore so easily seemed to slide off one side of his face. Her breath left her in one long, shaky sigh.

"I once knew a woman in Savannah whose name

was Cordero," Caleb murmured, his voice not quite steady. "Anita Cordero."

As still as he was, Mac could have been carved from wood. There was no expression on his face. And Sharon thought she might be the only person in Honoria who could read the emotion in his eyes. "Anita Cordero was my mother."

Caleb swallowed audibly. "Was?"

"She died three years ago."

"I'm very sorry to hear that." Caleb lifted a hand to wipe his mouth. His fingers shook. "Your—er—father. Is he still living?"

"I don't know. I never met him."

"Do you mind if I ask how old you are?"

"I'm thirty-three."

"My God." Caleb put out a hand to press it against the nearest wall.

Sharon reached out to him quickly. "Caleb?" She glanced worriedly at Mac. "He had a heart attack two years ago."

"No." Caleb held up his free hand. "I'm all right. Just...shaken."

Mac took a small step forward, looking worried. "Do we need to call for medical help?"

Still holding the wall, Caleb ignored the question. "Why did you come to Honoria, Mac?" he asked, his voice husky.

Mac looked at Sharon. She shrugged helplessly. He drew a deep breath. "I came to find some answers. I had no real plan about what to do with them once I found them."

Caleb couldn't seem to take his gaze off Mac's face. "You have your mother's features. Her eyes."

"I know." As if he was becoming overwhelmed by all the emotion in the room, Mac stuffed his hands in his pockets. "I don't imagine I look at all like my father's family."

Seeming to gather his strength, Caleb straightened, his voice steadier now. "Sharon, dear, I wonder if you would excuse us for a little—"

"No." Mac's tone was sharp as he took a step closer to her. "Sharon knows my story. She stays."

Sharon looked uncertainly from one man to the other. "I don't mind," she said. "We can talk later, Mac."

"No." He reached out to take her hand, and despite his almost arrogant tone, something about the gesture was oddly pleading. As if he needed her with him. There was no way, of course, that she could leave now. She nodded and curled her fingers around his.

Caleb glanced at those locked hands, and at Sharon's face for a moment. Then he turned to Mac. "I met Anita Cordero almost thirty-five years ago. I was consulting on a very lengthy, complicated legal case in Savannah, and it was necessary for me to stay in a hotel room for weeks at a time. My marriage was going through a difficult period and Anita became very special to me. I wanted to spend the rest of my life with her—and then my wife told me she was pregnant."

With Tara, Sharon thought, her heart in her throat. Dear God, Caleb McBride was Mac's father.

Caleb continued firmly. "My wife and I had tried for several years to have a baby, but we'd begun to believe it would never happen. Her announcement staggered me. She was carrying my first child—and I was in love with another woman. I told Anita everything. She told me I had to go home to my wife. She wouldn't break up a family, she said. She told me that we were never meant to be together. That the time we'd shared was never really ours. And then she asked me never to call her again. She made me promise I would never look back. And she became furious when I stupidly offered to send her money. She was a very strong-willed woman. And I was a very weak-willed man."

He must have been attracted to strong women, Sharon thought. Bobbie was one of the most domineering women she'd ever met. Everyone had always thought Caleb and Bobbie's marriage worked so well because he very contentedly allowed her to have her own way. Sharon had never dreamed that Caleb had concealed so much behind that fatherly-lawyer image he had perfected.

"She never told me about you," Caleb finished, looking straight into Mac's eyes. "I never knew."

So Mac's father hadn't deliberately abandoned him. He had never known he left a son behind when his love affair ended. Did knowing that ease any of the hurt and anger Mac had carried around for so long?

Mac sighed very faintly. "You never looked back." It wasn't a question.

"I tried very hard not to," Caleb corrected him. "It was all Anita asked of me. I've made a good life for myself here with my practice and my family, I'll admit that. But I can't say that I never looked back."

Mac's fingers tightened almost imperceptibly around Sharon's, as though seeking strength for what he needed to say next. "Just over two years ago, I lost my six-week-old son to a very rare genetic birth defect. A problem with his blood. The doctors told me the condition was hereditary, that it would have shown up somewhere in my family history. Does that sound familiar to you?"

Looking understandably distressed by Mac's loss, Caleb shook his head adamantly. "There's absolutely no history of genetic birth defects on either side of my family. I would know if there was."

Sharon hoped Mac had found some comfort in that reassurance. She couldn't imagine the pain he must have gone through when he'd lost his child. The anguish of not knowing whether it had been his absent father who had passed on that gene.

Still without expression, Mac nodded. "Then you've answered all the questions I had when I came here. There's no need for you to worry. I no longer need the revenge I once thought I wanted."

Caleb wiped his face with his hand again. "Mac—she named you Mac?"

"Miguel Luis. She called me Mac—after you, I

know now, though she never told me your name. When she died, I learned that my father was a McBride from Honoria. I didn't know until you told me that it was you, and not one of your brothers."

"So you literally came here on a private quest for answers. That must have taken a great deal of courage."

Mac shrugged. "I just needed to know."

"Your mother was a very special woman, Mac. I'm sorry I caused her, and you, so much pain with my weaknesses."

"My mother bore part of the blame—but you're right. She was very special. She gave me a good life."

"I'm happy to hear that. And now that we all know the truth—"

Mac broke in with a shake of his head. "My mother didn't want to break up your family, and neither do I. I've met all your children and your grandchildren. They're nice people. From what I've heard, your wife is a fine woman. There's no need to hurt any of them by stirring up the past. I plan to leave town soon. You needn't worry that I'll cause you any trouble."

Still holding Mac's hand, Sharon rested her free hand on his forearm, bringing them closer together. It had been a very gracious concession. She was as proud of him as she was saddened for him.

This time it was Caleb who shook his head. "I intend to tell Bobbie the whole story. Our children, too. Your siblings have a right to know that they have another brother, and you deserve to get to know them. I've lost thirty-three years of my eldest son's life. I don't want to waste any more time.''

Sharon felt her eyes well with fresh tears. The emotion in Caleb's voice was so strong, so touching that it went straight to her heart. Was Mac equally affected?

The gruffness of his voice told her that he was. ''I doubt that either your wife or Trevor would appreciate hearing you refer to me as your 'eldest son.'''

''Bobbie will have the most difficult time with it, of course,'' Caleb admitted honestly. ''But she's a strong woman with a few old secrets of her own. We've made a comfortable life together here. She won't throw it away easily. As for Trevor—all of my children have big, generous hearts. And there is nothing they value more than family. You are their brother, Mac. Once you get to know them, you'll understand how important that is to them.''

''And what about you?'' Mac challenged.

Caleb blinked rapidly. ''You're my son. Once you get to know *me,* you'll understand how important that is to me.''

Sharon could almost feel Mac begin to panic. ''I didn't come here to join your family,'' he said bluntly. ''I've gotten by just fine without a father, without siblings. It's too late for me to learn how to deal with them now. I think it would be best if we all just agree to keep this to ourselves.''

Caleb squared his shoulders, and Sharon realized

that Mac hadn't inherited all his stubbornness from his mother. "I let Anita talk me into leaving without looking back," he said. "I know now what a tragic mistake that was. I won't make it a second time. I'm telling my wife the truth. You do what you have to do, Mac—but I hope you'll choose to stay for a while. God knows you don't owe me a thing, but I'd like to find out if there's a chance you can ever forgive me."

Mac released Sharon's hand and stepped away from her, causing her arm to fall to her side. "I've hurt too many people in my life. I won't cause any more pain. You were all getting along just fine before I came here," he said, glancing at Sharon to include her. "You'll do the same again after I leave."

Sharon decided it was time for her to join the conversation. She faced Mac with her hands on her hips. "Don't you think it's up to us to decide how we were getting along before you came here? Maybe we think our lives will be better for having you in them."

"And if I think you're wrong?"

"Then maybe we'd like the right to try to change your mind." She stepped toward him and placed her hand on his rigid arm again. "You're a good man, Mac Cordero. You care about other people, even though you sometimes try to hide your feelings. But that stiff-necked pride of yours is only going to hurt you in the long run if you aren't very careful. It sounds as if you got it from your mother. But perhaps it would have been better for everyone if she hadn't let her own pride rule her actions.''

She knew she had taken a risk with even that slight criticism of his mother. To her relief, Mac didn't seem to take offense—maybe because he was simply too distracted by his own confused emotions.

''No one here is asking for any lasting commitments from you, Mac,'' she added gently. ''We only want the chance to get to know you better. To see what the future has to hold for us all.''

She hadn't forgotten that Caleb was there, that he heard every word she was saying. But reaching Mac now seemed much more important than protecting her own pride. Something told her that if she missed this chance, there might not be another one. And she wasn't willing to risk that.

''Maybe it's too late for me to be your father, Mac,'' Caleb added quietly. ''But I hope it's not too late for me to be your friend.''

Mac drew a deep breath, his shoulders seeming to relax a little. ''I need some time to think.''

''Of course.'' Caleb cleared his throat, then glanced at Sharon before looking back at Mac. ''It would take a very special man to win this fine young woman's heart. And a very foolish man to reject that gift. Since I have no right to offer you fatherly advice, I'll leave it at that.''

Mac only scowled, reminding Sharon very much at that moment of her notoriously stubborn younger brother.

''I'll see you both around,'' Caleb said after a

momentary pause, moving backward toward the door, his eyes still locked on Mac's face as if he was reluctant to look away. "I have some long-overdue things to take care of at home."

"Caleb—good luck." Sharon didn't know what else to say.

"Thank you, dear. Good luck to you, too."

Sharon suspected she was going to need it.

THE OLD HOUSE was almost eerily silent after Caleb left it. Filled with soundless echoes of raw, painful emotions. Sharon stood as still and quiet as one of the ghosts that probably haunted the place, watching Mac as though afraid he would disappear if she took her eyes off him.

He was filled with a sudden, bone-tired weariness. "I need a drink," he said. "I have some sodas in a cooler in the kitchen. Do you want one?"

She seemed only momentarily taken aback by the offer. "Yes, I'd like that."

He motioned for her to proceed him. He noted that she glanced over her shoulder a time or two on the way. Was she concerned that he would take the opportunity to escape while her back was turned? As tempting as that was in some ways, he had no intention of doing something like that. Not just yet.

The cooler was a small, electric unit he'd set in the kitchen to hold cold drinks for himself and the work crews. He didn't allow beer on his sites, but cold drinks, juices and water were always available. He noted automatically as he opened the door of the unit that the supply had been almost depleted. He would have to restock before the crew returned Monday morning.

"What do you want?" he asked Sharon.

She reached past him and took out a diet soda. He selected a beverage for himself, then closed the door. He popped the top on the can, then just stared at it, his thirst gone. Suddenly, he wasn't sure he could swallow.

"Mac?" Sharon set her own can on the plywood-covered countertop. "Are you okay?"

He avoided looking at her, uncertain what his expression might reveal. "I'm fine."

Very gently, she removed the untouched can from his lax fingers and set it beside her own. And then she went up on tiptoe and wrapped her arms tightly around him. He stiffened for a moment in surprise, but then gathered her closer and buried his face in her soft hair.

He was tired of fighting, tired of trying to resist her.

Without a word, she pressed a kiss to his throat. How could she know what he needed most right then? Could she actually read his mind, or had she learned him so well in such a short time?

She lifted her head to look at him, and pressed a cool hand against his warm cheek. Her smile was tremulous. Completely understanding. As if she knew what he was feeling even better than he did.

He lowered his mouth to hers, hesitating just before he made contact. She slid her hand to the back of his neck and brought their lips together. And he almost groaned with sheer pleasure. It had been days since he'd last kissed her. It felt like weeks.

Tenderness flared almost instantly into passion. Mac was almost consumed with the need to make love to her, to lose himself in her. To make the rest of the world disappear, leaving only the two of them in it.

Had he really thought he could walk away from her so easily? He knew now that he'd only been fooling himself.

He reached beneath the short hem of her dress, sliding his hands up her bare legs to her hips. His fingers curled in the fabric of her sheer panties, kneading her tight bottom. She really was perfect, he thought. Even her pale little appendectomy scar was perfect to him.

She moved in response to his touch, pressing against him, inflaming him further. The setting couldn't be more wrong for this. They were in a half-gutted old house, surrounded by the scent of sawdust. For Sharon, there should be flowers, candles, silk and lace. Someone better than a battered ex-cop with so much emotional baggage he practically needed a bellhop.

She didn't seem to care about any of that. Her mouth was as avid as his, her hands as greedy. And when he ripped off his shirt, draped it over the counter and lifted her onto it, she spread her knees eagerly so that he could step between them.

He took her there, on the counter, using protection

he carried in his pocket more from habit than antic-ipation. They didn't even undress, removing no more than necessary. It was rough and fast and awk-ward—and Mac had never needed anything more in his entire life.

His knees were weak when they finished. He had to brace himself against the counter on either side of her, his forehead resting against hers. His breathing was loud in his own ears, seeming to echo in the cavernous, empty kitchen.

When he was sure he could speak coherently, he said, "I didn't mean for that to happen."

Her arms were still around his neck, her face against his. "I know. But I'm glad it did."

He pulled back a few inches to look at her. "I didn't want gratitude from you before, Sharon. I don't want sympathy from you now."

She smiled and laid her hand against his face. "You always underestimate yourself."

He gave her a faint smile in return. "That isn't a mistake I'll ever make with you."

"See that you don't," she answered, her tone a little saucy.

He kissed her lingeringly, knowing he had just implicitly committed to staying in Honoria for a while. He didn't know what was going to happen, exactly—with the McBrides or with Sharon. But Sharon had asked him to give them all a chance to find out what the future held for them.

It seemed he still had at least one more question left to answer.

EPILOGUE

MAC STOOD in the master bedroom of the Garrett
house, surveying the room with deep satisfaction.
Above his head an old-fashioned ceiling fan turned
lazily, stirring the humid, late-August air. Early-
evening sunlight streamed through the windows and
the paned glass door beside the big fireplace, casting
a soft glow and extending his shadow across the
gleaming wooden floor.

It was a beautiful room, he thought, almost beg-
ging for furniture and occupancy. His team had done
a great job in here, as they had with the other parts
of the house that had been completed thus far. The
renovation was more than half finished. The place
would be ready for habitation by Christmas.

"I thought I would find you in here. This seems
to be your favorite place to think."

He turned with a smile to greet Sharon as she
walked into the room. She had changed out of the
fancy dress she'd worn to Trent's wedding earlier
that day, and now wore jeans and a T-shirt, as he
did. They had been invited to a casual dinner later
at Caleb and Bobbie McBride's house with Tara and
Trevor and their families. Trent and Annie had already left for their honeymoon. Sharon and Mac had

decided to meet here, since Mac had wanted to check on some things that had been done that morning.

"There's a peaceful feeling in here. It does help me think," he admitted. "I believe it's my favorite room in the house."

"It's definitely mine." She wandered over to the fireplace, as she often did, and rested her hand on the mantelpiece, looking inside as if she could visualize a fire burning there, even on a very warm day like this one.

She belonged in this room, he mused, watching her. It suited her perfectly. Just as he had discovered how well his bed suited her in their past few weeks together.

He would soon find out if she agreed with him.

She spoke before he could. "The wedding was lovely, wasn't it?"

He felt his mouth twist. "Flowers and music and cute little kids in ruffled dresses. They'd have been just as married if they'd stood in front of a justice of the peace wearing shorts. From the expression on Trent's face most of the morning, I think that's exactly what he would have preferred."

Sharon laughed softly. "You men just don't appreciate romance."

He shrugged.

Her amusement faded into sincerity. "Thank you for going with me, Mac. I know you were reluctant, but I thought it was important for you to be there.

And I think Trent was glad you came, even though he can't admit it just yet.''

Mac's newly discovered half brothers were still having trouble getting over their anger that Mac had deceived them so thoroughly when he'd first arrived in town. Jamie had told Mac that Trevor was having trouble learning to trust people again after the painful scandal with his first wife and their fickle Washington, D.C. cronies. What he had seen as betrayal on Mac's part—and Caleb's—had hit him hard.

Trent, too, was still reeling from so many changes in his life. The end of his air force career, the occasionally inconvenient physical limitations resulting from his accident, his new career as a carpenter, falling so deeply in love for the first time in his footloose life—the acceptance of a half brother, one who just happened to be his employer, hadn't been easy for him. He hadn't understood why Mac had felt it necessary to approach them with such subterfuge, rather than simply making his agenda known from the start. It had been Caleb who had asked his sons to forgive Mac—and to try to understand what Mac had been through. How much he had suffered while they had grown up so loved and protected by the father Mac had never known.

Mac didn't want their sympathy—but he was beginning to want their acceptance. He was tired of being alone. He needed family. And he thought they would get there, eventually. It would just take time and patience, on all their parts. Today had been a giant step in the right direction.

"No matter how he grumbled about all the fuss, I've never seen Trent look happier," Sharon said, fully convinced that everything would work out for the best now that the truth was out.

Trent had looked more than happy, Mac mused. He'd looked deeply, thoroughly satisfied—as if he'd just been given everything he'd ever wanted.

It had been an interesting day, all in all. Mac had been aware that he had drawn almost as much attention as the bride and groom, at least from the unrelated guests in attendance. He'd been aware of them watching him, looking in vain for resemblances between him and the McBrides. Watching him with Sharon, wondering what was going on between them. Eavesdropping on his conversations with Caleb and Bobbie, curious about *that* relationship, as well.

Mac knew they hadn't heard anything to start the rumor mills running again. He and the McBrides had been congenial, friendly, polite. As for Bobbie— well, he'd never met a woman exactly like her. Quite frankly, she rather terrified him. Once she'd gotten over the shock of finding out who he was, she had brusquely decided to accept him. And for Bobbie McBride, acceptance included full entitlement to giving advice and directions—all for his own good, of course.

Despite his healthy wariness of the woman, Mac actually liked her, oddly enough.

As for Caleb—he was trying very hard to figure out how to be a new father to a fully grown man.

Their relationship was still awkward, to say the least—but a bond had formed. Though he was still cautious, and still dealing with a lot of old anger, Mac was beginning to have a tenuous hope that the bond would only grow stronger during the years ahead. He would never have the relationship with Caleb that Trevor and Trent had, of course—but maybe they could form their own connection. And maybe it would be a bonus for both of them in the long run.

Tara had had the hardest time dealing with Caleb's actions thirty-three years ago. She had to know that it was only because of her arrival that Caleb and Bobbie had stayed together back then. Mac suspected that she had idolized her father, placed him on a pedestal that no mere human was worthy of, and it hadn't been easy for her to learn that Caleb had flaws just like everyone else. But Mac believed the wounds would heal, again with time. Already Tara was making friendly overtures toward him, letting him know she held no grudges against him for what had been done to all of them so long ago. She was a strong and gracious woman, and she had a heart big enough to accept another brother once the bruises faded.

It was a strong family with very close ties. They would survive this scandal, just as they had weathered so many other trials in the past.

"Did you notice how happy Annie looked that her mother came to her wedding?" Sharon asked, running a fingertip along the mantel as if looking for dust. "She wasn't sure her mother would have the courage to defy her father, who disapproves so strongly of Annie's marriage, but I could tell she was thrilled to see her there. Maybe that family is healing, as well. It's important for families to learn to forgive and move on. To be together. I know I was glad to have my mother and Brad with me today, our family all together again to celebrate our friends' good fortune."

She wasn't just talking about Annie Stewart's family, of course, or her own. She was referring to the McBrides, as well—letting Mac know, as she had so many times before, that she believed it would all work out for the best. Her unflagging optimism was one of the things he admired most about her.

Changing the subject, she glanced up at the slowly turning ceiling fan. "They've done a wonderful job in here, haven't they? And the rest of the house is really shaping up fast. It will be ready to put on the market in no time."

"Do you think I would have any trouble selling it?" he asked, watching her closely.

"No." She sighed wistfully. "I'm sure it will sell very quickly. It's such a beautiful home."

"Still lusting after it for yourself?"

She wrinkled her nose as he reminded her of that early conversation between them. "Don't I wish."

"Do you wish that, Sharon? Would you be happy living in this house?"

Her smile faded as she turned to him. "I'm not quite sure what you're asking."

He cleared his throat, oddly nervous now. "I'm asking if you'd like to live here. With me. In this house. As my wife."

It wasn't the most coherent proposal in history. Definitely not the most poetic. He'd probably just confirmed her earlier declaration that he had no appreciation for romance. But if sincerity carried any weight with her, it had come directly from his heart.

Apparently, earnestness was as touching to her as frills and flowers. Her eyes filled with tears.

"*Don't* cry," he ordered with quick male panic. And then added uncertainly, "Unless that's a good thing, of course."

She dashed at her cheek with one hand, smiling shakily. "That depends."

"What do you mean? I just proposed to you."

She stayed where she was, watching him with a puzzling air of expectancy.

"Well? Are you accepting or not?"

"I don't know."

He frowned at her. "What do you mean, you don't know? Why don't you know?"

"You haven't told me yet why you're asking."

He sighed. Apparently, she was going to insist on the frills, after all. Once again, he spoke from his soul. "I'm asking you to marry me because I love you. I fell in love with you when I pulled you out of that river and I've fallen more in love with you every day since. I expect I'll continue to fall harder every day I'm fortunate enough to spend with you in the future. I want you to be my friend, my partner, my lover, and the mother of my children. I will give you my absolute loyalty and undying affection in return. I will be a good son-in-law to your nice, ditzy mother, and a big brother and role model for Brad. I believe I have a lot to offer you, Sharon—but so much more to gain if you say yes.''

He'd started her tears flowing again, but he didn't try to stop them this time. He'd figured out that they were, indeed, a good thing.

"You had me when you told me you love me," she whispered. And then she threw herself into his arms.

"Is *this* a yes?" he asked, just to make sure.

"Yes. Definitely yes."

He covered her mouth with his before she could change her mind.

Romance is just one click away!

online book serials

➤ *Exclusive* to our web site, get caught up in both the daily and weekly online installments of new romance stories.

➤ Try the Writing Round Robin. Contribute a chapter to a story created by our members. Plus, winners will get prizes.

romantic travel

➤ Want to know where the best place to kiss in New York City is, or which restaurant in Los Angeles is the most romantic? Check out our Romantic Hot Spots for the scoop.

➤ Share your travel tips and stories with us on the romantic travel message boards.

romantic reading library

➤ Relax as you read our collection of Romantic Poetry.

➤ Take a peek at the Top 10 Most Romantic Lines!

Visit us online at

www.eHarlequin.com

on Women.com Networks

**Don't miss
an exciting opportunity
to save on the purchase of
Harlequin and Silhouette books!**

Buy any two Harlequin or
Silhouette books and save
$10.00 off future Harlequin
and Silhouette purchases

OR

buy any three
Harlequin or Silhouette books
and save **$20.00 off** future
Harlequin and Silhouette purchases.

*Watch for details
coming in October 2000!*

PHQ400

HARLEQUIN®
Makes any time special ™

Silhouette®
Where love comes alive ™

HARLEQUIN

Duets™